# AGED FOR SEDUCTION

## (A Tuscan Vineyard Cozy Mystery—Book Four)

### FIONA GRACE

## Fiona Grace

Debut author Fiona Grace is author of the LACEY DOYLE COZY MYSTERY series, comprising nine books (and counting); of the TUSCAN VINEYARD COZY MYSTERY series, comprising six books (and counting); of the DUBIOUS WITCH COZY MYSTERY series, comprising three books (and counting); of the BEACHFRONT BAKERY COZY MYSTERY series, comprising six books (and counting); and of the CATS AND DOGS COZY MYSTERY series, comprising three books (and counting).

Fiona would love to hear from you, so please visit www.fionagraceauthor.com to receive free ebooks, hear the latest news, and stay in touch.

ISBN: 978-1-0943-7360-7

## BOOKS BY FIONA GRACE

### LACEY DOYLE COZY MYSTERY
MURDER IN THE MANOR (Book#1)
DEATH AND A DOG (Book #2)
CRIME IN THE CAFE (Book #3)
VEXED ON A VISIT (Book #4)
KILLED WITH A KISS (Book #5)
PERISHED BY A PAINTING (Book #6)
SILENCED BY A SPELL (Book #7)
FRAMED BY A FORGERY (Book #8)
CATASTROPHE IN A CLOISTER (Book #9)

### TUSCAN VINEYARD COZY MYSTERY
AGED FOR MURDER (Book #1)
AGED FOR DEATH (Book #2)
AGED FOR MAYHEM (Book #3)
AGED FOR SEDUCTION (Book #4)
AGED FOR VENGEANCE (Book #5)
AGED FOR ACRIMONY (Book #6)

### DUBIOUS WITCH COZY MYSTERY
SKEPTIC IN SALEM: AN EPISODE OF MURDER (Book #1)
SKEPTIC IN SALEM: AN EPISODE OF CRIME (Book #2)
SKEPTIC IN SALEM: AN EPISODE OF DEATH (Book #3)

### BEACHFRONT BAKERY COZY MYSTERY
BEACHFRONT BAKERY: A KILLER CUPCAKE (Book #1)
BEACHFRONT BAKERY: A MURDEROUS MACARON (Book #2)
BEACHFRONT BAKERY: A PERILOUS CAKE POP (Book #3)
BEACHFRONT BAKERY: A DEADLY DANISH (Book #4)
BEACHFRONT BAKERY: A TREACHEROUS TART (Book #5)
BEACHFRONT BAKERY: A CALAMITOUS COOKIE (Book #6)

### CATS AND DOGS COZY MYSTERY

# CHAPTER ONE

Olivia Glass was beginning to panic.

She didn't have a clue what was scribbled on the handwritten list in front of her, and she was running short of time to figure it out.

"What does it say? Quick, quick!" Nadia, the vintner at La Leggenda winery, leaned across the tasting counter, drumming her nails on the polished wood. Impatience fizzed from every inch of her petite frame. Olivia could feel it like an electric force.

Frowning in concentration, Olivia peered at the writing. It was a messy scrawl, not helped by the fact the original had been blurrily screenshot before being emailed to the winery and printed out.

"I'm trying! Another minute and I'm sure I'll get it," Olivia reassured her.

Narrowing her blue eyes in concentration, Olivia angled the list so that it was in the beam of one of the elegant spotlights above the tasting counter.

The page was headed "Willing Lift." Or so Olivia had thought at first glance. It was only after a confused while that she'd realized this loopy, chaotic script actually said "Wedding List."

Since it was the list of requirements for the wedding venue, supplied by the bride-to-be, Olivia thought she should probably have figured that out earlier. It showed how bad the writing was!

"Okay. We've got the champagne flutes and the gold serviettes and the crystal beads," Olivia recapped, counting on her fingers. She had thought for quite a while that item read "crystal bears." Working it out had been a lucky save.

"Yes, yes, yes, we have all that, but I need the rest. I have to leave now," Nadia entreated. "These items must be purchased in Florence and the stores will close in an hour and a half."

Olivia felt like pulling out her blond hair in handfuls. Why had the bride-to-be scrawled these requirements down and not typed them out?

The list had been written on a letterhead titled "Big Bob's Debt Collectors, New Jersey, USA. You Ring, We Bring!"

Presumably, the bride-to-be worked for Big Bob? Why else would debt collector's stationery be used to compile a list of wedding

1

arrangements? And if she worked there, couldn't she use a printer? Olivia was sure she must be employed on the admin side—the "You Ring" and not on the kneecap-busting "We Bring" side of the business.

She was beginning to regret being the only English speaker at La Leggenda. That was why the list had ended up in the tasting room where she worked as sommelier. It had been passed from the handsome Marcello, the eldest of the Vescovis who owned this magnificent Tuscan winery, to Nadia, his younger sister, and then at the speed of light, on to her!

"Couldn't you stop in at a drugstore in Florence?" Olivia asked, as a brilliant idea struck. "I think you need to do that."

"A drugstore?" Nadia frowned, looking puzzled. "Why?"

"Because they're used to reading physicians' scrips. You know how bad doctors' handwriting is? I'm sure a pharmacist could interpret this at a glance."

Nadia snorted with laughter.

"Or I might come back with a bag of headache pills and hemorrhoid cream! No, Olivia, this is your job!"

"I could use a headache pill at this point," she complained, peering more closely at the jumbled writing again.

"Walls to be draped with—chiffon!" Olivia exclaimed in relief, as the scribble made sense at last. "Walls to be draped with chiffon which MUST BE—"

She stopped again. The last word had defeated her. And it was critically important. MUST BE what?

"It begins with a 'P,'" she stated after some intensive scrutiny.

"Pleated?" Nadia guessed helpfully.

"No, it looks like a shorter word than that," Olivia puzzled, wishing that the curlicues would form into a coherent shape.

"Pleated is not a long word," Nadia argued. "Shorter still? Plain? Pearl?"

"Pink!" Finally, it made sense. "Must be pink."

Nadia's mouth dropped open and she stared at Olivia in disbelief.

"Pink? For a wedding? Olivia, it is impossible! This is a marriage of adults, not the christening of a girl child."

Olivia shook her head, staring down at the page.

"I know, it doesn't make sense," she admitted. The vision of La Leggenda's restaurant draped in fuchsia chiffon was mind-boggling. But the more she looked at it, the less like any other word it seemed to be.

If she got this wrong, La Leggenda's first-ever tourism wedding would be ruined. She couldn't let that happen. And there was no time for another shopping trip. This was it, make or break.

Feeling flummoxed, Olivia wondered if she should turn the paper upside down and try reading it again.

Perhaps she needed to read it with fresh eyes. She raised her head for a moment, staring around the spacious tasting room, and turned to look behind her at the imposing display of oak barrels that formed a dramatic backdrop to the counter.

She turned back again hurriedly as, from the restaurant, came a disbelieving shriek.

"Pink? A five-tier wedding cake, frosted in baby pink? *Mio Dio*, it cannot be!"

Olivia recognized the outraged tones of Gabriella, the restaurant manager and her erstwhile rival.

Nadia tilted her head, listening.

"A pink cake? Can it be the theme color?" she asked incredulously.

"It sounds like it," Olivia agreed.

"Well, then. Pink it is. Pale pink chiffon, perhaps?"

"Yes, if the cake is baby pink, I guess the drapes should match." Olivia nodded.

"Unbelievable." Nadia rolled her eyes. "I had better go, because if the stores close, we will not have any pink at all."

She hurried out of the tasting room. As she opened the door, a blast of cold air rushed in. Olivia saw it was fully dark outside. A strong wind was howling, and she was pretty sure it would be raining, too. Winter had well and truly arrived.

Shivering, she ran over and closed the tall, stately door.

In the silence that followed, she could hear Marcello's voice from his office down the tiled corridor. He'd been barricaded in there all day, working through a massive list of logistics.

"White chairs, *per favore*. Blue-white, not cream, according to my instructions. Is that possible?"

Olivia could imagine him in there, leaning forward on his leather chair, his head tilted sideways so that a stray lock of dark hair fell over his handsome face—the strong jaw line accentuated by the warm glow of his desk lamp.

"Yes, a surround sound system for the after-party. I will email you the specs for the speakers. They seem very particular about the sound they want," she heard him say, sounding frazzled.

3

Olivia felt that way, too. This was the first large wedding that La Leggenda would be hosting, and she wasn't sure why Marcello had even proposed it. Did the winery need the money badly? She felt cold inside as she wondered if they'd landed in another financial predicament. Despite good sales in recent weeks, Olivia knew that the second vineyard near Pisa, which La Leggenda had recently purchased, had cost far more in upgrades and renovations than they'd expected.

Perhaps Marcello was planning ahead to take the winery through the lean days of mid-winter. After all, a wedding of more than one hundred guests was a massive event.

It was their first ever such function, and quite frankly, Olivia was dreading it.

In her previous life as an advertising accounts manager in Chicago, she had hated events. Not only were they a nightmare to organize, but the only predictable thing about them was their unpredictability. Bizarre and unforeseen things always ended up going catastrophically wrong at the last minute.

Olivia glanced down at the scrawled list again.

The hundred guests were all coming from America. In fact, the wealthy party was from New Jersey, which as a native New Yorker already worried her. She knew how picky—all right, that was a polite word—how obnoxious a group of wealthy American tourists could be in a foreign environment, if they weren't used to other countries' strange and different ways, and expected the same levels of service that they received at their local Ruby Tuesday. Especially if they had the notorious "Jersey attitude"!

Attitude or not, this bride sounded fussier than average. Olivia dreaded the tantrums that might ensue if the chiffon was the wrong pink, or the furniture had a hint of cream.

At that moment, Gabriella hurried into the tasting room, muttering angrily to herself. Her streaky, tortoiseshell hair had come loose from the swept-up do she'd sported that morning. Stray locks were dangling over her perfectly made up, although now rather smudged, face.

She headed toward Olivia and, for once, Olivia didn't feel her usual surge of defensiveness.

As Marcello's ex-girlfriend, who had kept her job after she and the handsome winery owner had broken up, Gabriella had resented Olivia from the start, sensing immediately that there was a romantic spark between her and Marcello. However, to Olivia's frustration, the spark had never flared into an actual romantic fire. Then, at the end of fall,

4

Marcello had confessed to her that although he wanted it to happen, he couldn't risk complicating their working relationship. As the head sommelier who also handled the winery's marketing, Olivia had become too valuable to La Leggenda.

She and Marcello had reluctantly agreed to stay friends, and Olivia was sure that Gabriella had sensed the change in their dynamic, with her finely tuned instincts.

At any rate, she'd been less hostile toward Olivia since then. Now, instead of the furious glower Olivia had been expecting, Gabriella rolled her eyes at her in a not-unfriendly way.

"This wedding!" she exclaimed. "I need to be paid more to deal with all of this. These people! Their demands! A pink wedding cake giving birth to many cupcakes? A personalized cupcake for every guest with their name on? There are one hundred and eight cupcakes. People will be drunk and take the wrong one and then what? And as for the wedding pizzas, I have never heard of such a stupid thing! Steak pizzas! Rib pizzas! Burger pizzas! Taco pizzas!"

She ran her perfectly manicured fingers through her hair.

"I know," Olivia agreed, amazed that she was able to speak with genuine empathy. "I'm worried the entire winery will be put off Americans after the wedding!"

Gabriella gave her a sly smile.

"Don't worry," she said in a conspiratorial tone. "I am already."

Olivia stared at her in consternation. Then Gabriella burst out laughing.

"I am joking," she explained. "Tell me, where is Jean-Pierre? We need to organize the wine list."

"I am here." The tall, temperamental French youth whom Olivia had recently hired as her assistant sommelier hurried through from the storage room. "There are many types of wine on this list that we do not have. Peach wine? Strawberry wine? Wine and Coke blend? How will we satisfy our guests?"

"We will supply labeled carafes of juice and soda, and they may mix their own," Gabriella decided.

"Good idea," Olivia agreed. "The basics should probably be our famous La Leggenda white blend, and the red blend that's heavy on the Merlot. Both of those are excellent quality wines that will appeal to the sophisticated palate of a wine lover as well as to the—"

She hesitated, not wanting to insult tourism visitors who also happened to be her fellow countrymen. Luckily, Gabriella had no such scruples.

"As well as the tasteless Philistines who will be attending this event," she spat. "Come, Jean-Pierre, let us work out how to arrange the carafes."

She whirled away, with Jean-Pierre following in her wake.

Olivia drew a deep breath. The wedding rehearsal would take place the day after tomorrow, and on Saturday, the wedding itself would be under way.

She let her breath out again slowly. In a short while it would all be over. Perhaps she was overdramatizing the situation, and there was no reason to dread it so much.

After all, it was just a wedding.

What could possibly go so badly wrong?

# CHAPTER TWO

It was fully dark when Olivia drove her elderly Fiat pickup through her farm's gateway. There was a gate, but since it was old and rather rusty, and at the bottom of her fix-up list, she had taken to leaving it open.

She breathed a sigh of happiness as she stopped the car outside the farmhouse. She never lost the feeling of gratitude and amazement that she was the owner of this twenty-acre farm, located on stony, hilly ground, but with a mysterious history and the most beautiful view in the whole of Tuscany.

How lucky she was to be living in this humble but homely abode, Olivia thought, turning off the windshield wipers and listening to the patter of rain on the car's roof, while admiring the faint outline of the farmhouse's stone walls. Even though she'd plunged most of her life savings into the dilapidated building and spent the rest on fixing it up, Olivia didn't regret it for a moment. It was an exotic world away from the neat but characterless apartment she'd owned in Chicago.

Olivia squeaked in surprise as a nose nudged her from behind.

It belonged to her adopted orange and white goat, Erba, who had started following Olivia home when she'd first begun working at the winery. Now, Erba commuted to and from La Leggenda with her. When it was sunny, they walked. In rain and storms, Erba traveled in the back of the car.

"Sorry, Erba! I've been dreaming and it's dinner time," Olivia apologized to her goat. "Time to feed you and put you to bed."

She scrambled out, pulling up her jacket's hood to protect her from the cold, spattering drizzle. Then she and Erba made a run for the farmhouse. Instead of going in the front door, Olivia rushed around to the back, where a brand new wooden Wendy house had been installed outside the kitchen courtyard.

"Inside!" Olivia encouraged her.

This luxurious lodging was Erba's new shelter. Olivia opened the door and Erba leaped onto the stack of straw while Olivia portioned out her dinner.

She'd had to ration Erba's grass, discovering that a too-rich diet had turned her goat into a head-butting whirlwind of excess energy. Now that she was on reduced alfalfa and grass hay, Erba was a delight to interact with again. Pretty, sociable, and full of character.

You couldn't ask for a better goat, Olivia thought, and she wasn't going to. One was quite enough!

She put the door on the hook so that Erba could go in and out. Then she followed the paved path that led to the kitchen courtyard and walked around the house to the front door again.

Olivia was adding to the length of stone paving every week, laying the cobbles and doing it herself. One day, her vision was to have a narrow stretch of cobbled pathway winding from the vine plantation, to the barn, to the house, perhaps even to the gate. That way, she could walk through her farm's stony terrain barefoot. Right now that seemed a crazy idea, but in summertime, she couldn't imagine anything more glorious than treading over cool, smooth cobbles in the summer heat.

From the other side of the front door, Olivia heard an impatient meow.

Her cat, Pirate, was eager for attention.

"Hello, little one!" After hurrying inside and closing the door against the cold, Olivia picked up the black-and-white cat, giving him a squish and rub against her chest as he purred loudly. Pirate was taming fast and, she had to admit, was becoming rather chunky. She couldn't believe that a few months ago, he had been totally feral, roaming wild around the farm and in urgent need of a few square meals.

Olivia mimed the actions of stashing him in a carrier.

Hmmm.

Although a visit to the vet was becoming a priority, Olivia still didn't think she was quite ready to stow Pirate in a carrier. Best case, she would end up permanently alienating the semi-tame feline. Worst case, she would end up losing a lot of blood and then permanently alienating aforesaid feline.

Olivia sighed. Cats weren't easy. She hadn't realized they were such complex creatures. Between Pirate and Erba, she felt her work was cut out for her.

As Olivia placed Pirate gently on the rug, her phone rang.

She was delighted to see her best friend, Charlotte, was calling, from back in the States.

"Hey, Charlotte!" Grinning with happiness, Olivia answered the call.

"It's so good to hear your voice, Olivia! Whenever I dial your number I start wishing I was in Tuscany again, on vacation with you. It seems so unfair that I had to go back and you got to stay," her friend joked.

Olivia imagined Charlotte at her tidy home office desk, with her new cat snoozing in the in-tray, and most probably, chilly morning rain spattering her clean, double-glazed window.

"How's Bagheera?" she asked. "Is he settling in well?"

"It's like he's always been here. It was such a good decision to adopt an adult cat," Charlotte enthused.

Locking the front door, Olivia walked through the hallway, which now showcased colorful local artwork on the walls. There was a watercolor of a balcony with red geraniums in the window box, a landscape with verdant hills in every shade of green below a bright summer sky, and her favorite—a still life of a decorative fruit bowl. She loved the intensity of the oranges, the soft pink of the peaches contrasting with the green figs, and the deep purple of the juicy-looking grapes.

"I can hear a jingle," Charlotte said. "Let me guess. You've just gotten into your house, and put your keys down on the table."

Olivia laughed. "You're telepathically brilliant," she said. "I'm lucky that Danilo gave me this beautiful hall table as a belated housewarming gift."

Olivia couldn't look at the exquisitely crafted table without thinking of Danilo—his warm, genuine smile, his toned, muscular build, his kindness and humor and handsome features and, of course, his hairstyles, the constantly changing, edgy looks crafted by his hairdressing apprentice niece.

Olivia smiled fondly down at it and caressed the smooth, polished wood with her palm.

"Now, I'm going into the kitchen to pour myself a glass of wine. It's been a long, long day, and boy do I need it. And I'm going to top up Pirate's food bowl. He's taken to clawing my ankles if I'm late refilling it."

Olivia poured herself a glass of sangiovese red and then drew the green plaid curtains, shutting out the spattering rain and making the warm kitchen feel even cozier.

"Why are you in such need of it?" Charlotte asked curiously. "It sounds like you might have a crisis there, or am I wrong?"

"We're hosting a wedding," Olivia shared. She poured kibble into Pirate's bowl before sitting down at the kitchen table. "Not just any wedding, though! A massive wedding with more than a hundred guests. It's the first time La Leggenda has done anything like this."

Charlotte gasped. "Oh, how romantic! It will be amazing for you to experience such a traditional event. Imagine being part of a real, live, Italian family wedding!"

Olivia sighed. If only.

"Actually, that's not going to happen. The party is from New Jersey."

"New Jersey? And they're coming to Tuscany?" Charlotte asked, sounding incredulous.

"There must be a family connection, I suppose. They're wealthy and demanding, and I'm dreading the entire affair. They've asked for the walls to be draped in pink chiffon, Charlotte. Pink. Chiffon. On the walls!"

There was a thoughtful pause.

Olivia took a big gulp of wine.

"It might still be fine," Charlotte volunteered, her voice ringing with fake enthusiasm. "After all, they'll probably be so blown away by the exotic setting that it will run without a hitch."

"I don't think so!" Olivia told her friend darkly. "It's going to be hellish."

"Well, I think you need to acknowledge that you're prejudiced against weddings. You've never liked them," Charlotte admonished her.

Olivia got to her feet. It was time to start preparing dinner.

"Me? Why?"

She opened the fridge, looking to see if dinner had perhaps made itself while she'd been at work. Nope, no such luck. She removed a packet of Parma ham, parmesan cheese, and a jar of artichoke hearts, noticing that, apart from these ingredients, the fridge was nearly empty. She needed to stock up on more of her favorite staples from the local supermarket and deli.

Charlotte sighed.

"Because, when you were twenty-two, you almost got married," her friend announced triumphantly. "You can't have forgotten? I feel it put you off weddings for life, not that I think it's a bad thing."

Olivia frowned. Charlotte had a memory like an elephant! What did the wild, foolhardy decisions in one's early twenties have to do with the sober maturity of age thirty-four, where she was now? Why was her best friend even reminding her of an episode in her life she'd all but forgotten, and wished had never happened?

Briskly, Olivia turned the kettle on and put a pot on the stove.

"That was youthful folly."

Even now, she didn't want to talk about it. But Charlotte clearly did.

"You were really engaged. Even if the ring looked like it came out of a Christmas cracker. I remember it was soon after you got a new job and moved to Chicago. It was so surprising to me, back in New York City, to hear about all your huge, sudden life changes. You didn't even tell me you were dating anyone. You called to say you were engaged!"

"It all happened very fast," Olivia muttered.

"What went wrong in the end? I know you canceled it at the last moment, because I literally arrived at the airport in my smart outfit and hat, and you messaged me to go home again. Remind me why?"

"It doesn't matter, Charlotte. I don't want to talk about it now."

Olivia poured boiling water into the pot, turned up the heat, and added linguine and a pinch of salt. Her fiancé's name had been Ward, but that was neither here nor there. It was certainly not relevant to the topic at hand, which Olivia was going to do her best to change, even if she suspected that distracting Charlotte would be like unfastening Velcro with her teeth.

Everyone had a Ward in their life, didn't they? That embarrassing detour into a future you should never have had, with a person you were never meant to stay with. Some people only learned by making mistakes, and Olivia knew from bitter experience she was one of them.

Stirring the pasta lightly with a wooden spoon, she sighed.

"You're right, though," she admitted. "It did put me off weddings."

Charlotte laughed.

"I'm sure this wedding will be different. They'll be lovely, normal people," she soothed. "This will be a perfect wedding. It will help you overcome your prejudices."

"Scars," Olivia corrected her friend.

"It will help heal your scars, and perhaps one day, you and Marcello will be walking down the aisle!"

Olivia rolled her eyes.

Even though she'd spent months dreaming about getting together with the most crushable boss in the world, the truth was that she and the handsome, dark-haired, blue-eyed Marcello were now firmly on a "friends only" basis.

It was an example to Olivia that Italian passion could, indeed, be restrained. Not an example she wanted to have, but then she hadn't had the chance to choose.

In any case, there was another reason why she was happy to be "friends only" with Marcello at this moment. She wondered briefly if she should share her romantic predicament with Charlotte.

Would things work out the way she longed for with the charming, friendly Danilo? She felt nervous just thinking about it.

Perhaps she should say nothing, and hope that next time she spoke to her best friend, she could surprise her with the exciting news that she and Danilo were an item.

Although, remembering that she also hadn't told Charlotte about her whirlwind relationship with Ward until he'd already bought the ring, Olivia worried that keeping her romantic situation to herself might jinx it. It would be better to explain now, she decided.

"I have to go!" Charlotte said, scuppering Olivia's plans for full disclosure. "I have a conference call that's started early. I'll chat with you again soon. Have a lovely evening!"

Smiling as she said goodbye, Olivia took the chopping board off the hook and sliced up the ham and artichokes. The pasta was perfectly cooked. Quickly, she drained it and assembled her simple but tasty dinner. Pasta with a liberal splash of olive oil and butter—artichokes and Parma ham, a dash of cream, and a very generous handful of Parmesan.

She sprinkled Italian parsley over the top, added salt and pepper, and took a moment to appreciate its tasty simplicity.

In fact, this dish was so pretty, it required photography, she decided, placing it on the counter and getting busy with her phone camera. Her friends back home in the States loved it when she published snapshots of her daily life, and she'd neglected the food side recently.

Olivia moved her wineglass into the frame and took a few more shots. That was definitely the finishing touch. The wine completed the picture perfectly!

With her culinary masterpiece immortalized on Instagram, Olivia headed through to the hallway. She decided to read while she ate her dinner, choosing from the bookshelf at the end of the hall where she kept her Italian literature stash. So far, it contained five children's books, three teen adventures, and two adult romances, as well as a dictionary and a large, heavy volume of grammar which was proving more difficult to tackle.

She might be a slow reader, but she was getting through the stories. In fact, she needed to go to the secondhand bookstore at the back of the coffee shop in the village and pick up a few more.

With a romance novel in her hand, she headed eagerly back to the kitchen, looking forward to digging into dinner.

But, as she twirled the first piece of pasta around her fork, she heard a loud, sharp knock at the front door.

Who could it be? She wasn't expecting anyone, and no friends would drop by unannounced, in the rain, at this hour of the evening. Was there a crisis brewing that she didn't yet know about?

Abandoning her meal, she hurried to the door.

# CHAPTER THREE

To Olivia's surprise, Nadia was standing outside. She was swathed in a bright blue coat, holding a white umbrella in one hand and a shopping bag in the other.

"*Salve!* I am dropping by your house without an announcement," Nadia said, delivering the almost-accurate English expression with a grin as rain spattered onto her umbrella.

"Come in, come in, you must be freezing," Olivia invited her. She ushered Nadia into the hallway. Why was she here? Olivia wondered. It was unusual for her to make a surprise visit.

"On the way back from Florence, I visited one of the bakeries in town. They had these cookies on special, and they gave me two boxes for the price of one. Would you like one? They are canestrelli, one of my favorites!"

She placed the bag on the hall table and rummaged through it.

"Oh, yes, please!" The deliciously simple cookies, with a subtle almond flavor, were covered in powdered sugar and absolutely addictive. In fact, Olivia was sure they were one of the main reasons why she was still five stubborn pounds over her target weight, which she now measured daily on her new bathroom scale.

"Here you are." Nadia passed her the box. "The trip was successful and I got everything I need. I also learned something interesting, by chance, while I was at the bakery."

Her dark eyes gleamed. Nadia loved local gossip.

"What did you learn?" Olivia asked, fascinated by what it might be.

"Well," Nadia said, leaning in conspiratorially, even though the only possible person who might overhear their conversation was Pirate. Curled on the rug by the fireplace, he had given Nadia an inquisitive glance before resuming the important job of sleeping.

"What?"

"We were not the first choice for this wedding!" Nadia announced in a stage whisper.

Olivia's eyebrows shot up.

"Really?"

Nadia nodded. "The party originally wanted to go to Sovestro in Poggio."

"They're very famous." Olivia remembered they were one of the leading wineries in Chianti, located on a huge and well-established estate. "How did you find that out?"

"Marcello was in Forno Collina bakery last weekend. While there, he took a phone call from the father of the bride. It was a long call and Dino the baker couldn't help overhearing one or two words."

In her expressive way, Nadia managed to imply that the baker had eavesdropped shamelessly on the conversation.

"Marcello apparently fought very hard for them to come here." Nadia continued.

"I wonder why it was so important to him," Olivia said. "I know it's a big-ticket event, but we're not short of money right now at La Leggenda. Are we?" she added anxiously.

Nadia shrugged. "I do not know why he fought so hard for it. Our balance sheet is healthy, yes. Still, perhaps Marcello feels this could be a new line of business we must compete for."

Her eyes blazed. Nadia lived to win!

"At any rate," Nadia continued, "I was wondering what Sovestro is like. I have never been there. I was thinking one of us should go and spy. Just out of curiosity." She spread her hands innocently. "And although I am busy the whole day tomorrow, it is your day off. Do you have plans, or are you free?"

Olivia had been planning to spend the day doing some laundry and housecleaning, as well as a trip to the village for the much-needed groceries.

She realized now that she had gotten her priorities all wrong. A full day of boring housework? What had she been thinking? Of course chores and shopping could wait, because spying was far more important. She was enthralled by the idea of traveling to this idyllic venue and seeing how it compared with theirs.

"I'd love to have a look," Olivia said. "I'll report back on anything I find, in case it could be helpful to us. I'm sure we can pick up some pointers."

"I hope we can. And now, I must run," Nadia said.

"Thank you for the cookies."

Olivia waited while the vintner grabbed her now-lighter shopping bag and picked up her umbrella. A moment later, she'd rushed out into the windy, rainy evening.

Olivia took the cookie box into the kitchen, thinking hard.

Sovestro was a renowned destination. It was a must-see for many visitors to the region. And it was famously romantic.

It would be wrong, she decided, to visit this magnificent location on her own.

She couldn't help feeling a flutter of nerves as she started to message Danilo.

Would he be available at such short notice? That was the first question that burned in her mind.

The second was even more critical and it made her mouth dry with apprehension. She resolved that the time had come. At this enchanting venue, she would share with Danilo how she felt about him.

This would mean plunging into her first-ever romantic relationship in her new home country. It was a huge and significant step for her to take.

Would Danilo feel the same way about her?

Olivia shook her head. This was too important for a message. What if he didn't see it until later? He might already have made other plans. In fact, every second that passed made it more likely he would already have organized his day.

Olivia dialed his number and waited, feeling breathless, until he answered.

"*Salve*, Olivia!" He sounded delighted that she'd called.

"I was wondering if you're busy tomorrow?" she asked.

"Me? Busy? Well," he paused. "Let me see, let me see."

Olivia fidgeted impatiently, wondering what Danilo was doing. Paging through his diary, or looking in his phone calendar perhaps. Clearly, his day was not entirely free, so how much time did he have? Would it be enough?

"Yes, I am busy," Danilo said decisively, and Olivia felt her heart thump into her boots. She'd left the invitation too late. Of course Danilo would have other commitments. The trip to Sovestro seemed far less exciting than it had a minute ago, but as she got ready to reply with a fake cheerful "Never mind," he spoke again.

"I am busy doing something with you?" he asked.

There was a question in his voice, and laughter, too. Danilo was such a tease!

"Well, yes, I was hoping so!" Now she was smiling, a grin that stretched from ear to ear.

"So, tell me. What are we doing and when?"

"We're going to Sovestro in Poggio. Nadia wants us to have a look around and assess the place. Including a wine tasting, of course."

"That sounds wonderful. What time shall I pick you up?"

Olivia felt bad. It was her invite and she had been about to suggest she pick him up, but now it would seem rude to decline his generous offer. Plus, being the passenger meant that she got to see a lot more of Tuscany as they drove.

"Nine o'clock?"

"It's a date," Danilo said.

Olivia disconnected, beaming happily. She couldn't remember the last time she'd looked forward to an outing so much. He'd said a date. A date! She waltzed around the kitchen, watched curiously by Pirate, who had woken up to scrutinize her odd behavior.

"Did you hear that, Pirate? We're going on a date!"

Emboldened by the success of her phone call, Olivia scooped the cat up from his fireside resting place and rocked him in her arms.

Pirate looked alarmed, but—and this was a significant but—he stayed calm and kept his claws sheathed. Great progress was being made in the cat-lifting department!

She gently placed him back in his spot, giving him an affectionate back rub to apologize for the interruption.

Then Olivia returned to her dinner and her book.

She couldn't have chosen a better read than an Italian romance novel, she decided, crossing her fingers that the loving words and emotional descriptions in the printed pages might become part of her real life day tomorrow.

# CHAPTER FOUR

At nine a.m. next morning, Olivia was ready—lipsticked, perfumed, and with an extra layer of hairspray to prevent her shoulder-length blond tresses from frizzing if the breeze picked up. Pleased that it was a fine, sunny day, she hurried outside as Danilo's pickup drove through the gate.

"You have a new hairstyle," Olivia observed, as he climbed out of the car. "Your niece has done great work. I love it!"

From the previous shade of purple, Danilo's hair had been returned to its natural dark, shiny color. The cut was amazing. With tapered sides cut close to his head, the strength of his jaw was emphasized. The longer top and fringe fell just above his dark brows, accentuating the brown gleam of his eyes. Thinking of her novel reading last night, Olivia decided he looked like a romantic hero. She was about to tell him that, but stopped before the words came out, feeling self-conscious. In fact, she was starting to blush.

"It's nice that it looks a bit more natural." Danilo grinned. "Although I can never trust it won't be pink next time."

He hugged her and then kissed her in the now-traditional Italian-American greeting they had worked out.

"Before we go, I would love to see your barn," he said. "Do you have time to show me?"

"Yes!" Olivia agreed, delighted that Danilo wanted to have a look at its progress. She was proud that it had been transformed from a rubbish dump into a proper winemaking building again.

It had taken months of hard work for Olivia and Danilo to reduce the heap of rubble that had dominated the barn's spacious interior. In the process, Olivia had found one intact bottle of wine, and a fragment of a far older bottle. There were still a few barrow-loads left, but since most of the barn was cleared, swept, and pristine, Olivia hadn't worked on the remainder of the pile for a couple of weeks.

"So, no more treasures so far?" Danilo asked as they headed up the hill to the imposing building.

"Nothing yet," Olivia admitted, disappointed. "I am still hoping I might find a key for the locked storage room in the hills, but I don't think it's likely, with so little left to remove."

"You can get a locksmith?"

Olivia made a face.

"It's a vintage lock. I sent a photo to a local firm, who told me it's a handmade lock and to construct a key for it would be very time consuming and expensive. And they would have to force the door first to take a proper look. I don't want to break it." She sighed. "Clearly, the lock and key were very special and I can't help wondering if the key might not be lost, but rather hidden somewhere. Maybe even in the farmhouse."

"Are you not tempted to search immediately?" Danilo turned to her, his dark eyes shining.

"Nooo!" Olivia protested. "I've come to an arrangement with the spiders in my farmhouse. If they stay out of sight, I pretend they don't exist and leave them alone. The problem is that in all the places a key might be hidden, a spider might also be waiting!" She wrapped her arms around herself dramatically. "Like the shelf above the fireplace. I can't even begin to find the courage to stick my hand into that narrow gap."

Olivia swatted a stray hair away from her face. Suddenly it felt like a crawling spider.

"This is a serious problem," Danilo sympathized. "That shelf is a dangerous place. I would be scared to shine a light inside. Imagine the eyes looking back!"

Danilo shivered theatrically, his eyes wide. He was a bigger arachnophobe than Olivia, if that was even possible.

Olivia wasn't going to admit to him that she had another, more important reason for leaving that isolated storeroom untouched. The truth was that she couldn't bear the disappointment if this secret building, hidden among trees in the forested hillside, proved to be empty. Its mystery was part of the romance of her farm. Locked, it was full of enthralling possibilities, and contained whatever she imagined.

Unlocked, it might only contain dust and sadness and old spider webs.

Danilo's face brightened as they rounded the corner of the barn.

"You have installed doors! What a difference! They are beautiful."

Olivia was delighted that Danilo thought her junkyard find suited the barn. She'd spent hours sanding and painting them and the massive, brand new hinges that supported them had cost almost as much as the old, weathered doors.

"They're so heavy the handyman had to bring three assistants to help him hang them," Olivia explained. "But they're solid and although they are old, I'm hoping they have a good few decades of use still in them."

"You have cared for them well." Danilo ran an approving finger over the smooth, cream-colored paint. "They should definitely last."

Olivia was thrilled by the compliment, especially since, as a carpenter and woodworker by trade, Danilo was giving his professional opinion on her hard work.

When she opened the door, though, he frowned, looking puzzled.

"Where is your goat, Olivia? Her bed was in the corner."

He pointed to the now empty, well-swept and dust-free area near the doorway.

"I bought a Wendy house for Erba. She's living near the herb garden now and she seems very happy there. I decided to move her out of the barn, because—" Olivia felt her face redden. She was embarrassed on her goat's behalf. Didn't they say "like pet, like owner"?

She took a deep breath. "Because Erba has an obsession with wine!" she confessed. "It's her only real vice now, since she's gotten over her head-butting phase. She started out preferring cheap wine but she's developing more expensive tastes. I'm worried if she was left in here overnight she'd knock the fermentation vats over and find a way to get into them."

As she spoke, she glanced around. Proving her words to be true, Erba was already peeking curiously through the doorway.

"You see? There she is."

"Yes, your wine is acting like a magnet," Danilo observed. "We must be quick." He walked toward the vats.

"So, this is my ice wine," Olivia said proudly. "Made from grapes frozen on the vine. It took me a whole day to walk around my farm and find every single wild grapevine."

She remembered how tired she'd been the next day, after roaming over the hilly landscape, bending and stretching to pick every single plump, frosty bunch of grapes and add them to the increasingly heavy container. Every so often, she'd had to lug it to the barn, decant the grapes into the chest freezer so that they would remain frozen in the barn's sheltered confines, and start again.

"So you say ice wine is a sweet wine?" Danilo asked. "Like noble late harvest?"

"Yes." Olivia gestured proudly to the two large steel vats where her wine was undergoing its first fermentation. Once this was complete, she planned to transfer it into the oak barrels that she'd placed against the barn's back wall. "It's sweet because the grapes are very ripe by the time the frost comes, and the ice crystals freeze up the water in the grapes. So it's not as sweet as a noble late harvest, but definitely not a dry wine. Refreshingly sweet. I'm hoping mine will have a hint of strawberry."

"It sounds delicious," Danilo agreed, inspecting the shiny vats. "You are off to a good start. Now, you must be patient. I think that is the worst part."

"It is! I've been having nightmares that the vats have exploded, or that they've leaked, or that I left the door open overnight and Erba got in."

Olivia whirled around to see her goat advancing eagerly on the closest vat. "Out! You see? She's drawn to it."

Olivia hustled her goat out of the barn. Winemaking inspection was over. Not that there had been much to inspect, except the vats containing her hopes and dreams for a unique and delicious wine.

Olivia made sure the barn doors were properly closed before they headed to Danilo's car. Climbing in, she inhaled the scent of coffee from the to-go cups. Danilo always did things properly. It made him such a fun traveling companion.

As they drove out, she saw a couple of letters wedged in the side of her open gate.

"Please can you stop so I can grab these before they get rained on or blown away," Olivia asked, buzzing down the window. She'd gotten used to chasing stray envelopes down the road, and drying wet pages in the warming drawer. "I need to invest in a post box."

She hadn't even realized that the mail would be delivered to this remote countryside farm, but it seemed the Italian mail service was tireless in their work. Given their dedication, Olivia hadn't wanted to buy an ordinary mailbox, but to look for one more fun. Wine-themed, or perhaps goat-themed. She hadn't had a chance to shop around, and as a result, was constantly rounding up her runaway letters.

Leaning out the window, she grasped the small bundle.

"A bank statement, a pamphlet about investments—I must contact the bank and tell them to email me these—and a postcard from my mother!" Olivia laughed. "No chance of getting that emailed."

Quickly, not wanting to interrupt their fun outing, she glanced at the postcard.

"She's taken to sending me cards every time she travels. I don't know where she even finds them. Are postcards still a thing? This is from a resort in the Catskills. She went there for a friend's sixtieth birthday, and she sent it two weeks ago. That's international post for you!"

Since Danilo was stopped at the intersection to the main road, Olivia quickly showed him the postcard, of a gorgeous lakeside view, while reading the back aloud.

"*Hello, Olivia. Here we are, having a wonderful time. This resort has an excellent wine cellar. Last night we drank a Spumante Sweet sparkling wine from California.*"

Olivia rolled her eyes. "My mother doesn't share the same taste in wine I do, but she's trying to develop her repertoire," she explained to Danilo before continuing. "*I wish you were here, angel, and can't wait for your crazy jaunt in Italy to come to an end. There's a magnificent apartment for sale in town, just ten minutes' drive from us. It has views over the whole city and would be ideal for your new home! Your father caught a sixteen-inch fish yesterday, but released it. Perhaps he will catch it again today! Much love.*"

Olivia felt as if she needed to roll her eyes even harder after getting through that missive. Her mother's constant belief that Olivia would return "back home" was becoming tiresome, but she knew from experience there was no easy way of derailing her from the topic. Apart from staying in Italy and hopefully making a long-term success of her job and her winery-to-be.

Thank goodness the postcard was between Danilo and her so that he couldn't see her fed-up expression, Olivia thought.

"Mothers!" she said with a sigh, lowering the card. She actually didn't know where to start in explaining Mrs. Glass's quirky and stubborn character to Danilo. It would take the whole day.

She expected Danilo to offer laughing sympathy, but to her surprise, as he pulled onto the main road, he was oddly quiet and unsmiling. In fact, he didn't even acknowledge her words. It was as if she wasn't in the car at all.

Olivia felt a pang of unease. Why was Danilo suddenly so withdrawn, and why was the usually outspoken man not telling her what was bothering him?

She started to worry that their perfect day was going wrong.

# CHAPTER FIVE

As they neared the medieval town of San Gimignano where the winery was located, Olivia managed to put aside her worries about Danilo's unusual quietness. The town was enchanting, and possessed a fairytale character all of its own. Set in a rolling, mysterious-looking landscape, it was studded with stone buildings including a number of dramatic towers that seemed to glow in the low winter light.

She remembered from her reading that San Gimignano, known as the Town of the Fine Towers, was also referred to as the Manhattan of Tuscany thanks to its impressive skyline. What a thrill to view it in person, Olivia thought, sticking her arm out the window to get the perfect shot on her phone as they approached.

There was a luxurious-looking hotel at the foot of the hill, where Olivia was entranced to see a large, turquoise-blue swimming pool in pride of place among the historic stone buildings. She could imagine how this would appeal to visitors in the summer months.

Beyond the hotel was the small, family-owned Guardastelle vineyard. The neat rows of vines combed the hillside, rising from a bed of morning mist in the valley below.

Being in the middle of Italy's famous Chianti region, it was no surprise that this winery specialized in Chiantis, and Olivia couldn't wait to sample their quality wines.

"I read on their website that the tasting includes a vineyard tour, as well as olive oil tasting and snacks. Shall we do the tour?"

"A good idea," Danilo agreed. "That will occupy us for the whole morning."

He drove up the gravel driveway, lined with neatly trimmed hedges and flower beds that even in winter, looked colorful and welcoming. Olivia could imagine in summertime they would be filled with blossoms of every hue.

When they climbed out of the car, Olivia saw a smiling, curly-haired woman waiting at the winery's entrance. "Welcome to Guardastelle," she greeted them warmly. "I am Ricky, the sommelier. Are you here for the tasting, or the full vineyard tour?"

"The full tour, please," Olivia said, glancing at Danilo to check he was as excited as she was, and feeling disappointed to see that once again, he looked solemn and preoccupied.

She couldn't wait to head out into the vineyards and see how this estate farmed their grapes. She was sure she would pick up some valuable pointers for her own vines, and hoped that this educational tour would cheer Danilo up and help him forget his worries.

"Come this way. I will take you around the estate now. At this time of the year, we do not get so many people wanting to tour. Most prefer to sit inside, taste, and enjoy some food. I am pleased to have the chance to see my own vines, even though there are no grapes growing at this time!" She laughed.

"I notice you have a few north-facing fields," Danilo said, as the bubbly woman led the way, following a gravel path toward the first vineyard.

"That is so." Ricky smiled. "It took us a long while to work out which grapes preferred the north slopes, and which ones—obviously many more—loved the southern slopes. It was a good learning process for us, as we were able to get inside the heart of our grape plantations, and find out where they really wanted to be. Our production doubled when we solved this puzzle."

Olivia was captivated. This was incredibly useful information. The upside was that grapes would thrive in exactly the right locality for their characteristics. The downside, of course, was that it would probably take her another ten years to figure out her own farm. But every year would help. Knowing this would allow her to progress faster with her very hilly terrain which had a few north-facing slopes. Now, Olivia felt optimistic she could make use of them.

"Apart from sangiovese, which grapes do you use the most?" Olivia asked.

"Canaiolo nero, which is a fruity grape with a softer acidity, and ciliegiolo. They add freshness and liveliness to wine, and are particularly suitable for wines that will be consumed earlier, and not stored for long. Of course, colorino is also used to give a dark, rich color to our wines," Ricky explained.

When they reached the bottom of the slope, the checkerboard of vines gave way to a well-established grove of olive trees. These represented the second staple crop of Sovestro. They were a major producer and exporter of olive oil, and a tasting table was set up under an ancient, sprawling olive tree.

Olivia loved olive oil, and a day didn't ever go by without her consuming it in some form—as a flavorful salad dressing, drizzled onto bread or pasta, or used to add rich brownness to braised or broiled meat. What a treat to be able to taste this oil while standing in the shade of one of the trees it had come from. She thought having a tasting table set up was a wonderful idea, and something that they could offer at La Leggenda. It would add another dimension to their offering, and also provide a special experience for the guests who preferred not to drink wine.

As she savored the oils, dipping chunks of bread in each one to absorb the flavor and also the texture, Olivia felt as if she'd been transported a million miles away from all her worries.

With the simple perfection of the finely made oils, the pillowy bread with its crunchy crust, the golden bowls seeming to be filled with liquid sunlight, she felt as if she'd taken her own vacation, far away from the worries of reality.

"Are you enjoying our recce?" she asked Danilo.

"A recce?"

Although Danilo's English was good, there were certain terms he wasn't familiar with.

"It's short for 'reconnaissance.' It's originally an Army term. You visit a place to check it out."

As she was speaking, the word *ricognizione* jumped into her mind. She was sure this was the Italian word, which she must have picked up from her reading. If only she was brave enough to say it out loud, but she was sure her accent would sound stupid and awkward, instead of musical and attractive, like Danilo's spoken English.

Danilo nodded.

Feeling increasingly anxious, Olivia tried to draw more conversation out of him. She hoped that talking would cheer him up, and although she didn't want to ask outright, perhaps he might even share what was bothering him.

"How's your business going?" she asked him, hoping he would have exciting projects on the go, and that speaking about them might lift his mood. He could be busy with anything from crafting a child's doll house, to installing the shop fittings for a smart new store.

"It is going well," he said. "I have orders lined up for the next three months, two shops in neighboring towns to refit, and I am currently busy with a set of dining room chairs in a fantastic quality of mahogany. They are going to be beautiful."

26

To her relief, speaking about his passion and his trade, Danilo seemed more positive.

"Did you study woodworking at school? How did you learn the craft?" she asked.

"I used to spend hours doing it on weekends as a youngster. My dad was an engineer, and was forever tinkering with projects and ideas in his shed. I picked up that passion for inventing and creating from him. In fact, I also studied engineering, and then life took me in a new direction. I worked on huge container ships, sailing the oceans, for close to ten years."

"Really?" Olivia was fascinated. This was a side of Danilo's life she'd never known about, or even imagined.

She took another piece of bread, dipping it in the golden oil and munching as she listened to his story.

"The pay was excellent. I always wanted to make my fortune while adventuring, and this was my chance. It was different than I expected, though, being on a ship in the middle of a vast ocean. Container ships do not stop at any of the pretty ports, like cruise ships do. And I was far away from Tuscany, and from friends, from our hills and villages and vineyards," he said, sounding regretful.

Olivia nodded, understanding how he must have felt. Staring around, she found that she couldn't imagine saying goodbye to this exquisite landscape. Not for any length of time—certainly not for ten years!

"It must have been an adventure, but difficult," she suggested.

"Yes. That describes it nicely. I was happy, yet sad."

"Why did you come back?" she asked, but Danilo shrugged, and Olivia saw to her concern that his frown had returned.

"Various reasons. None that would make for good conversation now," he said abruptly.

Olivia bit her lip. She'd thought she was getting somewhere, and now Danilo seemed to have landed firmly back in his bad mood again.

"Are you ready for the wine tasting now?" Ricky asked, and Olivia stood up, glad that the uncomfortable silence had been interrupted.

"Yes. In fact, I can't wait," she said, and Ricky smiled.

"We have three wines available for tasting today. Two Chianti varieties and our white blend."

Olivia was impressed when Ricky poured the wine. Never mind tasting portions—at this winery, full, generous glasses were supplied.

The second Chianti was her favorite of the day. Fruity, large, bold, and managing to be almost, but not quite, brash, she felt that if the wine was a real-life character, she would have had a serious crush on it.

Danilo sighed, tilting his glass to admire the ruby glow of his portion. Olivia felt happy to see he was appreciating the wine. Perhaps his mood was finally lifting. If these excellent wines didn't improve it, she had no idea what could.

"Magnifico," he said. "One day, I dream of making a wine of this quality from my vines."

"How long have you been making your own wine for?" she asked.

"This is only my second year. The first year I made a mistake and ruined the entire batch."

Olivia shook her head in sympathy. It was every winemaker's nightmare when that happened.

"I make such small quantities that it is really no more than a hobby," Danilo explained. "Something else to do with my hands, in between sawing, sanding, and polishing. I think I prefer woodworking, though, as it is more predictable. Each year as I begin making my homemade wine, my worries begin at the same time."

"I sympathize," Olivia said. She guessed the process would never become easy and would always be fraught with anxiety, whether you were making a few bottles for home consumption, or aiming to become a commercial vineyard.

She drained the last delightful sip of Chianti.

As soon as they had finished, their attentive host was ready to guide them on the next step of their tasting tour.

"There will be a light lunch with cold meats, homemade bread and pasta, olives and local honey, and more wine of your choice, up at the main building." Ricky smiled. "If you continue along this path, it is a scenic walk, and the views are spectacular."

The word *spettacolare* leaped into Olivia's mind. She was starting to automatically translate from English to Italian. That must mean solid progress in her language learning journey.

Olivia thanked her again before she and Danilo headed along the path. What a treat to be strolling through this exquisite estate on such a perfect winter's day. As she stared out over the vistas that opened up with each twist and turn the path took, Olivia was reminded again why she'd fallen so deeply in love with Tuscany.

And, thinking about affairs of the heart, as they admired the views, Olivia slipped her arm around Danilo's waist. When he wrapped his arm around her in return, his touch made her heart beat faster, and Olivia wondered if Danilo was thinking the same way she was—that here, in this idyllic destination, was the right moment for their relationship to reach the next level.

Perhaps that was why he had been so quiet all day, Olivia suddenly realized. After all, starting a romance with a good friend was a big step to take, as the friendship could be jeopardized if it didn't work out. Perhaps he was as worried as she about the outcome.

That must be it! Olivia felt massively relieved to have worked out the reason for Danilo's strange behavior.

She decided to take the lead. After all, she was the one who'd suggested the outing.

Her opportunity came a few minutes later, when the treed path curved once again and they reached a clearing that provided the most breathtaking view yet.

"Every time we climb higher, these lookout points become more amazing," Olivia shared. She twined her arm around Danilo's waist again, feeling her heart soar as he embraced her in turn.

"It is a treat to be here. It reminds me again why I returned to this region," Danilo confessed. "It is easy to fall in love with the life and landscapes here."

There, he'd said it. The word "love."

"I think I'm falling for more than that," she said softly. "Danilo, I've wanted to tell you how I feel for a while. And I think now's the right time."

Olivia turned to him, feeling him instinctively draw closer to her. She felt breathless with the expectation of what her words would bring. She'd noticed his mouth of course, but had never taken in how perfectly sculpted his lips were. Now, he wasn't smiling, but was staring down at her with an expression that was serious and intense and—and something else.

Olivia closed her eyes, knowing that the next moment would bring the kiss she'd been waiting for, and it would change her whole world. She was sure Danilo must be able to feel how fast her heart was hammering. Starting a new relationship was exciting and wonderful— but it was also stressful and nerve-racking, she remembered.

Especially when the kiss she'd been expecting didn't come!

Olivia's eyes flew open in concern.

Danilo was staring out over the view, his head raised as if he hadn't noticed or taken in her body language.

He stood in silence and his jaw looked set and firm.

He'd understood what she meant, Olivia was certain of it. Understood, and rejected her invitation to take things further.

Now, Olivia felt as if her stomach had tumbled all the way down that steep, panoramic hill, and ended up in the scenic, winding river at the bottom.

She felt her cheeks burn with embarrassment. Quickly, she let go of him.

"My goodness, I felt dizzy there for a moment," she said hurriedly, trying to explain her actions in a way that wouldn't cause even more awkwardness. "All that wonderful wine tasting, and then looking out over this steep hill—phew. I hope I didn't grab you too hard, as I felt I was about to fall down the hillside." She fanned her face energetically. "Let's get a move on. I'm sure some food will settle my stomach."

Staring firmly in front of her, she powered up the path ahead of Danilo.

She wasn't sure how she would eat the food she'd spoken so enthusiastically about. Her appetite had sunk to the bottom of that pretty, winding river, too. She had no idea when, or if, she'd get it back again after that romantic moment had turned into such an appalling disaster.

What had gone wrong, she wasn't sure!

She must have misread the dynamic between them completely and now felt like the biggest idiot in the whole of Tuscany.

"Lunch!" she announced in tones of fake cheerfulness, heading into the wine tasting hall.

She'd set such a pace up the hill that she'd outdistanced Danilo. Olivia had already sat down before he made his way inside. Or maybe he'd held back deliberately to put some distance between them, she thought.

Olivia wasn't certain of much. In her confusion, all she was sure of was that in terms of romance, this outing had been the biggest possible catastrophe.

Even so, she knew she couldn't show him how hurt and upset his rejection had left her. That would make things far worse. Although she was shaking with shock and felt like crying, Olivia resolved to put on a brave face.

Somehow, she would have to force down a whole plate of food to prove how well she felt after her momentary dizziness on the hillside.

After that, she had no idea what to do.

She'd never imagined that the day out, which she'd had such high hopes for, would end in such bitter disappointment. Clearly, Danilo didn't want to get romantically involved with her and was also not willing to share his reasons.

She might never find out why, and worst of all, after this disaster, she had no idea whether they could resume the warm, easy friendship that had meant so much to her.

Or had her reckless foray into romance destroyed that too?

# CHAPTER SIX

Olivia woke the next morning to the sound of cold, spattering rain.

"Aaargh," she sighed, sitting up and staring at the chilly downpour. Like her romantic life, the weather had taken a drastic turn for the worse.

"Pirate, I have no idea what to do," she confessed to her cat in a shaking voice.

Stroking him, she felt glad of the comfort his soft fur provided, and his sweet new habit of rubbing his head against her hand. At least her cat's loyalty was unwavering. Pirate was taming into a wonderful feline companion. In fact, having his entertaining black-and-white presence in her life was making Olivia wonder why she'd never had a cat before.

They were the best pets. The best! She could see that Pirate sympathized with her predicament.

"I don't know if Danilo and I can still be friends. At the moment it feels too awkward, and I'm too hurt. I might say something I'd regret. I don't think there's any coming back from what happened yesterday. I'm not even sure *what* happened, or why," she confided to her understanding feline.

Climbing out of bed, she did her best to put her gloomy thoughts aside. Today was the wedding rehearsal. It was likely to be a long, demanding day and she'd be astounded if it went without any hitches.

At least she'd be too busy to worry about Danilo.

After getting dressed and doing her hair extra smartly, Olivia headed downstairs and gave her goat an extra portion of carrots. She topped up Pirate's kibble and water, so that he wouldn't go hungry if she arrived back late. Sitting in her kitchen, she drank a cup of coffee, trying not to think about the fact that Danilo had given her this packet of beans.

Then she stepped out of the farmhouse, taking a deep breath of the fresh, tangy air which to Olivia always seemed to carry the undertone of herbs.

"I just have to make the best of it," she reminded herself. "Things happen for a reason. Perhaps we can start again. Rebuild our friendship."

She swung her purse over her shoulder, locked the door, and headed purposefully for her car. Erba jumped in the back, she scrambled into the front, and they drove to work.

As soon as she pulled up in the parking lot, she saw the place was already abuzz. Two catering trucks were parked outside the restaurant entrance, and Olivia was sure that Gabriella must have been toiling over her stoves for hours already. Marcello's SUV was covered in frost, which told Olivia he must have been out and about before sunrise.

As she slammed her car door, she was greeted by a shouted, "Hello!"

Jean-Pierre had arrived.

The lanky, passionate young Frenchman looked every inch the part. His dark hair was neatly gelled, and he wore black pants and a smart gray and white striped dress shirt.

"Is this not wonderful?" Jean-Pierre said breathlessly. "Our first big wedding is almost here! Imagine if we can do more such events?"

Was this the difference being twenty-one and thirty-four? Olivia wondered. She was burdened by concerns about what the day would bring. And yet, dewy-eyed Jean-Pierre was bursting with hope and optimism.

Olivia decided she needed to follow his lead.

"It's going to be an exciting day," she agreed, heading into the winery, which was already cozily warm. Fires burned in the hallway and tasting room hearths, with piles of wood stacked near each. Olivia was beginning to understand why Marcello had started so early. There were a multitude of details to consider.

Antonio, the younger Vescovi brother, was supervising the layout of tables and chairs in the restaurant. It looked magnificent. Twelve eight-seater tables were symmetrically arranged in the spacious room. Along the back wall was the bridal table, seating twelve. The white-covered tables and blue-white chairs, each with a pale pink ribbon knotted around their back, looked welcoming and elegant. The bright furniture gave the restaurant a warm and friendly ambience.

The ceremony itself would take place in the restaurant's covered verandah area. Rows of neatly arranged chairs had been set up, and Marcello and Antonio had constructed a flower-twined archway for the bride and groom to stand underneath. With the glass sliding doors around the verandah closed, this would be a cozy place for the couple to say their vows while everyone was treated to a panoramic view of the Tuscan countryside beyond.

Olivia was amazed that all the chairs and tables fitted perfectly into the allocated sections. It meant that La Leggenda was versatile enough to accommodate large groups on such occasions.

Thinking back to yesterday at Sovestro, not that she wanted to think about it ever again, Olivia realized that La Leggenda was substantially bigger. Although it was stunningly beautiful and exceptionally friendly, she didn't think that the boutique winery in Poggio could have accommodated the same numbers so easily. Probably, Marcello had used the extra space as his main selling point.

"What shall we do first?" Jean-Pierre asked eagerly.

"We need to get the wines ready, set out everything for the after-party, and make sure the table decorations are perfect."

As they worked their way through the long list of chores, Olivia found that the time flew by. There was so much to do. The tasting room floor had to be mopped and polished, the hundreds of wine glasses set out, and the party's music playlist compiled. In the restaurant, the fancy menus needed straightening in their holders and the crystal beads strewn over the tables. They did look pretty, Olivia thought.

Sidling up beside her, Jean-Pierre glanced meaningfully in the direction of the kitchen.

"Something smells so good in there! I am starving!"

Olivia suddenly realized how hungry she was. Delicious smells were wafting from the kitchen. Gabriella had devised a sumptuous menu. As well as preparing the three-course dinner for the twenty rehearsal guests, she was also cooking most of the food for the full wedding party, to be reheated and presented for the main meal tomorrow.

Unable to stop herself, Olivia peeked into the kitchen, drawn by the mouthwatering aroma of baking bread. Inside, organized chaos prevailed. Crusty ciabatta loaves were set to cool on the counter, and inside the ovens, rows of slow-roasted free range chickens were cooking to a state of flavorful tenderness.

Gabriella herself was stirring a pot of polenta, frowning in concentration as she poured in what must have been a pint of cream and a brick of grated Parmesan. Olivia was certain it would pair perfectly with the other elements of the main course—roasted Mediterranean vegetables to accompany the chicken, and gravy laced with red sangiovese wine.

"Can we steal a small pizza?" Jean-Pierre whispered, peeking over her shoulder.

Topped with mini burger patties, rib meat, tacos, and chunks of steak, the pizza bases looked perfectly browned. The cheese was gooey and melty, and Olivia had tasted Gabriella's tomato reduction before and knew it was a flavor-packed triumph.

The problem was that they were on trays close to where Gabriella was working, together with the other, more traditional starters—Parma ham and melon skewers, bowls of olives with herbs and chunks of feta, and green asparagus spears with a creamy dipping sauce.

Gabriella turned and saw her peeking.

"The cake's incredible!" Olivia commented hurriedly, walking into the kitchen to stand on her opposite side. "It's a work of art. I'm sure the bride will be thrilled."

The multi-tiered cake was set on a shelf on the far side of the kitchen. It had been frosted in pale pink and festooned with edible glitter. Perched atop the smallest layer, a miniature bride and groom figurine surveyed the kitchen. Olivia thought that even at this far distance, the bride's expression and attitude seemed disdainful.

Gabriella shrugged, waving her spoon expressively.

"Through the grapevine, I have heard that this bride is—how you say in English? Bridezilla? She will find something she does not like, and make a fuss."

Olivia's eyes widened. How had Gabriella discovered this? Perhaps someone had warned her while discussing the food arrangements.

"Surely she can't find any fault," Olivia protested. "The tables are decorated down to the last footnote, this food is a feast fit for royalty, Marcello has organized the sound system for the party afterwards, and I've put together a fabulous playlist. What is there to complain about?"

"We all need to be careful," Gabriella warned darkly. "Things could very easily go wrong."

Glancing innocently past Gabriella, Olivia saw that Jean-Pierre had been successful. He was disappearing from the kitchen and heading toward the tasting room with a small stack of the pizzas stashed inside his jacket.

Hungrily, Olivia hurried to join him, straightening one of the pink menu cards on the silver place mats as she passed.

*"Angelique Miller and Terenzio Jones Welcome You To Share Their Special Day!"*

Terenzio sounded Italian so she guessed this was why the party had chosen Tuscany. Perhaps he or his mother had even been born in Italy. That fact made Olivia feel better, because with an Italian background, he would understand the local customs and might even speak the language. That would be helpful, especially since he was marrying Bridezilla with all her unreasonable demands.

In the tasting room, Olivia accepted two of the five mini pizzas that Jean-Pierre had stolen. Hiding out behind the counter, they stuffed their faces with the tasty treats.

After she'd wiped her fingers and checked her lipstick, Olivia glanced at the clock on the wall and saw that it was already four-thirty p.m. In half an hour, the rehearsal party would start to arrive.

In fact, sooner! To her alarm, Olivia saw a blond woman march in.

She was wearing a white fluffy jacket over a pastel-colored gown that looked designer and expensive. Her hair was a symphony of tonged curls. Her sandals sparkled with Swarovski crystals.

With a start, Olivia realized that the tilt of this woman's chin was identical to the figurine on the cake! Gabriella must have worked for hours over the frosting artwork, working from a photograph, and knowing her, Olivia was sure there had been more than a little malice in her faithful interpretation.

An older woman with a similar hairstyle, who was clearly her mother, walked by her side. Following behind was a portly, stern-faced man that Olivia guessed was the father of the bride.

"Hello!" Olivia rushed to greet her. "You must be Angelique. Welcome to La Leggenda. I'm Olivia Glass, the sommelier."

"Hi, Olivia!" To her relief, Angelique sounded normal and in fact, very sweet. "It's wonderful to be here. These are my parents, Karen and Malcolm Miller."

"Welcome, welcome!" Olivia enthused, but Karen was frowning.

"We booked an authentic Italian experience. I wasn't aware that there were going to be American staff here."

Malcolm nodded. "I'm beginning to think we should have stayed in New Jersey!" he said, giving a humorless chuckle. "It would have been cheaper, too!"

"Er—we're multinational," Olivia explained hurriedly, her heart plummeting as she feared she would inadvertently wreck this joyous occasion. "I help with any communication needs as well as serving wine, as we have a lot of international tourists visiting the estate. This is Jean-Pierre, my colleague." Hurriedly, she waved her assistant over, hoping that his exuberantly French accent would not further disappoint the Millers in their search for authentic Italy.

"Well, it's lovely to meet you, Olivia, and how thoughtful of the winery to have hired an English speaker," Angelique said. "Not that we need one, as Terenzio is very fluent in Italian."

"Yes, yes, exactly, he knows many of the words," her mother agreed, but she was distracted by Jean-Pierre's effervescent welcome.

"*Bonjour, buon giorno,* beautiful people, welcome to the winery," her assistant announced.

Clearly, his French panache had saved the day because the Millers' expressions brightened.

"Come this way, with me, so that we may introduce you to Marcello, the oldest of the Vescovis who own this estate," Jean-Pierre invited them. "He will be delighted to meet you, but has been momentarily delayed in his office while resolving a tiny issue with the chocolate fountain, which the suppliers were not aware should have used pink chocolate. It is all in order now and I believe the delivery van is on the way."

Jean-Pierre beckoned them toward the office, but Angelique lagged behind.

"I just want to check that all the table decorations are as they should be," she confided to Olivia in a sugary stage whisper. "I know my parents are all about the international experience, but I personally feel that if instructions get lost in translation, it'll be a disaster waiting to happen. And"—she lowered her voice even more—"I don't trust Continentals!"

Olivia blinked, not sure what to say in response to this at all. It was better to keep her mouth shut and simply smile, she decided.

"In fact, I'm relieved to find you here," Angelique continued. "You will be my go-to person so that I don't have to waste any time repeating myself to someone who misunderstands me—or deliberately refuses to understand!" She gave a tinkly laugh.

Olivia smiled again, hoping the expression gave away none of her consternation. This woman, who appeared saccharine sweet, was a demon in curvy, blond guise. And worse still, she'd just appointed Olivia as her BFF and go-to person if she had a quibble with any of the distrustful Continentals who comprised the winery's entire remaining staff!

"I hope I can help everything run smoothly," Olivia replied diplomatically. Anything to make this a success. "I understand how much this means to you. You want the very best for all your guests and to enjoy your special day!"

Angelique's pink lips curved in a sweet smile. To Olivia's relief, she'd said exactly the right thing to placate her. In fact, Angelique slipped a friendly arm around her waist.

"I can see you understand how things are!" she praised Olivia, while pacing toward the restaurant. There, she gazed intently at the tables.

"If I could draw your attention to one small detail." Angelique pointed a coral-manicured finger at the display. "I see you have festooned the tables with crystal beads. They are very pretty and I'm not saying you should remove them, but where are the crystal bears I asked for?"

"Crystal bears?" Olivia goggled at her in horror. She'd spent hours staring at that scrawled list and had still gotten it wrong. How was that even possible? Who in their right mind would actually want crystal bears as part of their wedding décor? Crystal? Bears? What? The?

Nadia had shopped yesterday. The budget had been blown to smithereens, and every person at the winery would be packing twenty-four hours of work into an eighteen-hour day tomorrow.

"You know, it seems that there were unfortunately no crystal bears to be found in Florence," she tried nervously. "I understand that in this local part of the world, it's all about the beads. It's not the same as back in New Jersey."

Angelique considered her words, still with that saccharine smile in place.

Then she squeezed Olivia's waist. Olivia tried not to flinch as her pointy nails dug in.

"I understand," she said.

Olivia's stomach flip-flopped in relief. Prematurely, as it happened.

"However," Angelique added, and now her voice was like icy sugar. Or sugar laced with arsenic. At any rate, there was a highly unpleasant note audible in her light, high-pitched tone.

"However, this is my wedding." She tapped her finger on her chest in case Olivia was under the misconception that it was anyone else's wedding. "And I want things the way I want them. Remember, I work for debt collectors. Mornings only. I do it to keep myself busy, not because I need the salary."

Her smile was syrupy as she leaned forward and whispered in Olivia's ear.

"They know nasty, and I've learned it from them, and I won't hesitate to get nasty with you, if anything should go wrong."

Whirling around, she headed toward Jean-Pierre and her parents, crying out, "Wait for me! I want to be the first to shake Marcello's hand!"

Olivia stared down at the shocking pink serviette, folded into the shape of a swan.

She'd just landed herself in a terrible predicament. Her new BFF would have the knives, or kneecap busters, out for her personally if anything was not up to scratch.

There was an hour to go until the rehearsal and twenty-three hours until the wedding began.

Was there any way of saving this worsening situation?

# CHAPTER SEVEN

Olivia didn't have time to dwell on the serious and unsolvable crystal bear predicament. From the entrance hall, a chorus of excited women's voices rang out. More guests had arrived, and anxiety flared inside Olivia as she hurried over, her plastic smile glued in place. She hoped the new arrivals weren't as hell bent on having a totally authentic experience.

Olivia met six breathless, giggling young women at the door.

"Hello! We're late!" the tallest and slimmest of the six greeted her. "We were supposed to get here before Angelique, but we took a wrong turn and ended up in some tiny village with walls on either side of the road. We dented the rental car about eight times trying to turn around. This area is so confusing and small! My name's Cassidy."

"Hi, Cassidy," Olivia greeted the friendly brunette. Luckily, Cassidy didn't blink at her American accent.

"This is Jewel." Cassidy squeezed the shoulder of the plump, red-haired woman on her right. "And this is Dinah." She slung a friendly arm around the petite, dark-haired woman on her left. "This is Molly and this is Madeline, and this is Miranda." She waved at the three chestnut-haired women following, who ranged from tall to short. "We're so stoked to be here! First time in Italy for all of us, isn't it, ladies?"

"We're gonna have such a party!" Jewel announced, shaking back her gorgeous, russet locks.

"Well," Dinah cautioned, "our first job is to look after our wonderful bride. Let's not forget that, girlfriends!"

All the others looked taken aback, as if they'd forgotten that was on the agenda at all.

Privately, Olivia didn't think Angelique needed looking after. If anything, the bridesmaids' role should be to protect the general public, starting with herself, from the psychopathic blonde.

Crystal bears? Where to begin!

What kind of bears did the bride-to-be even want?

Polar? Koala? Teddy? Gummy?

40

Olivia was too scared to ask for specifications. Any details would only reduce her chances of finding something that might possibly fit the bill.

She dragged herself back to her current situation, aware the bridesmaids were watching her expectantly.

"Angelique is over there." She pointed to the corridor, where she could hear the sound of voices raised in welcome. Marcello's voice rang out, deep and resonant. She was sure with his good looks and gorgeous accent he would impress the scary Angelique and her hard-to-please parents.

The bridesmaids rushed off and Olivia stared after them with interest. They couldn't have been more different in height, shape, and coloring. She sure hoped there wasn't a one-cut-fits-all bridesmaids dress.

Olivia had never been a bridesmaid. Perhaps her early near-miss with marriage had scarred her, and her friends had sensed that she was not the right person for the job.

Standing in the tasting room, she remembered that she, too, had been an excited bride-to-be, for a very brief while. After a two-month whirlwind romance, she and the dashing, twenty-three-year-old Ward had set a wedding date and made arrangements. Olivia recalled her mother had been delighted, yet worried. After all, it was a *wedding*—so *exciting*! And to such a *nice* and *well-mannered, in fact very charming* young man! But Olivia was so *young*, and was she certain about this *lifelong commitment*? Did he and she not want to *live together* for a while, even though some might *frown upon it*, to *make sure*?

It was one of the times her mother had, in fact, had a point. She'd been totally right and twenty-two-year-old Olivia had been completely wrong. She'd been blown away by Ward's handsome looks, and his affable charm, and his ability to become instant best buddies with everyone he met. All her friends had adored him! As it turned out, that had not, in fact, been a good thing.

Olivia wrenched her mind away from the memories because more guests were walking in.

This tall, firm-jawed, and muscle-bound man striding toward her must surely be the groom. He was very handsome, and as he gazed confidently around him, Olivia sensed that he knew it. With a start, she realized he reminded her of Ward.

Yet again, Olivia had to derail her thoughts. What on earth was she doing, harking back to such a tumultuous time in her life? Perhaps the

41

catastrophe with Danilo yesterday had caused her to dwell on other romantic disasters. She told herself firmly to stop it. All her energy must be focused on the wedding party and their needs.

With a smile, she stepped forward.

"Terenzio Jones? Welcome to La Leggenda."

"Or, as his friends and parents call him, Terence," one of the young men following him joked. "I'm his brother, Lance. These are Terence's best friends, Kyle, Rog, and Don."

Terenzio—or Terence—pointedly ignored his brother's input as he clasped her hand in a firm, almost crushing grasp.

His parents were heading straight over to where Marcello was addressing the bride's family and bridesmaids. They hadn't bothered to greet her at all. Although she could see a family likeness in the tall, graying Mr. Jones, Mrs. Jones looked much younger than her husband and nothing like Terenzio. Olivia wondered if she was his stepmother.

"Angelique said she wanted crystal bears on the tables. I'm sourcing them tomorrow," Olivia told Terenzio, hoping he didn't notice her redden at this promise that might be just hot air. "I was wondering what significance they have for you two, to guide me in choosing the perfect pieces?"

Terenzio looked confused.

"Bears?" he asked.

"Yes."

He replied rather rudely. "And I must know this, how? Maybe she thought they'd look good. She's picky about what she likes. I don't know why she wants bears, but if she wants bears, I'd recommend sourcing the right bears, and the right sizes, and the right quantities! Or else!"

He grinned at her—a supercilious expression—before sauntering over to join the others.

"*Buenos giornos*," she heard him say.

Olivia looked around in surprise.

Was Terenzio joking? This was a very basic Italian greeting, which she'd managed to pick up on her very first day. And he'd gotten it completely wrong! She'd thought he was Italian and had even picked up a trace of accent over and above the strong New Jersey drawl. Was that accent fake, and was Terenzio, possibly christened Terence, pretending?

Marcello stared at him and Olivia saw confusion flit briefly across his face before he grasped what the groom was attempting to say.

"*Buon giorno*," he replied with a warm smile.

"I feel delighted to be among my fellow countrymen again! Ever since my great-great-great-grandfather arrived from Italy and landed on American shores after disembarking from the—the—from one of the important ships back then, I feel I have never lost my roots," Terenzio pontificated. "I feel such a strong affinity with this place it's almost as if I have been here before. Cellular memory! I believe one of my ancestors was in charge of this winery! More than likely he was your great-great-great-grandfather's boss." He grinned conspiratorially at Marcello. "Most probably, you should be paying me some commission on your wines!"

Since La Leggenda's main building had been constructed by the family in the early 1900s, and Terenzio was sixth-generation American, that was all but impossible. Olivia didn't know what to say as Terenzio turned and marched down the corridor.

"I remember an herb garden being down here. I feel it in my genes."

He returned a moment later, looking puzzled.

"I see it is a men's restroom now. But anyway, I feel you are part of my Italian brotherhood. I am sure we made the right choice coming here, even though only time will tell, and we will reserve judgment until after the wedding. Then we will see if you guys have truly given us the best experience, without messing up or doing anything wrong." His chin jutted aggressively as he spoke.

"We welcome you, and will do everything to make your special day most memorable," Marcello emphasized.

Olivia wondered if he was starting to regret having fought so hard to host this event. She knew she was. Terenzio seemed arrogant and dislikeable. What with his critical attitude, Angelique's sugar-coated threats, and her obnoxious and hard-to-please parents, she was dreading that this wedding would end up being an expensive, acrimonious disaster.

The guests had only just arrived, and she was already fretting about how she could do damage control if the worst happened.

This did not bode well, Olivia feared.

# CHAPTER EIGHT

Dragging her thoughts away from the disturbing attitude of the bride, groom, and parents, Olivia saw more guests were arriving. She and Jean-Pierre rushed over to welcome the blond duo who looked like Angelique's brother and sister. They were escorting two gray-haired ladies who seemed to be the grandmothers of the bride and groom. This truly was a multigenerational wedding. At least that was traditional, Olivia thought, even if none of the guests had set foot in Tuscany before.

And, to her relief, both the grandmas were smiling and looked pleased to be here.

With a click, Antonio activated the sound system.

"Welcome, welcome! We will be playing some light music while you finalize the arrangements for tomorrow, rehearse your ceremony, and enjoy some drinks. Dinner will be served at seven p.m. in the restaurant, followed by a wonderful party here in the tasting room."

The murmur of conversation suddenly became muted and expectant. Olivia hoped that the wedding party were abandoning their critical demeanors and picking up on the venue's incredible ambience.

Watching the families as they headed through to the verandah, Olivia started feeling more optimistic. She could hear them exclaiming as they discovered the archway and took in the views. The atmosphere had warmed up and the vibe seemed more positive now. She was certain dinner would be mouthwatering, and with any luck, this rehearsal would go without a hitch.

Remembering that pre-rehearsal drinks must now be served, she rushed through to the restaurant and filled a tray with glasses of white, red, rosé, and sparkling wine, together with a pitcher of fruit juice for those who preferred to mix their flavors.

Olivia circulated among the guests on the verandah, enjoying the babble of voices, the shrieks of laughter, and the cries of delight as people noticed some of the small details the La Leggenda team had worked so hard over. Finally, she began to relax. This was what she had visualized the rehearsal would be like. Of course there would be a

44

few stumbling blocks at the start. That didn't mean it would ruin the entire wedding weekend.

Firmly, Olivia pushed the thoughts of crystal bears to the back of her mind. If Angelique had a good enough experience tonight, perhaps she would forget all about them.

"Wine? Metodo Classico?" she asked Terenzio.

"Do you have sparkling wine?" he asked.

"Yes, that's Metodo—" Thinking fast, Olivia changed what she was going to say. "Yes, here you are. Italian champagne."

"Italian champagne. Champagno Italiano!" He raised his glass and clinked with his friends, spilling some of the sparkling wine on Olivia's shoulder.

With both hands on the tray, she couldn't do anything and just had to let it soak in, while feeling irritated.

Then a stern finger tapped Olivia's shoulder blade and she and the tray turned carefully around.

"Hello, young lady. I am Terence's grandmother, Brittany Jones. My family usually refers to me as Gramma B, but he has asked that people call me Nonna for this event."

The forceful-looking, purple-haired woman sounded as if she was all out of patience with her grandson's pretentious ways and his fixation on appearing as Italian as possible.

"What can I get you to drink?" Olivia changed the topic to a happier one. "We have fruit juices and sodas available, or I could even make you a cup of tea."

Gramma B, aka Nonna, snorted.

"Tea! Do you not have whiskey? My nightly tipple is a whiskey and soda. Double whiskey, easy on the soda, one cube of ice if your water's drinkable here. If not, hold the ice, I'm up often enough at night without the runs." She cackled.

"Yes, yes!" Olivia found herself grinning with pleasure at Nonna's straightforwardness. "I'll get you the whiskey straight away. Our water is high quality and you can safely have ice with any drink you choose," she reassured her.

Putting down the tray, she hastened to the bar and fixed Nonna her drink, pouring generously and guessing that skimping on the whiskey would have even worse consequences than being unable to provide crystal bears.

After handing Nonna her whiskey, Olivia attended to the other grandma.

Angelique's grandmother, Petra, had the same quiet way about her as her granddaughter but Olivia sensed she was a softer character. She was also rather deaf.

"What would you like to drink?" Olivia asked, smiling.

"The pink?" Granny Petra peered into the restaurant. "Well, dear, I can't say I like the pink. I don't approve, and have always felt weddings should be white. When I was a girl, that was the norm."

Olivia decided to try another angle.

"Would you like some wine? Champagne? Lemonade?"

"Lemonade, thank you."

Olivia brought the lemonade, and as the rehearsal run-through began, she refilled the trays and put the final touches to the after-party venue.

The rehearsal ran surprisingly smoothly. Either the guests didn't care as much as they thought they did after a glass of wine, or else they magically got everything right the first time. Either way, all the preparations and practice were soon wrapped up. People gravitated to the bar where Paolo, bartender for the night, was doing a brisk trade, particularly in beers and whiskey. Gabriella began carrying the trays of starters from the warming oven and the fridge and setting them out on the tables. Antonio turned the lights down a notch, and the music up a little, and a festive atmosphere filled the winery.

As everyone sat down for dinner, Olivia hovered in the doorway, watching the celebrations in relief. After a rocky start, proceedings had smoothed out. Perhaps she'd been wrong to dread this occasion so much.

It was turning into a happy, joyous, and seamless experience, she was starting to realize.

The starters were a huge hit. Everyone guzzled the pizzas, and Olivia started to feel guilty that she'd conspired with Jean Pierre to steal a few of them. She was comforted by the fact that there was so much food to follow that the diners would not regret having had a few pizzas less than they'd wanted.

With the food gone, she helped a pleased-looking Gabriella carry empty plates back to the kitchen. Olivia had thought that the main entrees would follow immediately, but instead the guests made their way to the bar again.

It was getting decidedly louder in here, Olivia realized. Twenty people were making noise enough for fifty. The bridesmaids were screaming with laughter as they downed a round of Bailey's shots. The

46

groomsmen were guffawing at the punch line of a joke told by Terenzio.

Luckily the older generations were heading back to the table with their drinks, talking ever more loudly as the general noise levels increased.

Olivia overhead Terenzio's father conversing with Angelique's mother.

"My company is 'Wines of the World,' but we do beer and spirits too, and luxury cigars. We've been in business for more than three decades now, and in the past few years, we have grown phenomenally and added five new countries to our network."

The two passed by and Olivia didn't catch any more of the conversation, but what she had heard was enough. So Marcello had an ulterior motive for fighting to host this event, and a very important one. It sounded as if Mr. Jones was an influential businessman in the world of wine. If he took on La Leggenda, it could open up many new markets for their wines to be distributed in the States.

It all seemed to be going well as the sumptuous main course was devoured. The hum and babble of conversation was a pleasing sign. The families were mingling, laughter rang out. Olivia glanced at Angelique and Terenzio. Their heads were pressed together, deep in conversation and seemingly oblivious to everything around them.

Would she ever find real love? she wondered sadly. Her thoughts returned to Danilo with confusion and regret. They'd been speeding toward romance, springboarding from a solid grounding of friendship. Why had their budding relationship crashed and burned?

"Dessert!" Gabriella announced.

She'd made an extra layer of the pink iced cake, enough for twenty. She carried it in, with a massive sparkler sizzling above it, for the bride to cut the first slice. Behind her, Paolo followed, distributing bowls of tiramisu and double chocolate gelato.

Olivia was filled with relief as she watched everyone guzzle down their desserts. Dinner had gone smoothly and the menu had been perfect. It was almost time for the after-party.

"We have everything?" she asked Jean-Pierre. "The pink shooters, the bowls of chocolates, the wine set out?" Once again, she surveyed the room.

"Yes, and yes," he confirmed.

"Do we have cabs on speed dial ready to take guests back to their hotels?"

"We have a cab company standing by," Jean-Pierre confirmed. "They are waiting to be called."

Needing a breath of air after having been indoors the entire day, Olivia walked across the tasting room and made her way outside into the cold and breezy night. To her surprise, she saw there were a number of rental cars outside. She hoped the guests would agree to take cabs back home, and that insisting on this wouldn't cause any friction or unpleasantness.

As she stood, enjoying the freshness, Olivia heard a mischievous giggle from the opposite side of the parking lot, close to the restaurant. The high-pitched sound was brought to her clearly by the gusting wind. It was followed by a man's deep chuckle.

"You're so bad!" a woman's voice whispered. "We must go back in!"

It seemed romance was in the air. Olivia peered into the darkness, trying to make out who the speakers were, but they were too far away and all she saw were two shadowy shapes heading back inside.

"Don't let them see us together. Meet me later," she heard the man mutter as they disappeared from sight.

Olivia's gasped, feeling her anxiety surge back again.

Even though his voice had been little more than a low mutter, she thought she recognized the distinctive arrogance and New Jersey drawl of the bridegroom, Terenzio Miller.

# CHAPTER NINE

Olivia felt beside herself with worry as she hurried back to the tasting room. She peered over to the far archway to see if she could make out who'd walked in through the restaurant entrance, but the thronging crowds at the bar blocked her view. Even so, she was certain that there was trouble afoot.

Perhaps she'd been wrong, she tried to convince herself. The speaker might have been Lance. Although she hadn't spoken with him as much, brothers sounded similar.

Didn't they?

Olivia made a determined effort to be present in the moment and not to stew in her doubts. There wasn't time to fret about something she might have misheard or misunderstood. Following dinner's massive success, she needed to make sure that the after-party provided an unforgettable experience for the wedding rehearsal group.

She was pleased by how breathtaking the venue looked.

The large space was flanked with tables on which the La Leggenda wines and sparkling wines had been set out, together with the pink shooters. Fairy lights were strung across the ceiling and Marcello had even procured a set of laser lights.

"What about the music playlist? Is that going to start now?" Jean-Pierre asked.

"Yes, I've put a lot of thought into it!" Olivia said. She was proud of the sound journey that guests would enjoy, which she'd spent a lot of the afternoon compiling. "It starts off with the eighties because—well, who doesn't love dancing to Bon Jovi and Cyndi Lauper and Foreigner? They're so catchy and multigenerational. And REM, and Sting, and Elton John, and I even included a Metallica number!"

Olivia had to admit it, she adored eighties music. Unlike the hair and fashion of the decade, the music was pure gold.

"And then?" Jean-Pierre asked.

"And then I included Heart and Aerosmith and Queen—of course!"

"And after that?" Jean-Pierre asked, looking puzzled.

"Then U2, and the Bangles, and Whitney Houston, and George Michael!"

Jean-Pierre nodded, frowning. "So still the eighties?"

"Oh, yes," Olivia said. "I really want to get people dancing!"

"Are there any songs apart from the eighties?" Jean-Pierre asked carefully.

"Of course. After my eighties playlist is finished—" She paused, trying to remember how she'd planned the sequence.

"Everyone goes home?" Jean-Pierre ventured.

"No, no. Then we move to the sixties for a few of the most stunning hits of yesteryear. And after that we accelerate into modern times with some of the biggest hits from the 2000s which segue seamlessly into a selection of great high-energy dance music. Probably the grandparents will have gone to bed by then so I chose some fabulous mixes and honestly, it's so edgy. And that's how it finishes. I estimate the entire playlist will take about two hours and by then people will be tired. Especially with the wedding tomorrow!"

Jean-Pierre nodded, checking his watch. "It is nine p.m. now. I am sure by eleven p.m. people will be ready for bed."

Olivia waited eagerly as the wedding party headed into the tasting room, talking and laughing. Angelique and Terenzio led the way, hand in hand. They headed straight for the shooters.

It was time to get the music going. She pressed Play and dimmed the lights, activating the lasers and watching their beams jet around the room.

As the first song began, Olivia watched eagerly, waiting for the catchy tune to send the guests, young and old, flocking onto the dance floor.

Her smile disappeared as Terenzio turned and headed over to the tasting counter, looking exasperated. He was followed closely by Angelique and two of his groomsmen.

"What is this? Who chose this rubbish?" He jabbed the Stop button. "What the hell? This isn't party music!"

"Uh—it's a musical journey. We can fast forward. There's some high-energy dance toward the end of the sequence," Olivia said. She felt affronted by his criticism. She'd put so much love and care into the choices.

Terenzio looked down his nose at her.

"Musical journey? You're just the assistant wine server. What the hell do you know about dance? Tomorrow night, keep your ignorant hands off this sound system," he sneered insultingly at her. One of his friends sniggered from behind him.

Olivia felt smoke coming out of her ears. What was he implying?

With her temper surging, she was about to snap out that he had the brain of a sixteen-year-old and that the barstool he was leaning on had more Italian heritage than he did.

"He is just being rude," Jean-Pierre whispered.

Thankfully, Jean-Pierre's support allowed Olivia to clutch at her self-control.

"There's a port on the side if you want to plug your phone in and use your own music," she told Terenzio coldly.

"Here we go!" Terenzio connected his phone and pressed a few buttons.

Olivia jumped as hard rap blared from the speakers.

Grinning meanly at her, Terenzio turned the volume up to head-splitting levels.

Olivia had to use all her self-control not to stick her fingers in her ears. This music was awful! She was worried that everyone except Terenzio would be appalled by the eardrum-bursting beat.

Terenzio swaggered onto the dance floor, catching Angelique by her waist and pulling her along with him as he showed off some smooth dance moves.

Jean-Pierre was trying to say something to her but over the thumping noise, all Olivia could see were his lips moving.

She reached for the volume control and turned it down a modicum, watching Terenzio carefully. Luckily he had his back to her and didn't notice the slight, but life-saving, reduction in sound.

"What did you say?" she yelled to Jean-Pierre. Now, her voice was just audible.

"I said, these people are mad!" Jean-Pierre tapped his head expressively.

"I know!"

But to Olivia's surprise, the parents and grandparents didn't seem to mind. They scattered to the corners of the room, where the sound was quieter and Olivia's strategically placed seating allowed them to sit comfortably.

They seemed content with the skull-shatttering blast.

Olivia reached over and turned it down a little more.

This time, Terenzio's head whipped around. Quickly, Olivia looked the other way.

"They have already finished the wine!" Jean-Pierre tapped her shoulder.

"What?" She'd thought she'd set out more than enough for the evening! The glasses had been emptied in only a few minutes.

"They were having a drinking game," Jean-Pierre yelled into her ear, pointing to the groomsmen. "I think the guy farthest away won. He drank eight glasses."

Olivia stared in amazement as Terenzio's brother, Lance, punched the air in triumph in front of a disgruntled-looking Kyle, Rog, and Don.

The glasses were only halfway filled and Lance was a big man, but she was starting to worry how the evening was going to play out.

"More wine!" he shouted, turning to her and waving his hands.

Olivia abandoned her war of attrition with the volume dial and hurried to refill the glasses. Thanks to the blaring rap, she couldn't hear herself think, let alone communicate with Jean-Pierre.

She rummaged in the fridge, topped up a fresh tray of glasses, and placed them on the table where they were instantly grabbed up. With yells and catcalls, another round of the drinking game was taking place. This time, it seemed to be bridesmaids versus groomsmen, and Olivia suspected that the ladies were going to win. Jewel in particular looked to be in strong form and was knocking back the wine as if it was cool water on a hot summer day.

"Hey, waiter boy!" Terenzio roared, leaning over the counter again. He was addressing Jean-Pierre, who looked startled and none too pleased by the term. "Give me a bottle of champagne, would you? I'm fed up with these glasses!"

With his eyes almost bulging out of his head, Jean-Pierre stomped over with the bottle.

Terenzio shook it violently and then loosened the wire. The cork burst from the bottle with the force of a guided missile. It hit one of the laser lights, which promptly fell and shattered on the floor. Sparkling wine spurted and foamed from the bottle and Terenzio showered guests with it as if he was a winning Formula One driver.

"Waitress! More wine!"

This time, the rude summons from Lance was directed at her. Olivia tore her attention away from the Metodo Classico drama and hurried to fill glasses. These people were impatient for their drinks. She was amazed they were still thirsty.

She made three more breathless trips with a brimming tray before the guests' appetite finally started abating.

Olivia felt exhausted, and her head was pounding.

She started back toward the tasting counter, but as she passed the corridor to Marcello's office, she glanced down it.

His office door was open and the light was on. It represented a quiet refuge, if only for a moment.

Olivia headed down the corridor and into the office but stopped abruptly at the door.

Marcello was in there.

He was reclining in his chair, a half-finished glass of wine in his hand, with his back to the door while staring out the window at the darkened view. The scattered lights of farmhouses, and the village in the far distance, added sparks of detail to the darkness.

Marcello swung round on his chair when he heard her clear her throat, nearly spilling his wine.

His face looked as grim as she'd ever seen. What had gone wrong?

# CHAPTER TEN

"Olivia, I am sorry," Marcello said, but his rueful smile didn't reach his eyes. "I did not hear you. Is everything all right out there?"

Olivia sidled into the office, desperate for a chance to rest her aching legs, even if only for a minute. To her relief, Marcello gestured to the chair on the other side of the desk.

"Please, have a seat."

Olivia collapsed onto the cushion. What an exhausting night!

"I sneaked in here for a break," she admitted. "They're drinking like crazy in the tasting room, and it's getting out of control."

Marcello had a framed aerial photo of La Leggenda on the side wall of his office, and Olivia caught sight of her reflection in the darkened glass. She was appalled. Her mascara was smudged, her eyeliner had pooled under her eyes, her hair was wisping out of the neat ponytail she'd tied it in, hanging around her too-pale face as if she'd just walked off the set of a zombie movie!

"Er," Olivia said. She wished she'd brought her purse in with her but it was behind the counter. "Do you have a Kleenex?"

"Sure."

Marcello's expression softened as he passed her a pack of facial tissues.

Olivia couldn't help thinking how weird it was that a month or two ago, sitting in the office with Marcello this way would have felt like an intimate moment.

Now, their agreement to stay friends meant that it no longer felt as if the atmosphere between them was electrically charged—although the brush of his skin against hers still gave her a thrill of warmth.

She licked the Kleenex surreptitiously and then dabbed at the smudges under her eyes. She glanced in the makeshift mirror again. Success. She didn't look as much like a raccoon as before. Romantic arrangement shelved or not, she wanted to appear her best in front of her boss.

"You seem upset," she ventured.

Marcello pushed his fingertips against his temple, as if trying to ease a throbbing headache.

"I feel this entire wedding was a bad decision," he shared. "I made it for the wrong reasons."

"You did?" Olivia asked, startled. "Why? What were the reasons?"

Marcello pressed his lips together, making his handsome face look uncharacteristically hard, before he spoke again.

"The groom's father is a major importer of wines and spirits. I thought—I hoped—that if we hosted the wedding here it would create a relationship between us and open the door for La Leggenda's wines to be distributed more widely through the United States," Marcello confessed.

Olivia nodded, feeling worried. Her guess had been right, but Marcello was speaking about this as if it was the past tense.

"And?" she encouraged. "Have you had the chance?"

Marcello looked briefly furious. "I spoke to him during dinner. I did not ask him outright but instead simply told him I would love to know more about his business, in case we could work together in the future."

"What did he say?" Olivia asked, frowning.

Marcello sighed. "He laughed at me. As did his son."

"What?" Olivia said incredulously.

Marcello nodded. "He said that we were priced way beyond what he would consider. In fact, he insulted our wines by calling them overpriced. He said that Italian wines were the poor cousin of Europe and if we weren't dirt cheap, he wasn't interested. Then his son, Terence, jeered at me, saying that his father had achieved a monopoly with many of the largest wine stores, and that he would inherit the business in a few more years, and that I would have to beg and scrape like a poor cousin would do, if I even wanted a meeting."

Olivia clapped her hand over her mouth in horror. What hurtful comments both father and son had made! Especially seeing they had chosen to host their family wedding at this venue, and the groom was on a mission to prove his six-generations-back Italian heritage!

"It sounds like Mr. Jones is more of a racketeer than a merchant!" she exclaimed. "What a nasty man. When I first saw him, I thought he looked shady. Like someone who has made a lot of money doing unsavory deals."

Marcello nodded.

"I think you are correct. I think he has gained some dominance in the market and is using it to drive down prices, while making maximum profit. That is not good business and it cannot last!"

His voice rose to a shout at the last words and Olivia felt her heart stop. She'd never seen Marcello so smolderingly angry. She guessed his strong sense of fairness made this impossible for him to stomach.

Olivia was about to suggest that they both have some wine and talk it over. Anything to avoid going back to the after-party. Plus, she sensed Marcello needed to vent further, and hadn't yet gotten everything off his chest.

But as she started speaking, Olivia heard a scream and a massive crash from the tasting room.

"I'd better go!" She leaped to her aching feet and limped hurriedly out of Marcello's office. What had happened? she wondered, as she ran into the tasting room. What new disaster would she have to deal with now?

The dancers were screaming and shrieking, backing away from a rapidly widening circle in the center of the dance floor. Seeing Jean-Pierre rushing away from the scene, Olivia caught up with him. Calling to him was impossible as Terenzio must have turned the sound up again after she left.

She grabbed his sleeve to stop him.

"What has happened?" she yelled. She felt bad for having abandoned the action for even a minute. This was a volatile situation.

"Two of the groomsmen were juggling with bottles of Metodo Classico. It was a competition, I think." Jean-Pierre waved his arms in consternation. "At the same time, each dropped both! All have exploded. The floor is covered in broken glass and champagne!"

Olivia's mouth fell open as she took in the extent of this disaster. The dance floor had become a sea of broken glass, the laser lights casting garish, flashing reflections off the spilled wine.

How was it possible for a sophisticated family event to have degenerated so fast? she asked herself incredulously. And a more serious question—given the rapidly escalating level of drunkenness, were things going to get any worse?

Urgent damage control was going to be needed to prevent this.

"Let's grab some mops!" she yelled.

Olivia raced to the back storage room and yanked open the broom cupboard in the righthand corner.

The brooms, mops, and dustpans inside were used occasionally when a guest knocked over a glass in their enthusiasm, or in the very rare event that a bottle was dropped.

56

Now, Olivia grabbed every implement she could find. She shoved a mop and broom toward Jean-Pierre, keeping one of each aside for herself.

She was relieved to see that Paolo, the head waiter, was hurrying into the tasting room to help. All hands were going to be needed to clear up this mess of spilled liquid and shattered glass.

She turned up the lights and turned down the music, before hurrying onto the dance floor. The wild knot of revelers had dispersed. A few dedicated dancers were still jiving on the borders. The glass had exploded over a wide area and her shoe crunched over a shard almost immediately.

"Sweep it into the center," she advised. "It's the best way to make sure all the glass is picked up, and we can bring in the vacuum cleaner to help clean up the liquid."

Working feverishly, Olivia swept and mopped, hunting down all the stray fragments and splinters.

What madness, she thought irritably. The bridesmaids and groomsmen were being totally irresponsible. This was not socially acceptable behavior in any country. She wished she could grab Terenzio by his shiny, dark, gelled quiff, and yell into his ear exactly what she thought of him and his destructive ways.

Perhaps the worst was over, Olivia decided, trying to avoid getting angrier by thinking positively. The drinkers had caused enough destruction to brag about it afterward, and with any luck, going outside would sober them up and ramp down their wild behavior. Therefore, the rest of the evening should pass smoothly.

Being her own reassuring voice of reason calmed her annoyance and gave her a much-needed boost of energy, and the clean-up was finished in a few more minutes.

Leaning tiredly on her mop on the now-abandoned dance floor, Olivia narrowed her eyes against the lasers zigzagging above.

Then, from the winery's entrance, she heard a piercing scream.

Olivia spun toward the sound, feeling stunned. She thought the worst had happened, but clearly she was wrong.

She rushed to the door to find out what new catastrophe these reckless partygoers had caused.

# CHAPTER ELEVEN

Glancing helplessly at Jean Pierre as she hurtled to the main entrance, Olivia could see the unspoken message pass between them.

*What on earth have these maniacs gotten up to now?*

Never mind overtime, she was starting to think she needed danger pay to manage this crazy group!

She skidded to a stop as she saw Angelique standing in the foyer.

Her mouth was open, ready to scream again. Her face was crimson, her eyes were red, her fists were bunched in fury. As Olivia watched in horror, Angelique looked around, clearly needing to vent her anger in a more physical way.

She grabbed a huge glass vase filled with pink roses and raised it above her head.

"No, no, no!" Olivia entreated. She'd cleaned up enough broken glass to last her a lifetime! Rushing forward, she grabbed the heavy, slippery rim in an attempt to prevent Angelique from hurling it to the floor.

A deluge of icy water cascaded over Olivia's head, followed by the light thuds of several roses.

Blinking and gasping at the cold shock, Olivia was starting to seriously regret her life choices. At least the vase had been saved, she thought, even if her hairdo was history. Another pair of strong hands grasped it. Jean-Pierre had come to her rescue.

Shaking back her sodden hair, Olivia stepped over the puddle to stand next to Angelique.

The young blonde was screaming uncontrollably, and when Olivia tried to gently take her arm, she shoved her away.

Olivia tried again, placing her wet, cold palm on the girl's heaving shoulders.

"It's okay," she soothed. "It's all right. I think everything has gotten a little out of hand. Take your time. Tell me what happened."

Out of the corner of her eye, she saw Jean-Pierre place the empty vase safely under one of the tables, before gathering up the fallen blooms. Other people were arriving, alerted by the commotion. Angelique's parents were hurrying toward the foyer looking anxious, and her brother was marching purposefully across the dance floor to join them.

Angelique turned to her and Olivia saw pure rage in her eyes.

"I went outside while you were cleaning up," she hissed. "And what did I see but that useless, womanizing Terence kissing Alice. My own sister!"

Mrs. Miller uttered a small shriek.

With a jolt, Olivia remembered the low-voiced conversation she'd overheard outside. She'd feared the worst and it had happened. The speaker must have been Terence.

Jean-Pierre frowned in confusion.

"But how could he have done that? You are marrying each other tomorrow, no?" he asked. "

"Not anymore!" Angelique yelled.

Olivia heard another, louder shriek from behind her as Mrs. Miller took in this shocking announcement.

She and Jean-Pierre stared at each other in horror. This put the whole wedding in jeopardy. How could such a thing have happened? Olivia agonized.

"Was it a friendly kiss? Perhaps he meant it as a brother," Jean-Pierre suggested in hopeful tones.

"What do you mean by that?" Angelique's brother asked threateningly.

Massaging Angelique's shoulders, Olivia felt panic rising inside her. She had no clue how to deal with this situation, and worse still, it was giving her unwanted flashbacks.

Angelique seemed glad of Jean-Pierre's question. It provided an opportunity for her to share what Olivia realized were extremely strong, albeit recently formed, opinions.

"He had his face mashed against hers! I saw clearly. His revolting, ugly, lying face. And it was not in any way a brotherly kiss."

Olivia pushed the memories of her pre-wedding catastrophe with Ward out of her mind. Now was not the time to dwell on long-forgotten bad decisions, but rather to try and manage this one.

"Why would he do such a thing?" Jean-Pierre asked, sounding puzzled.

"Because he's a devious, underhanded cheater," Angelique announced to Olivia, Jean-Pierre, and the wider world. "Because he can't be trusted, he's a stinking, lying coward. I should never have agreed to marry him or believed there was any good in him! He's faker than a—than a plastic Gucci purse! My Moschino travel bag has more Italian roots than he does. He's a sneaky, slimy, oily, pretentious—"

Luckily, at this point, Angelique ran out of air. Olivia didn't think for a minute that she'd run out of words. She was certain the blonde had plenty more of those in store. But as she gasped in a breath, she started sobbing again.

"It's absolutely unacceptable, and I agree with you," Olivia found herself shouting. "His behavior tonight has been atrocious. Shameful, in fact! He's been rude to me and my assistant, and in my experience, if you treat strangers badly, you don't treat your friends any different. Cheating is out of line and he deserves to be punished for it. And if that means not marrying you, well, it's his own fault. He brought it upon himself!"

Olivia had hoped to be the voice of reason, and was astonished to find these furious words spilling out of her mouth.

She couldn't stop thinking of the moment when she had walked into Ward's hotel room on their wedding morning. She'd waited until he had gone down to breakfast and quickly obtained an access key from reception. They were staying in separate rooms at the Holiday Inn, but Olivia had wanted to surprise Ward with a buttonhole for his suit, and a handwritten note.

She'd planned to leave her gift romantically for him on the bed and then hustle back to her own room to start getting ready.

Never in her wildest dreams had she expected to find her friend and bridesmaid Hayley actually *in* the bed, staring at Olivia in horror.

Like Angelique, she hadn't been short of words. Her ensuing hysterics had brought neighboring guests out of their rooms, the manager from reception, and eventually, Ward from the breakfast room.

Olivia had thrown the buttonhole at him, called the wedding off then and there, and stormed out of the Holiday Inn. No wonder she'd blocked the entire sorry episode from her mind! It was embarrassing to think she'd made such an error of judgment. She should have realized how fake Ward's charm was, and how he'd never really meant most of what he'd said. He'd been a narcissist. She was sure Terence was, too.

"You made a mistake in trusting your fiancé," she told Angelique. "Some people aren't trustworthy and they lie!"

Olivia could hear the anger in her own voice. After all these years, she was still furious about what Ward had done. And she'd had enough of Terence. With his irresponsible drinking, and spilling champagne on her, and treating her like a slave, and insulting Marcello, there wasn't enough money in the world to make this party worthwhile.

An angry male voice shouted agreement.

"Where is he? I'm going to find him and beat him up!"

Glancing up, Olivia saw Angelique's brother standing there. He looked livid and his florid cheeks were flushed deep red. "How dare he do such a thing? It's his fault, not Alice's. He must have taken advantage of her!"

"Oh, no, you're wrong there, Lysander!" another aggressive voice shouted out from behind him.

Lysander? As Olivia was taking in his odd name, she saw the groomsmen Kyle and Rog had joined the fray, together with Terence's brother, Lance.

"Alice is a tart! She probably tried to seduce him!"

"Terence—I mean, Terenzio—is a good guy! He'd never do anything like that!"

"Are you looking for a fight, Lysander?"

The four turned to face each other, all flexing their muscles, apart from Lance, who was holding an open bottle of white wine in one hand and a slice of cake in the other. Kyle, however, was already rolling up his sleeves, and Olivia dreaded that a fight was imminent.

She should have spoken differently and not lost her temper and inflamed the situation! She wished they could all be back in the drunken rap party. It had been uncontrollable and crazy, but at least everyone had been enjoying themselves. This was a massive crisis and she was in way over her head.

"Let's go and sit down," she announced as loud as she could so that the guests could all hear. "We need to discuss this calmly. There could be a—a reason for it. Maybe he thought she was you?"

"No way!" Angelique spat, finding her breath again. "It was deliberate and intentional and he knew what he was doing!"

"Come. It's cold out here in the entrance hall."

Well, she was cold, anyway. In her drenched top, she was starting to shiver. There were heaters in the restaurant as well as the roaring fire, she remembered.

Olivia ushered Angelique to the safety of the pink-draped restaurant, with the retinue of followers bringing up the rear. Lysander and the groomsmen were muttering aggressively to each other, and didn't look eager to smooth out their differences at all.

Angelique's Granny Petra was sitting at the table closest to the fireplace, drinking a sherry. Even though she was deaf, Olivia didn't want to upset the elderly woman with this drama. Instead, she headed for the table by the biggest heater, and sat with her back to it.

Plates of cake and assorted chocolates had been placed on the tables. Despite the tension of the moment, Olivia stared longingly at the sweet treats. Starvation, she remembered, was an inevitable consequence of organizing events.

At the bar, the chocolate fountain was cascading sickly-looking ripples of pink gunk. Looking at that helped curb Olivia's hunger.

"Sweetheart, I'm sure Alice couldn't have done such a thing," Angelique's mother reassured her. "Do you want some tea? Or water? We can sort this out, I'm sure."

Olivia winced. She could have told Mrs. Miller that saying this was a bad idea. Angelique turned on her in a fury.

"Are you calling me a liar? Terence is the liar. And the wedding's off! That's my final decision!"

At the exact moment Angelique made this announcement, someone turned the music down.

Her words rang through the restaurant. Everybody's head snapped around.

In another moment, they were surrounded by a circle of guests. Some looked horrified, others fascinated. Terenzio's Gramma B, aka Nonna, looked hungry.

"Cake, anyone?" she said, taking a piece for herself before passing the plate around.

"He was cheating on me! With my own sister!" Angelique lamented.

Olivia was struggling to find the right consoling words, but at that moment, Terenzio strolled into the restaurant and she froze in apprehension.

He had a casual half-smile on his handsome face. His hair was tousled and Olivia had an uneasy vision of Alice running her fingers through it.

"Hey, everyone! What's up?" he asked casually.

Angelique leaped to her feet, tottering on her fancy heels. Olivia grabbed her arm and helped her to balance. Cassidy rushed into the restaurant behind Terence and headed straight for Angelique, taking her hand supportively.

"Don't you dare come near me. You cheater! I saw you out there with Alice," Angelique spat.

Terence blanched, looking briefly horrified.

Then, showing remarkable resilience, he recovered his poise.

"Wrong, sweetheart! You are the love of my life. I wasn't kissing Alice. In fact, I was whispering to her how much I adore you. My bambino."

Olivia cringed, hoping that neither Alice nor her family would pick up that Terence had mistakenly called her a young boy child.

"You were in a clinch with her. I know what that looks like," Angelique hissed. "Stop lying. Get lost!"

"Yes, you get out of here," Bristling with wrath, Angelique's father leaped to his feet. "You have upset my baby girl and she now wants to call everything off. Do you know how much money we spent on this jaunt, which you insisted must be in Italy because of your so-called roots? This is an absolute disaster. I invested in this believing my precious daughter would be safe with you. Now, I'm not even sure it's tax-deductible. Is it, honey?"

He turned to his wife, but she was in tears, her head buried in her hands.

Terence's face had turned thunderous.

"You don't believe my version?" he shouted.

"There is no way I'm swallowing that pack of lies," Mr. Miller retaliated, ignoring the angry cry from Terence's father, who was hurrying over to join the fray, and the threatening growls from the groomsmen.

"Well, in that case, fine! Fine! I'm not sure I want to be ashoshi—associated with a family who doeshn't trust me!"

Terence slurred out the words, his drinking jag finally catching up with him.

He grabbed a full bottle of red wine from the display on the bar and began marching out with it.

Then he stopped and stared at the bottle myopically, as if coming to a complicated and difficult conclusion.

Brushing past his father, Terence veered to the tasting counter and grabbed one of the corkscrews that Olivia had left out. Although La Leggenda's white wines and rosés were screw-top, their reds, like many other wineries', were still traditionally corked.

Implement in hand, Terence half-strode, half-staggered to the winery's door and vanished into the night.

"Now look what you've done," Terence's father barked, sounding militant. "You've insulted him without hearing him out. Probably, he just needs to have his version believed."

He glared at Angelique's father, who sat down with his arms folded and scowled at him in return.

"I don't care if he never comes back!" Angelique shrieked. "I hate him and I wish he was dead!"

Her words echoed around the restaurant.

Olivia had no words. She exchanged a helpless glance with Jean-Pierre. Looking up, she saw Gabriella watching in fascination from the kitchen. Marcello, probably alerted by the music stopping, had emerged from his office and was standing at the entrance to the corridor. He looked furious.

"My poor boy, with so many people conspiring against him," Terence's father said wrathfully.

Shaking off the concerned hands of the three chestnut-haired bridesmaids, Angelique stood up. "Go away. I hate you all, too. You've probably all kissed him! I want to go home!"

She flounced out through the restaurant's side door with Cassidy running after her, shouting for her to stop.

"Where is Alice, anyway?" Mrs. Miller asked, wiping her eyes. "And where is Jewel?"

"I don't know where Alice is, but I saw Jewel run to the ladies' restroom a moment ago." Gramma B cackled. "She didn't look very healthy. I think she was regretting that eighth glass of wine."

"I'll go and find Alice," Dinah, the remaining bridesmaid, said. She hurried out of the restaurant.

Olivia stared again at the plate of snacks. At this stress-filled moment, it seemed to be screaming her name.

She needed a minute to collect her thoughts, and while she did so, she was going to have a sugar fix. She reached over and took a piece of wedding cake, richly studded with fruit and cherries, and thickly iced in pink, with a white layer of marzipan inside.

She ate a small bite, and then another, remembering that she'd donated her engagement ring to a charity fair after discovering how Ward had cheated on her. She'd never seen or heard from him again. He'd moved on, but Olivia was sure he had never changed his ways.

In what seemed like no time at all, the cake was gone. Glancing up as she wiped the crumbs from her mouth, she saw Marcello had disappeared. The two sets of parents were sitting on opposite sides of

64

the restaurant, whispering together and occasionally glaring at the other. Jean-Pierre was collecting used glasses from the tasting room, and Gabriella had retreated to the kitchen from where the delicious aroma of coffee was emanating. She'd clearly resolved to ignore all the drama and stick to the evening's schedule, which dictated that at eleven p.m., tea and coffee would be served.

Olivia decided to round up the guests and suggest that everyone come back inside for coffee. Probably it would be a good thing to have caffeine's sobering influence. It might help to redeem this terrible situation, although she wasn't sure how.

She headed to the tasting room and grabbed her phone. As she turned on the flashlight, she felt like a boarding-school matron heading out to round up a bunch of unruly students.

The freezing night air made Olivia flinch. The wind was gusting through her still-damp hair and she wished she'd brought her coat as well as her phone.

Shivering her way around the paved path to the parking lot, Olivia planned to return to the winery via the main entrance, calling inside everyone she found along the way.

As she walked through the parking lot, with the beam dancing from side to side, she was surprised how empty of people it was. Only the large rental SUVs the wedding party had hired occupied the pristine paving.

Passing one of them, located under a discreet spotlight, Olivia noticed a shape in the back.

She hesitated and looked again, peering through the tinted glass.

Was that Terence? She thought she recognized the now-mussed silhouette of that perfectly gelled quiff.

Had he passed out there? Olivia sighed, wishing that his reckless drinking habits could have caught up with him a half-hour earlier and saved them all so much heartache!

Suddenly, she remembered that bottle of wine. If Terence had passed out, the red wine could have spilled all over the car's interior, or else it might tip over at any moment.

She'd better rescue the bottle, she decided, or it would turn into a messy disaster.

*Another* messy disaster, she thought, trying the car's back door.

To her relief, it opened. Shining her light inside, she couldn't see or smell any spilled wine. The rental company would be glad about that, she thought.

As Olivia stared at the slumped man in puzzlement, she realized two more things.

Firstly, Terence was lying strangely still. There was none of the belabored snoring she'd expected to hear from a young, passed-out male who had drunk enough for an elephant.

Secondly, the corkscrew was no longer in his hand.

It was—it was…

Olivia let out a brief, shocked cry as her brain pieced together what her astonished eyes were seeing.

The corkscrew was jutting out of Terence's neck.

# CHAPTER TWELVE

Clapping her hands over her mouth, Olivia stumbled back from the gruesome spectacle. She only stopped when her backside collided with the car parked next door.

She leaned against it, feeling weak, and as if she was going to throw up.

Without any doubt, this was murder. Terence was dead. Emotions had boiled over, tensions had snapped, and someone at this party had killed him.

"This can't be happening!" she whispered.

When she'd wondered if anything else could go wrong, she'd never dreamed of this catastrophe.

Before she knew it, Olivia found herself racing away from the scene, tottering through the darkness on cotton-wool legs. She didn't want to look at that again, ever! She wanted to collect Erba and drive back to her farm right now, leaving behind the chaotic mess and the warring families and this shocking sight.

It was only when she reached the restaurant door that she realized this was an even worse decision.

She'd found the body! She couldn't run home, and was responsible for what happened next. Somewhere out there, a killer had gotten away with a crime and was hoping that he, or she, would never be found.

Breathing rapidly, Olivia turned around and forced herself back to the car.

Call the police, she decided. That was what a sensible person would do. She had to become that person, and fast, before it was too late. In fact, that should have been her very first move, before she broke and ran for it.

She fumbled in her jacket pocket, grateful that she'd brought her phone along with her. Although she thought longingly about heading to the safe refuge of Marcello's office, Olivia knew had to make the call right here, right now, in the parking lot. Every moment counted.

She couldn't look at that awful sight a moment longer, though.

Olivia pushed the car door closed with her foot.

"I'd like to speak to the detective in charge, please," she said as her call connected. She spoke as softly as possible, suddenly aware that the killer might be hiding nearby.

"I am calling from La Leggenda winery to report a murder," she said, as soon as the male detective answered her call.

Quickly, Olivia gave the details, including the vehicle's number plate. She tried to keep her voice as calm as possible but she could hear how she was squeaking out the details, reading the number plate wrong, even mispronouncing the road name. Worst of all, Olivia knew that her confused account would be recorded for all to hear, and that her incoherence might be perceived as suspicious.

Finally, the ordeal of reporting the crime was over.

"*Grazie,*" she whispered. She disconnected and stared wide-eyed into the darkness, dreading that the killer might suddenly pop up from behind a car, or emerge from one of the terra cotta planters that were set at the winery's four corners.

But the parking lot was quiet, even though there was plenty of noise further away. Faint cries resonated from the lobby, and she picked up the faraway sound of an argument, as well as the music which someone had turned on again.

She should try to assemble the guests now, she decided. That way, they would all be in one room when the police arrived.

She was trembling all over as she headed into the winery via the restaurant.

"Can everyone come in here, please?" she called.

Deep in discussion, Angelique's parents ignored her completely. Even Gabriella, adding whipped cream to an Irish coffee at the bar, didn't raise her head.

Olivia realized her voice had been little more than a breathy cry.

Remembering that the public address system include a loudspeaker, she decided to use it.

She headed over to the microphone, switched it on, and spoke with more authority.

"CAN EVERYONE PLEASE COME IN HERE?"

The words blasted out, rattling the windows. Olivia was surprised plaster didn't shower from the ceiling. A head-splitting howl of feedback followed her thunderous announcement.

The music stopped abruptly, and Olivia heard the distinctive tinkle of breaking glass.

Terence's stepmother had been so startled she'd dropped her champagne flute.

The thirty-something-year-old socialite turned and glared at her.

"What do you think you are doing? We're not cutting this event short. I don't care what time you plan on closing, we're the customers here. Leave us alone, and get back to your job," she ordered. "Boy, bring me another glass of Classico a la Methodo." She snapped her fingers at Jean-Pierre.

"Exactly." Terence's father nodded firmly as he marched back into the restaurant carrying a glass of sangiovese. He was followed by the three chestnut-haired bridesmaids, who had briefly returned to the dance floor after the drama had played out. "We call the shots here. Somebody clean up this mess."

"I will clean the breakage, and then bring you your drink!" Brandishing a dustpan and brush, Jean-Pierre sprinted loyally into action.

Olivia decided to ignore the Joneses. After all, this was a massive emergency.

She turned the volume down slightly and tried again.

"CAN EVERYONE PLEASE COME INTO THE RESTAURANT IMMEDIATELY?"

Gabriella, placing the coffee on a tray, frowned at her as if she was disturbing the peace.

Two of the groomsmen arrived at the restaurant's entrance.

"Want a career in showbiz?" Kyle taunted Olivia. "Don't give up your day job!"

"Give us a song!" Rog jeered.

Olivia stared at them, feeling exasperated. Why was nobody understanding the seriousness of this situation?

Jean-Pierre finished sweeping the glass. He carried the dustpan and brush away, and returned with a brimming flute of sparkling wine.

A few people trickled in. Gramma B was holding another, larger whiskey. Alice and Lysander walked in, arguing in subdued voices with each other.

Then, from outside, came the rapidly approaching blare of sirens.

"Wait a minute!" Terence's stepmother sounded outraged. "You called the cops on us? I don't believe what I'm hearing. We booked this venue for the evening. I don't care if we ran late. We will stay as long as we like!"

"Exactly," Kyle agreed. "You should be arrested for being such a party pooper."

"THAT IS NOT WHY I CALLED YOU ALL HERE!" In her temper, Olivia had forgotten that she was still clutching the loudspeaker. "I CALLED YOU ALL HERE BECAUSE THE GROOM IS DEAD. HE HAS BEEN MURDERED, AND THE POLICE ARE COMING TO INVESTIGATE!"

Too late, she realized that her words hadn't just reached the Joneses but had boomed around the entire winery. Appalled, Olivia stabbed at the Off switch, jumping as, with a crash, Gabriella dropped the tray of Irish coffee.

Gathering up his dustpan and mop again, Jean-Pierre hurtled in her direction.

Terence's stepmother leaped up, her chair clattering down behind her.

"No!" she screamed. "Impossible! All our friends have already flown here, expecting the event of the year. Our story was going to be featured in *Elite Traveler*. They promised us four pages. This wedding has to take place. This must be a lie!" She turned to her husband, sobbing. "Is it a lie?'

Looking stunned, Terence's father shook his head slowly.

Kyle and Rog rushed toward Olivia.

"Murdered? How?" Rog shouted at her.

They looked like a two-man lynch mob and Olivia was relieved that the sirens were now screaming right outside the winery.

Abruptly, the noise cut off.

The next moment, there was an official clatter of feet from outside the main entrance.

Detective Caputi marched in, accompanied by two plainclothes detectives and a uniformed officer.

She glared at Olivia as if she'd been the direct cause of all of this inconvenience.

Olivia stared nervously back at the slim, stern, smartly suited detective who was her nemesis. After their last encounter, where Olivia had narrowly escaped being arrested, she'd hoped never to see her again. The detective's steel-gray bob was shorter and sharper than she remembered. Olivia was sure that, at this hour of the night, her temper was, too.

With every shiny hair in place and flawless lipstick on her unsmiling mouth, she didn't look as if she'd been dragged out of bed by the call. Olivia wondered if she ever slept!

After searing Olivia with her unfriendly gaze, Detective Caputi directed it at everyone else in the room.

"*Buona sera,*" she said, in a tone of voice that told everyone it clearly wasn't a good evening at all. "I see this is a wedding party. Where are you all staying?"

It was as if the headmistress had walked in. The groomsmen looked at the floor. Mrs. Jones stared at Detective Caputi in repentant silence.

Olivia couldn't help thinking that they all looked remarkably sober. She didn't know whether it was thanks to the shock of the murder, or the arrival of the scary detective. One way or another, the events of the past fifteen minutes had done the job that gallons of strong coffee and eight hours' sleep would have struggled to do.

It was the father of the bride who finally spoke.

"All of our party is staying at La Locanda."

"That would be the five-star hotel beyond Collina town?" the detective asked sharply.

"Er, yes. About ten minutes' drive from here."

Caputi looked at him sternly.

"You were planning to take a cab back, no?"

"Um—yes, absolutely." Mr. Jones looked at the array of empty glasses. "A cab. After the party. Yes."

"All the rental vehicles will remain where they are." She turned to her officer. "Call cabs to take these guests back to the hotel now." Then, addressing the group at large, she added, "You will write your names and room numbers down in this notebook. Do not leave the hotel, or in fact your assigned rooms, when you return. I will interview you as soon as we have concluded our business here."

She handed the notebook to the closest guest.

Olivia watched in awe. Detective Caputi had been wasted in the police force, she decided. She should have been in charge of an expensive private school. The only sound in the room was the scratch of the pen on the page. Nobody was even crying anymore, not even Terence's stepmother. In any case, Olivia suspected, her intense grief had been due to the fact that the wedding wouldn't get the four-page spread in *Elite Traveler*. She wasn't sure that the woman had much love for her stepson at all!

71

Even Gramma B appeared calm. Sipping on her whiskey expressionlessly, she glanced from time to time at Lance.

"Were there any witnesses to the crime?" the detective asked.

The group was silent. Everyone glanced guiltily at each other.

"No? And who discovered the body?"

Everyone's gaze swiveled to Olivia.

She blinked rapidly as she realized the implications of her presence in the parking lot at the worst possible time.

"You?" the detective said, in a tone that didn't sound surprised at all. "Of course it was," she added. She stared at Olivia with a considering expression, then nodded emphatically, as if she had confirmed her own suspicions.

# CHAPTER THIRTEEN

Olivia perched on the edge of the seat in the restaurant where the detective had ordered her to wait. She watched the last of the previously drunk and disorderly wedding party file soberly outside and climbed into the waiting cabs.

Watching at the door, Detective Caputi muttered something under her breath. Olivia thought it sounded like *"Grazie a Dio."* She couldn't blame the detective. She, too, was glad to see the back of them, but worried that she was now the detective's sole focus.

She relaxed slightly as Caputi marched out, clearly doing a hands-on job to ensure everyone departed in an orderly fashion. Even though she wasn't hungry at all, Olivia found herself reaching for one of the silver forks and digging it into a slice of the wedding cake. She was a stress eater. As she munched automatically, she felt grateful for the sugar hit. The past few hours had been a long, exhausting, emotional rollercoaster.

Quickly, she swallowed her mouthful and put the fork down as the detective returned.

"Who else from this winery was on site at the time of the murder?" she snapped.

To Olivia's relief, she heard Marcello's deep voice from behind her. Although he looked as stressed as Olivia felt, his tone was strong and authoritative.

"Olivia and the assistant sommelier Jean-Pierre were working with the rehearsal party," he explained. "I was in my office most of the night. Paolo, the barman, and Gabriella, our restaurant manager, were serving guests throughout the evening, and did not leave the restaurant premises."

The scary gray-haired policewoman nodded. "Gabriella and Paolo may go. You can sit down, and Jean-Pierre as well."

Olivia was glad to have Jean-Pierre by her side. He crept around the table and edged into his seat, clearly as intimidated by Caputi as she was. Marcello sat opposite. Olivia could see he was making a huge effort to remain calm and in control.

"Give me an account of what happened this evening. This was the rehearsal, you said? So, family and friends, but not the full wedding party?" the detective asked.

"That is correct," Marcello agreed.

Olivia took a deep breath. As the most senior staff member who'd been on site the entire evening, she knew she would have to give the first account of what had happened.

"The wedding party was from New Jersey," she explained. "This was their first time in Tuscany. I'm not sure how well the two families knew each other but I would say they were not well acquainted. Both sides seemed wealthy and entitled and were quick to get nasty if things weren't how they wanted them."

No matter how unreasonable the demands, she thought resentfully. The crystal bear episode still rankled! That had been a total abuse of power on Angelique's part.

Olivia was encouraged to see Marcello and Jean-Pierre nodding enthusiastically in agreement as she spoke.

She wasn't sure how Detective Caputi was taking her story. The policewoman was disturbingly hard to read. Olivia would have hated to sit opposite her at a poker table. Not that sitting opposite her at an investigation table was any better.

Detective Caputi had a terrible habit of defaulting to Olivia as the prime suspect whenever she was unfortunate enough to be caught up in a murder case. Therefore, it was imperative to plant the seeds in the detective's mind that one of the wedding party must have committed this crime. Gathering her thoughts, she continued.

"Everything went without a hitch until after dinner. Then they started partying and it got out of hand. They were drinking like crazy. I actually didn't know people could drink so much!" She gestured to the kitchen, where ranks of used glasses were stacked on the counters. "As they drank more and more, I could see that everyone was letting their true feelings come out. The bride's family had issues with the groom's family and vice versa. The groomsmen were on a complete mission of destruction. They smashed four Metodo Classico bottles while trying to juggle them. And just after we'd cleaned up all that mess, the bride discovered the groom outside, kissing her maid of honor, who's also her sister."

Detective Caputi's lips tightened disapprovingly as she scribbled notes on her pad. Olivia hoped that after this vivid description and sharp insight into the family dynamics, the policewoman's sights would now be firmly set on finding the suspect from among the wedding party.

"What happened after the bride discovered this?" Caputi asked.

Uh-oh, Olivia thought. Her version had been progressing smoothly, but now, she had to admit, there was some rocky ground to navigate. If only she hadn't been such a loudmouth and vented her feelings in front of so many people! All of them would tell the police what she'd said, so she might as well admit to it upfront.

"Well, I took a firm stand against Terence's bad behavior," she tried, but already the detective had looked up from her notes and was staring at her with narrowed eyes.

"And how, exactly, did you do that?"

Not by killing him, Olivia wanted to protest, but knew blurting that out would only make things worse.

"Verbally," Olivia said, trying to keep her voice calm and reasonable. As opposed to manually, with a corkscrew, she thought with a chill. "I criticized him in harsh terms, in front of a large group of the guests. You see, I'm very anti that sort of behavior." She shrugged deprecatingly, to try and soften the impact of her words. "Personal experience. You could say I have baggage."

As soon as she'd spoken, Olivia started regretting it. Baggage? What had possessed her to use that word? Why on earth was she handing the policewoman more and more reasons why she might have been motivated to commit the crime?

"What exactly did you say when you criticized him?" Caputi asked, watching her closely.

"I said I hoped he got what he deserved," Olivia explained, feeling as if she'd dug a huge hole for herself, and then jumped inside, and then thrown the spade out! "I find it's very helpful to speak my mind and get things off my chest. I felt calm and tranquil after that! No baggage left at all!" She hoped that this further explanation would set things straight, but as she gazed appealingly at the detective, she was sure it hadn't.

She knew Caputi was now firmly focused on what else Olivia might have done. Shouting out that she hoped Terence got what he deserved was by far the worst thing she could have said. If only she'd been psychic and had known what would play out later in the evening.

Olivia felt another chill that had nothing to do with her still-damp blouse. Even though she couldn't read the detective's mind, she felt sure that she was thinking a sommelier would be skilled in handling corkscrews. This was another reason why she might suspect Olivia all the more.

"Were there any other incidents prior to that? Any disagreements or clashes?" Caputi asked.

As she spoke, she looked at all of them sternly, as if daring them to withhold any information.

"Terence was very rude to both of us before that!" Jean-Pierre exclaimed, glancing at Olivia.

Then he clapped a hand over his mouth as if regretting what he had just said.

Olivia felt like burying her head in her hands. Things had already been heading in the wrong direction, and now Jean-Pierre's outspokenness was turning this interview into a complete disaster.

"There seemed to be many petty disagreements among the guests. I noted them as I served wine," Jean-Pierre continued, and Olivia breathed a sigh of relief that he'd gotten back onto firmer ground.

"And after?" Caputi asked, clearly not letting petty disagreements derail her from the stronger motive Jean-Pierre and Olivia would have had after being personally insulted by the victim.

Marcello cleared his throat, speaking with an air of calm authority.

"The groom left the winery, and in front of many onlookers, the bride declared that she hated him and wished he was dead."

Caputi didn't often give away her emotions, but Olivia saw her perfectly plucked eyebrows shoot up at this bombshell.

"Is that so?" she asked.

Olivia and Jean-Pierre both nodded eagerly.

"That is significant," the detective said in reluctant tones. Then she drew herself up and glared at Olivia.

"A murdered American is an international crisis. The pressure will be on my team to solve this as fast as possible."

Was this a subtle plea for help? Olivia wondered if she should offer her assistance. Probably, the detective could use it. Weren't all police departments understaffed and overworked? And after all, she'd had good success with her past investigations. On the other hand, she didn't want to offend Caputi or hint that she thought she was incapable!

As she was mentally wording a discreet, professional-sounding offer, the detective spoke again.

"We do not need any members of the public interfering in this," she emphasized. "Untrained people acting impulsively and not following protocol could compromise our whole investigation. Also, meddling in a murder investigation might place your life at risk."

She was only talking to Olivia now. She wasn't even glancing sideways at Marcello or Jean-Pierre. Clearly, Caputi didn't want her help at all and in fact was warning her off.

Olivia felt relieved she hadn't made her offer, as it would have put the detective in an even worse mood.

Despite the warning, Olivia was sure that the police wouldn't mind if she asked a few innocent questions here and there—would they? After all, that wasn't the same as actual investigation. She'd wanted to visit Hotel La Locanda for a while. She might inadvertently bump into one or two of the wedding party while she toured its famously lavish facilities.

The detective's eyes narrowed and Olivia realized that she was actually reading her mind.

"All of you three are still suspects at this time," Caputi said deliberately.

She said all three, Olivia thought with a surge of annoyance, but Detective Caputi's eyes were fixed only on Olivia.

Tapping her pen thoughtfully on the table, the detective continued.

"I understand that you need to work and the winery must continue operations. Therefore, I am not going to restrict you to your homes."

Olivia felt a surge of hope, but it was quickly crushed by her next words.

"You may travel between your homes and this winery. You may go nowhere else until our investigation is concluded." Caputi's voice was like ice. "Not to any other location than home or work. Should you do so, and should I discover you elsewhere, I will assume that you are guilty of this crime, and you will be immediately arrested!"

The detective sounded triumphant as she delivered this bombshell.

# CHAPTER FOURTEEN

As the detective announced her repressive ultimatum, Olivia felt breathless with shock. This was unjust. It seemed as if Caputi was trying to entrap her into breaking these tyrannical rules, so she could end up arresting her.

Beside her, Jean-Pierre whimpered in despair. She remembered that he had recently joined the village soccer team. They practiced five times a week, at the local junior school grounds. Missing practice might mean being dropped from the team, and she knew how important it was for him to be part of the social life of his new home village.

This was downright cruel.

Even as Olivia seethed with anger, she realized that Detective Caputi was waiting for her to protest against these restrictions. Then, she would most probably arrest Olivia straight away for defying orders. Her only hope was to agree.

"But—" she said, as she remembered her almost-empty fridge and larder.

"What?" the detective snapped.

"I was just wondering about going to the shops?" Surely an innocent trip to the village would be allowed?

The detective's voice scythed her.

"No shops! You can get groceries delivered!"

Olivia stared at her, perplexed. She wasn't sure the local stores did deliveries. Was Detective Caputi intending her to starve to death?

She sighed in frustration. She'd have to find out if the stores could deliver at such short notice. Maybe they could bring supplies to the winery while she was at work. With these inhumane fetters in place, she couldn't even stop by the local restaurant and grab a to-go pizza.

Briefly, Olivia thought of Danilo. In other circumstances—like, two days ago when her whole world was different, she would have called him up and given him a list. He would have brought the groceries to her, along with a smile and a bottle of wine and most likely, a few treats that weren't on the list.

Then she would have cooked dinner for them to enjoy together in her warm kitchen.

Olivia felt a pang of bitter sadness as she recalled that terrible day out. It was to have been a romantic adventure. She wished she knew what had happened. Danilo hadn't called since then and she didn't feel she could call him after he had been the one to take such a giant step back.

He was clearly resetting the boundaries of their relationship, only right now, it seemed that they were moving all the way to "nonexistent."

Olivia knew she would struggle to go back to the original friendship. Some things couldn't be unmade or undone. Too much had happened between them, gradually bringing them closer and weaving a web of emotional entanglement.

A fragile web, as it turned out.

Maybe, having decided he wasn't ready for romance, or whatever his reason had been, Danilo had chosen to call it quits altogether.

Detective Caputi finished scribbling her notes and stood up. The scrape of her chair wrenched Olivia out of her gloomy musings and back to her uncomfortable reality.

"Go only home, or else," the detective reminded her in frigid tones.

For once, Olivia didn't feel the usual chill of dread at these threatening words. She was too busy listening to an odd, barely audible sound she'd just noticed.

During the interview, her attention had been too focused on her own predicament to worry about anything else. But now, this weird buzzing noise was grabbing her attention. What was it?

Olivia stood up, turned, and walked in a curious zigzag line across the room. This was where it was coming from. The far corner, next to the fireplace.

She drew in a sharp breath as she stared down.

"Detective?" she called in a high voice. "Detective, I need your help here!"

She glanced around to see the policewoman regarding her suspiciously.

"Do you have any space in your car?" Olivia asked. "Or should we call another cab?"

The detective hurried over, her shoes clicking on the warm, earthen tiles.

She gave an astonished snort as she stared in the direction of Olivia's pointing finger.

Granny Petra was curled on the mat, snoring ecstatically, with five empty sherry glasses lined up in front of her on the terra-cotta-tiled hearth.

"I think the Millers must have forgotten her," Olivia explained. "I don't know how long she's been there. What should we do?"

The detective sounded at the end of her tether as she barked out an instruction to her police sergeant.

The tall man hurried over and gathered the elderly woman up in his arms.

She didn't even wake, just giggled and muttered something unintelligible.

"I'm not sure what her room number is," Olivia said. "Perhaps one of the family will know?"

Realizing she was shifting anxiously from foot to foot, she stopped herself and stood still.

"Come, now," Detective Caputi commanded her sergeant. She stomped to the exit, as if her patience had reached a snapping point.

Olivia felt briefly sympathetic toward her. She was sure the detective would be busy the whole night. With nineteen guests to interview, she didn't foresee her wrapping up before morning.

Olivia jumped as a warm hand clasped her shoulder.

Marcello stood behind her.

"I wanted to thank you," he said. He spoke in a low voice, sounding relieved.

"You did? For what?"

Marcello pressed his lips together thoughtfully before he continued.

"For not telling the detective that the groom's father rejected my business offer. It would have complicated things. I do not want the police to look in the wrong direction."

"That's no problem," Olivia said, although she feared the police were already doing exactly that. "There were so many bigger issues that it didn't even occur to me to mention it."

"I believe family politics was the cause of this tragedy," Marcello agreed.

But as he walked away, Olivia couldn't help frowning in concern.

What would happen when Mr. Miller told the detective he'd refused the offer, to the amusement of his son? That would make the handsome winery owner a prime suspect. He'd be at the top of the list with Olivia. She knew Caputi would believe the rude rejection of a business proposal with its loss of pride and profits to be a bigger issue than simmering family tensions.

And, Olivia acknowledged with a chill, perhaps Caputi would be right.

She'd never seen Marcello so angry. Had he snapped, and unleashed his passionate Italian rage?

When she realized what a compelling motive Marcello had, Detective Caputi might arrest him immediately. He could end up in jail, accused of a dastardly crime. That meant the pressure was on.

Olivia decided she had no choice. She would be forced to investigate this herself, despite the dire threats she'd received! She needed to clear her own name, it was a matter of urgency to clear Marcello's, and most important of all, Jean-Pierre had to get back to his soccer practice before the team found someone else.

There wasn't a moment to lose.

First thing in the morning, she would have to fling herself into an intensive investigation, even if it meant defying orders, risking arrest, and going head to head with the detective.

Venturing straight into the dragon's den, Olivia hoped she would manage to avoid the teeth and flames she knew were waiting there.

# CHAPTER FIFTEEN

Olivia woke well before her alarm the next morning. Surfacing from a restless and uneasy slumber, she replayed yesterday's events in her mind as she stared up into the darkness.

How could she have prevented yesterday's tragic outcome, she wondered? If she could turn back the clock, what would she have done differently?

Then, switching to a more realistic angle, she began mulling over the events of the previous night. Was there anything she had noticed during that chaotic evening that could provide a clue to the murderer's identity?

As she replayed events in her mind, a terrible realization hit her.

Olivia sat bolt upright in bed, her heart hammering with shock.

That corkscrew was her favorite one! She had used it to open all the bottles of red wine for the party. That tool would have her fingerprints all over it.

"Help!" Olivia cried, clutching the bedcovers as shivers prickled her spine. This evidence was going to incriminate her, despite her innocence. Thanks to all her hard work and planning and diligent preparation, she would be locked up as soon as the police dusted down that tool.

She scrambled out of bed and drew back the curtains, staring at the gray, cloudy sky.

The winery was closed today due to the wedding that should have been happening, but Olivia decided to go in early anyway. She knew everyone would be working hard to tidy the mess, so that they could open for business as usual on Sunday.

She got dressed, fed Erba, and headed out of the front door with the goat gamboling alongside, pleased to be walking to work. Olivia felt jealous. Erba was a free goat, who could roam where she pleased. Her movements weren't restricted by a terrifying detective.

"You're a lucky animal," Olivia told her, bending forward to scratch her back in mid-scamper.

Jean-Pierre arrived at the same time she did, and they headed into the tasting room where the air was fragrant with the aroma of freshly brewed coffee. Marcello and Antonio were busy dismantling the tables and loudspeakers.

Glancing into the restaurant, Olivia saw that the pink chiffon had been removed from the walls. Nadia was busy cramming it into a trash bag with what seemed like unnecessary force.

"Good morning," Olivia said, trying to sound bright and cheery. "What can I do to help?"

Marcello looked around, his face warming at her words.

"You can pack the unused wine bottles away, and update the computer so that our stock is accurate." Moving toward her, he squeezed her arm gently. "I have told everyone what happened. They all know what a disaster last night was, and what we are facing now."

He returned to the sound system, unplugging cables carefully as he disconnected the giant speakers.

Glad to have a job to do, Olivia headed into the restaurant, with Jean-Pierre trailing behind her. Melancholy oozed from the expressive Frenchman. His shoulders were bowed, and Olivia thought that even his dark, wavy hair looked subdued.

She was taken aback to be greeted by a hostile snort as she walked into the restaurant.

Gabriella, stacking coffee cups, glared at her.

"So there you are. I hope you are proud of yourself."

Olivia gaped at her. What had happened to teamwork and unity? Why had Gabriella escalated their conflict all the way back up to vendetta level?"

"Why?" she asked.

"Because now we have another murder," Gabriella hissed. "How many more do you think you can cause, before people stop visiting us? I need my tables full, and they will be empty if people are afraid to come here!"

"But—it wasn't my fault," Olivia protested. Never mind blaming her for having caused the killing, Gabriella was practically accusing her of wielding the corkscrew. It was hugely unfair.

Clearly, she wasn't going to get an apology or even a compromise. Gabriella flounced back to the kitchen, tossing her hair, which this morning was artfully curled over her shoulders.

Grimacing in consternation, Olivia had no idea whether Gabriella genuinely believed this was true, or if she was using it as an excuse to resume hostilities. Either way, the restaurant felt like an unfriendly place now. The sulfurous fumes of resentment emanating from Gabriella's kitchen lair were almost tangible.

Olivia set about her job, collecting and sorting the bottles and then making a list. Once the bottles had filled a case, Jean-Pierre carried it back to the tasting room and unpacked it, while Olivia updated the computer records. Then they headed back and began the process again. She was glad that this work required constant mental focus as well as physical effort, as it kept her thoughts occupied and distracted her from her predicament.

As opposed to Gabriella, who was doing nothing more than stirring a sauce, and most probably marinating in her own animosity, Olivia thought, taking a quick break to glance sourly at the kitchen where she could hear vigorous, and in fact aggressive, scraping noises.

Then, from behind her, she heard a stern throat clearing.

She recognized the sound only too well.

Feeling as if her heart had stopped, she spun round.

Detective Caputi stood there, glowering at her.

Olivia's first, rather random thought was that the detective couldn't possibly have slept. It wasn't yet nine a.m. and she could only have arrived at the hotel after midnight.

Given this timeframe, Olivia was alarmed by how sharp-eyed and alert she looked. She thought it provided more proof that Detective Caputi might not be entirely human.

"Olivia Glass, I must speak to you in private," the detective announced.

Jean-Pierre hotfooted it back into the tasting room, clearly relieved that he wasn't in her crosshairs. Out of the corner of her eye, Olivia saw Gabriella peek out from the kitchen, looking gleeful.

"Come outside," the detective continued inexorably.

With her heart accelerating, Olivia realized what this was about.

It was the fingerprints. Those incriminating prints, all over the corkscrew. The detective wasn't even going to ask questions, but would arrest her immediately.

She followed her out on leaden feet.

"I know what this is about," she stated, trying to sound calm and in control of the situation. Of course, she failed dismally. Even she could hear that she sounded petrified.

"What would that be?"

"The—the murder weapon. The corkscrew. I know I was the last person to handle it." Too late, Olivia realized her slip-up. "Well, not the last person, of course. The third last, actually, because the groom took it outside and then someone else—er—used it. But I know my prints are probably on it. It was my favorite one, as it worked the best and was by far the sharpest. All corkscrews have their own character."

Quickly, she closed her mouth. In her nervousness she was beginning to babble. In present company, that was unwise.

The detective stared at her.

"As it happens, the corkscrew was wiped clean of all prints," she said.

"Oh! Was it? My goodness."

Olivia didn't know what to say. She felt herself going red. The lack of prints didn't help the police at all, but she could see it didn't help her either.

"A very convenient action. Particularly since, as you have said, you were aware how sharp it was, and that your prints would be on it. This is highly suspicious." The detective regarded her closely. "When did you do this? Did you use your shirt or jacket to wipe it?"

"What?" Olivia asked, alarmed. She felt skewered by Caputi's relentless gaze. Was she being formally accused? It sounded like it, despite the lack of prints. "I didn't touch the corkscrew when I saw his body! I didn't touch him, either!"

"Many of the guests reported that you were in conflict with Terence Jones throughout the evening," Caputi continued malevolently. "You had an argument about the music earlier in the night. You didn't tell me that. Why? Are you concealing evidence?"

"I—I didn't mention it because I forgot all about it. He did insult my choice of music, which was hurtful, because everybody loves the eighties and I think personally it would have created a far more congenial vibe. But I was too busy to worry about that for long." Once again, Olivia felt firmly on the back foot.

"I believe he insulted you repeatedly."

"No, he didn't. Well, only once. He was too busy drinking and dancing the rest of the time."

"At least two witnesses have stated clearly that they saw you follow Terence Jones out of the restaurant."

"No, that's totally untrue." Now Olivia was on firmer ground. In fact, she felt the beginnings of righteous indignation. "If they said so, they are either lying or misremembering. I'll tell you exactly what happened. Terence went out. He was so drunk he was reeling. Then Angelique told us all what she thought of him, and she went out.

85

Everyone dispersed, but I stayed where I was and I ate a piece of wedding cake."

"Cake? At such a time?" Disbelief dripped from Caputi's voice.

Olivia shrugged. "I'm a stress eater."

"And why did you not go and help?"

"I had already! When Angelique came into the winery, screaming that she'd seen Terence kissing Alice, I was the first to run to her, with Jean-Pierre right behind me. She was furious, and picked up a huge glass vase. I tried to stop her from smashing it, so the water spilled all over me! My blouse was soaked and freezing cold. I decided we should all talk about this calmly, so I walked Angelique to the restaurant and sat with my back to one of the heaters, drying it. After Terence left and she ran out, I ate a piece of cake while I calmed down and thought about what to do."

What more could she say? Olivia agonized. Clearly, the detective was doing her best to pressure Olivia into confessing. But she couldn't confess to something she hadn't done!

As if reading her mind, the detective continued. Olivia thought she sounded slightly disappointed.

"Although some eyewitnesses did indeed make those observations, others were confused and could not confirm this happened," Detective Caputi continued. "People were drinking, their memories were hazy, and many of the guests became very emotional as the evening unfolded. Therefore, I will need to re-interview a number of them before I can take this further."

She needed to re-interview? Olivia felt a sliver of hope. It sounded as if she was not going to be arrested. At any rate, not yet.

"You are still a prime suspect who had the motive and the opportunity to commit this crime. If you are guilty, I will uncover the facts. In the meantime, do not get involved." Detective Caputi pointed a stern finger at Olivia. "This is not a game. The murder of an international visitor has put our department under huge pressure from the top. It is essential that we complete the investigation speedily, and that you do not interfere, or attempt to frame anyone else."

Caputi's words sounded as if they had been carved from ice. Olivia felt a shiver run between her shoulder blades that had nothing to do with the intensifying breeze.

"I understand," she reassured the detective.

Caputi nodded sternly.

Olivia was expecting her to head into the winery, but instead the detective stomped over to her steel-gray Fiat and climbed inside.

A moment later, she drove away, leaving Olivia gaping in concern.

She'd come all the way back just for that? It was more than a veiled threat. It had been a direct attempt to obtain a confession.

It seemed the only thing standing between Olivia and the waiting police cell was that nobody could recall exactly what had happened last night and everyone had given a different story.

Her fate now hinged on the flimsy memories of eighteen roaringly drunk guests, and one snoozing grandma.

# CHAPTER SIXTEEN

As Detective Caputi's gray Fiat disappeared from sight, Olivia felt resolve build inside her. Even though she would be directly defying the detective's serious threats, she needed to get to the hotel where the wedding party was staying, and confront Angelique. It was highly suspicious that she had run out of the restaurant soon after Terence had left, refusing all offers of help from her bridesmaids. And she had the strongest motive by far.

Olivia packed up the last case of wine, glad to be walking out of the unfriendly environment of the restaurant. Back in the storage room she unpacked the bottles and headed to the office to make the final updates on the computer.

Then she began making notes. When she reached the hotel, she would need to question Angelique extensively. Her thoughts must be in order, so that she could work as quickly as possible.

*"Where did you go when you left the restaurant?"* Olivia wrote. That would be her first question. Then, *"Was anyone with you?"*

At that moment, the door to the storage room banged open.

"Ugh, ugh, ugh! I feel ill! I am going to throw up," a loud, French-accented voice groaned.

Olivia scrambled up and hurried out of the small office.

"Jean-Pierre, are you all right?" she called, as she rushed past the cool, tall shelves of wine.

*"Non, non!* I am going to perish from sickness." Reaching him, she saw he looked pale green. "I have just had to clean the ladies' restroom! The whole bathroom was covered in sick. Covered!" He shuddered. "And my stomach is not strong."

"Oh, that's terrible!"

Quickly, Olivia reached into the fridge and grabbed a can of ginger ale, one of the last survivors of the wedding soda stash.

She poured it into a glass and added lots of ice.

"Ginger's supposed to be good for nausea. Come into the back office and sit down and sip it slowly. That must have been the worst job to do!"

Jean-Pierre collapsed into a chair.

Olivia watched him, feeling worried, as he slowly sipped the drink. Gradually, his color changed from green, to sheet white, and then a faint pink reappeared in his cheeks.

"I feel a little better now," he declared.

He peered down at Olivia's notes. "What are you doing?" he asked curiously.

Even though discretion was paramount, Olivia decided she could trust her assistant.

"I am writing down some thoughts and questions I have about what happened last night," she said.

"Ah!" Jean-Pierre said. He looked at her inquiringly.

"It's for my own personal closure. I am not doing any investigation," Olivia said in firm tones.

"Oh, *non, non!*" Jean-Pierre waved his arms expressively before downing the last gulp of ginger ale. "Absolutely not. I would not dream of doing that either, but can see how you need your thoughts to be in order." He lowered his voice. "In fact, I, too, have been trying to reach closure by recalling how things were. Until I was told to clean the bathroom. Then I was not able to think clearly for a while."

Olivia was comforted that she and Jean-Pierre were on exactly the same page. She closed her notebook and put it, and her pen, back in her purse.

"What are you going to do now?" Jean-Pierre asked.

"I am going to go home," Olivia stated firmly. "I will stay there as instructed, and think about this some more."

She headed out of the winery and detoured past the goat dairy to pick Erba up.

As they walked home, Olivia found herself immersed in thought, so preoccupied she didn't even gaze around her to take in the vista of hills and vineyards and cedar trees. The rural landscape seemed to hold a different beauty every day, depending on the light and the sun and the season.

Today, Olivia did no more than glance at the verdant landscape before fixing her gaze on the road ahead. She had a serious problem to solve and needed to give it urgent attention. How on earth was she going to arrive at the hotel, which would be filled with police detectives including Caputi, without being spotted?

It seemed impossible. Was she going to have to abandon her mission before it even began?

It was only when she was striding up the steep hill that led to her farm's gate that an answer came to Olivia.

"Of course!" she exclaimed to Erba. "I can do it, if I make myself look different enough! I can't take you along, though. Unfortunately you'd be a total giveaway. You stay here and guard the farm. If Detective Caputi arrives, tell her I've just left for work!"

Hurrying into the farmhouse, Olivia raided her wardrobe, watched curiously by Pirate, who was reclining on the bed with his white paws in the air and his black tail dangling off the edge of the covers.

At the back of the wardrobe was a large, tan coat that she'd bought on a sale before realizing it was too big and heavy and she was never going to wear it.

Together with the oversized pair of sunglasses that she'd brought from the States, and also never worn because they were too heavy and left dents in her nose, this would form the basis of her disguise, Olivia decided.

She needed a hat. Her blond hair was far too conspicuous. Searching through drawers, Olivia came up with a black beanie that she'd forgotten she'd ever owned. It was large and remarkably ugly. As she pulled the knitted monstrosity into place, Olivia was reminded all over again of why she'd decided that a cold head was better than this shapeless covering.

For now, it was perfect. It completely hid her hair.

"I think I have a black scarf, too, Pirate."

Reaching into the wardrobe again, Olivia added it to her ensemble.

"What do you think?" she asked the cat.

He stared at her impassively. Olivia had the clear impression her cat thought she was mad.

"I need to be a different shape," Olivia decided.

She took out three sweaters and pulled them on, one after the other, before adding the coat.

Then she scrutinized her reflection in the full-length mirror before nodding admiringly. She looked nothing like herself. Nothing! Her hair was hidden, she appeared twenty pounds heavier, and the sunglasses made her look like a typical tourist.

"Pirate, if I get arrested, I'll call Danilo and ask him to come and feed you," she promised her cat. "He doesn't love me, but I'm sure he loves you. And now, I'm heading to the hotel."

As she said that, her confidence in her disguise evaporated and a hundred butterflies took wing in her stomach.

Going downstairs, she opened the front door and glanced apprehensively around, expecting to hear a gleeful cry as Detective Caputi rushed over with the handcuffs.

All she saw was Erba. She'd headed up to the barn and was nosing at the door hopefully, clearly smelling the wine. Olivia knew that if her goat managed to get inside, those steel vats wouldn't stand a chance! In fact, she'd probably arrive back to find her head peeking drunkenly out of the closest one.

Quickly, Olivia lumbered over in her cumbersome outfit to double check the doors were secure. Then, she waddled back again and, with some difficulty, climbed into her car.

This disguise was not only bulky, it was swelteringly hot. She was starting to wish that winters in Tuscany were colder. After turning her car's A/C to its lowest setting, Olivia drove cautiously out of the farmhouse.

She stopped outside the gate and checked the road carefully.

No other cars were nearby. But had the detective stationed a police officer en route? It would be just the kind of sneaky maneuver Olivia would expect from her.

Although she racked her brains, she couldn't remember if the police had the exact details of her car. Hopefully not. And fortunately for her, she'd chosen a common make of vehicle in an unobtrusive color.

At the time she'd bought the car, Olivia had wished it could be bright, pillar-box red. Now, she couldn't be more thankful for its dull, ordinary grayness that might well save her skin in this tense situation.

She headed into the medieval town, too preoccupied to glance at the majestic, crumbling walls of the ruined castle at its entrance. All she was looking out for were police officers.

With its narrow roads, Collina was always busy with traffic and Olivia grew even more edgy as she waited to pass a large, badly parked tour bus. She didn't want to be stopped in this busy, public spot, but there was no other way to the hotel without driving for miles around a long circular route. La Locanda was a couple of miles further on along this very road, in the scenic countryside beyond the village.

Distracted by the tour bus, Olivia swerved at the last minute to avoid a portly man on a bicycle. Pot-bellied and with a handlebar mustache, he had a cycling helmet wedged low on his head and was wearing sports sunglasses.

Olivia twisted the wheel to stop the car careening into the opposite wall. She gave an apologetic wave, hoping the large-bellied rider had noticed it, although he didn't seem to be looking anywhere except the ground.

Olivia felt terrible about this near miss. She'd almost mowed down an innocent cyclist! She needed to pay attention. Now was not the time to lose focus.

She concentrated hard for the rest of the short drive, but by the time she reached the hotel, her butterflies numbered in the thousands.

If she had any sense, she'd turn back again.

"I have no sense whatsoever," Olivia muttered, turning into the hotel's main gate. Despite the dangers, she was committed to search for the killer now.

# CHAPTER SEVENTEEN

La Locanda was a stately, five-story building, set in large, immaculately maintained grounds. Glancing admiringly at the profusion of color in the flower beds as she cruised up the long gravel drive, Olivia was certain that the owners aimed to give the feeling of year-round summer in this smart, five-star establishment.

Luckily the hotel had separate parking at its golf course entrance. Deciding this would give her a better chance of surviving this reckless quest, Olivia stopped at the golf course, hiding her car behind a large minibus so there was no chance of Detective Caputi noticing it. Then she headed up to the main entrance on foot.

She was puffing by the time she reached the imposing gateway. Checking the hotel's parking lot thoroughly, she didn't see Detective Caputi's car. It didn't mean the detective hadn't used a different car this time, or that she might arrive any minute.

She hoped her disguise would hold up!

Heading into the hotel, Olivia tried to look familiar with the spacious, airy, and high-ceilinged building, as if she'd been there many times before. She didn't want anyone rushing over to try and help her.

The first person she saw was a uniformed police officer standing near the front desk.

Olivia's heart jumped into her mouth. Was he going to see straight through her disguise and arrest her on the spot?

He seemed to be watching the staircase and elevator, rather than the front entrance. So she guessed that his main role was to stop the wedding guests from trying to do a runner.

Where would Angelique be staying?

In the honeymoon suite, obviously! Olivia breathed a sigh of relief as she saw the signboard next to the elevator. The suite was on the top floor and must command a panoramic view.

Olivia headed to the elevator in a businesslike way, as if she was a guest who had just returned from a healthy walk. Luckily, the hotel receptionist was busy checking in a new arrival and was too distracted to notice her.

Before she could climb inside, she heard the stomp of footsteps from a side corridor. Angelique's brother Lysander rounded the corner. He'd been working out. He wore a vest and gym shorts, and his blond hair was dark with sweat.

He headed for the elevator.

Hyperventilating, Olivia turned away and marched in the opposite direction. She did not need to bump into this aggressive individual! She couldn't help remembering how he'd threatened to beat Terence up as soon as he'd heard what had happened.

Olivia pretended a sudden interest in the display on the far wall, which was a framed collage of signed photographs from celebrities who'd stayed there. As she surveyed the display, she was enchanted to see that the great Pavarotti himself had stayed in the Presidential Suite during the 1990s.

Staring fixedly at his dark-haired, smiling face, Olivia tried not to think about what might happen if Lysander's perspiring finger jabbed her in the back, and he accused her of arriving here to spy.

The elevator pinged and the doors whooshed closed. Only then did she dare to look around. To her relief, the lobby was now Lysander-free.

Olivia headed back to the elevator, hoping Lysander hadn't forgotten anything. Imagine if she came face to face with him when the doors opened!

Luckily, the elevator was empty when it arrived. Pressing the button for the top floor, she rode up in solitude.

The honeymoon suite was halfway down the bright, tiled corridor which had narrow, arched windows along its length. Light spilled through, making the terra-cotta tiles seem to glow. In between each window were framed pieces of art that looked original and expensive. As she hurried by, Olivia's gaze was caught by the evocative, misty pinks and greens of a framed painting by the young Milanese artist Serena Vestrucci.

Olivia loved her work. How she wished she was here under different circumstances, so she could stop and admire the gorgeous swirls of colors and textures that made up this artist's mysterious interpretation of a landscape.

With a firm shake of her head, she moved on to the honeymoon suite. Before she could lose her nerve, she knocked on the door.

"What is it?" a petulant voice called from within. "I don't need my bed made! Someone already did that!"

"Minibar stock take," Olivia muttered, trying to sound Italian.

She heard footsteps padding across the carpet and a moment later, Angelique wrenched the door open impatiently.

"Come—" she began, before staring at Olivia in surprise.

"You're not from the hotel! Where are you from? Who are you?" she asked as Olivia pushed her way inside.

Quickly, she removed her dark glasses and closed the door.

"I'm from the winery," she whispered. "Remember me? I said Terence should be punished for what he did to you!"

Angelique brightened.

"Oh, great! Are you the one who punished him, then?"

Horrified by the bride-no-longer-to-be's misconception, Olivia hastened to set the record straight.

"No, no! Absolutely not." Deciding she should start by being polite and sympathetic in this delicate situation, she added, "I'm very sorry for your loss."

Angelique shrugged. "What loss? You expect me to forgive him for what he did, just because he was murdered?"

Alarmed by the other woman's attitude, and wondering if it confirmed her guilt, Olivia hastened to explain the reason for her innocent arrival in this fancy suite.

"I discovered the body, but I wasn't the one who committed the crime. I'm trying to find out who was, and that's why I've come here."

Perching on the white lace coverlet of the enormous four-poster bed, Angelique stared at her suspiciously for a few moments.

"Are you trying to force me to confess? I know that I am a suspect, because of telling everyone I wished he was dead."

Olivia shook her head.

Angelique hadn't asked her to sit down, but even so, she took a seat on the cute red velvet love seat opposite the bed. Standing up was making her seem like Detective Caputi, and she didn't want Angelique to feel threatened.

"I had the same thing happen to me on my wedding morning. I mean, the groom cheating on me. Not being murdered."

"Really?" Angelique sounded friendlier.

"I went to his hotel room to leave a gift after he'd gone to breakfast. And there, in his bed, I found my friend and bridesmaid!"

Angelique looked horrified.

"Two women were there?"

"No, no, just one."

"Oh." Angelique paused. "Well, one's bad enough!" she said firmly.

"I thought so too. I threw Ward's gift at him and shouted a lot of bad things before calling the wedding off. I'm sure I told him I wished he was dead, too. It's what you say in the heat of the moment. It's probably obligatory when you discover such a thing," Olivia explained.

Angelique seemed mollified by Olivia's words. She walked over to the mini bar and peered inside.

"Peanuts? Beef jerky? Chocolate?"

She chose a three-pack of Ferrero Rocher and unwrapped one of the gold foils.

"Actually, I'd love a chocolate," Olivia said. She didn't think she could possibly eat it now, she was feeling too nervous about having to make a sudden run for it. But she thought it would be a friendly gesture to accept the sweet treat. She needed to build trust between her and the bride-no-longer-to-be.

Angelique handed her the rest of the pack.

"Where did you go when you went outside?" Olivia asked, remembering the questions she'd written down. She reminded herself to listen carefully to the answers and to think about what Angelique was keeping back, as well as what she was sharing.

"Well, I stormed out." Sitting on the bed again, Angelique bit the chocolate in half. "I was so angry, I planned to walk the whole way back to the hotel and from there, get a cab to the airport. That was what was in my mind. In fact, I was heading out of the parking lot and down the driveway. But then Cassidy called out to me."

Olivia nodded. That was question two answered: Who was with you? She remembered how the tall brunette had raced after her upset friend.

"So you two stayed together?"

"Yes. Cassidy tried to persuade me it would be better not to leave the winery, as we might get lost."

"And did you agree to that?" Olivia pressured her, needing more detail.

"Well, sort of. I told her there was no way that I was going back inside. I mean, would you have?"

Olivia shook her head. "I would also have needed to get some air for a while."

"So, instead of heading out of the estate, we went for a walk on the inside roads to calm down. It was very dark, so I'm not sure what route we took, but we found a path leading to the back of the winery. Then we walked for a while, came back, got lost again, and ended up at the goat dairy."

"I see."

Angelique nodded. "Cassidy probably remembers it better. I was so angry I wasn't thinking or looking. Just walking."

Well, in view of what had happened, that sounded reasonable. Probably, it would have been more suspicious if Angelique had given an accurate step by step account of her journey around the winery.

However, although the blonde couldn't provide any more information, Olivia knew she had to get to Cassidy urgently and confirm the story. If Cassidy could provide clearer details—and only if—then both women would have an alibi.

Doubts set in again as Olivia put the chocolate in her pocket. There wasn't going to be such a thing as a reliable witness after the massive quantities of wine and emotion that had surged yesterday. And thanks to the crystal bear episode Olivia knew that Angelique was manipulative and could have forced Cassidy to lie on her behalf.

This interview with Cassidy would be critical, and she would have to look out for any signs that Cassidy might be covering for her friend, or hiding the truth.

"Do you know which room Cassidy is staying in?" Olivia asked. "And anyone else?" she added hopefully.

"Cassidy is in room 301. My brother is in room 309 and my revolting sister, who I never want to see again, is next door to Cassidy. The other bridesmaids are on the second floor, but I'm not sure which rooms. My parents are at the end of the corridor on this top floor. I think most of the groomsmen have rooms on the fourth floor."

"That's so helpful. Thank you," Olivia said, delving in her coat's inner pocket for the small notebook she'd brought with her and jotting the information down.

"Tell me," she added, trying to sound casual, "do you have an idea who could have done this?"

Angelique sighed.

"I've been thinking it over and I have decided it was either Kyle or Rog."

Olivia felt startled. The groom's friends? Why did Angelique suspect them?

"Is there a reason for that?" she asked carefully.

"Well, I feel they both had anger issues. I think they were jealous of Terence." She lowered her voice. "There was this not-so-nice side to him, you see, which I couldn't help but notice sometimes. When I was at breakfast yesterday morning, I was getting my eggs made. They do it behind this screen, and there's an egg lady who does whatever you want. Scrambled, poached, fried, or omelet."

"I see," Olivia said.

"I was behind the screen, getting a cheese and mushroom omelet, when I heard Terence bragging to his group that he was going to take over his dad's business soon, and be super-wealthy. He said he was a business guru who'd studied all the latest information, and that if any of his friends wanted a job he wouldn't show them any favors and they'd have to beg and scrape just the same as everyone else."

Olivia remembered that Terence had used the term "beg and scrape" when insulting Marcello as well. He had seemed to like it.

"Who was in the group?" she asked.

"Well, all the guys in the wedding party. All the groomsmen, as well as Terence's brother."

"Lance is younger?" Olivia asked, needing to get the facts straight.

"Yes. Lance is two and a half years younger than Terence and he never lets—" Angelique corrected herself hurriedly. "Terence never used to let him forget it. Honestly, when I look back at his behavior, I'm sorry that I fell so hard for his looks and didn't focus more on his personality and actions. Then, all of this could have been avoided."

Olivia nodded understandingly. Given the scenario Angelique had described, she thought Lance, as Terence's younger brother, had an even bigger motive than the groomsmen. He could have planned to do the deed at the wedding, hoping that in the foreign setting and with so many other suspects, he would get away with it. She would need to be very careful when interviewing Lance, Olivia decided.

Olivia didn't think Terence would have made a success of his father's business. Perhaps he'd read *How to Lose Friends and Influence People*. Or maybe, Olivia mused, *The Seven Habits of Highly Effective Victims*.

"Well, thank you so much. What you've said has been really helpful. If you have any other ideas, will you call me?" she asked.

"Of course. Let me write your number down, and you can take mine, too."

Angelique rummaged in her purse. Olivia guessed she was searching for one of her debt collection business cards, but she never got the chance to hand it over.

At that moment, somebody rapped loudly on the door.

# CHAPTER EIGHTEEN

Olivia stared at Angelique in horror. Her heart jumped into her scarf-wrapped throat. This was a disaster! She was trapped in here, with nowhere to hide.

She spun around, desperately scouting the spacious room. The crimson velvet seat had spindly legs and offered no useful cover. The king-size bed's solid base reached almost to the floor. The red curtains were artfully held back by cords and tassels, and couldn't conceal a toddler, never mind a trench-coat-wrapped Olivia.

The bathroom didn't have a door. Olivia could have lamented the modern, broadminded openness of the European design that had only an archway, with the claw-footed bath beyond. The toilet cubicle on the far side had a frosted glass door, but you could still see if someone was inside or not. Plus, whoever was entering the room might need to use the bathroom!

"In here! In here!" Angelique hissed.

She propelled Olivia over to the large wooden wardrobe as the knock sounded again, this time even louder and more impatient.

Was there enough space in this modestly sized wardrobe?

Olivia hesitated, but a determined shove from Angelique sent her scrambling into the restrictive space.

Angelique slammed the door, but thanks to Olivia's bulky clothing, it didn't close properly. A crack of light was visible. Olivia shifted back, trying to solve this problem, but when she moved, the floor creaked alarmingly.

She froze. Better just to stay where she was, flattened—as far as being flat in her stifling coat and jersey layers was possible—against the wardrobe's back wall. She resolved to try not to move at all. Or to breathe.

Olivia snapped her mouth closed as she heard Angelique unlatch the door.

"Hello, Daddy," she said.

At least it wasn't Detective Caputi. Small mercies, Olivia thought.

"Hey, my baby girl. I was on my way to the rooftop cocktail lounge and thought I would check in on you," he said. "Your mother's joining me there for an early lunch, but she's taking a walk around the grounds with Granny first. They wanted to explore the hotel's maze and the vineyard and the golf course. Granny wanted to play croquet on the front lawn, but they'll probably do that this afternoon if the weather holds. I've got a game of tennis organized with Lysander, but if it rains we can book one of the squash courts instead."

"You can always go for a swim in the heated pool," Angelique suggested.

Her father sighed. "It's preposterous that we are being held hostage here. I feel so trapped! I am sure you do, too. It's unacceptable. Not only has that detective seized your passport, but she's stationed someone in the lobby to make sure none of us take any luggage out!"

"Yes, Daddy," Angelique said. "I feel very claustrophobic. I felt like I was in prison the whole time during my four-mile jog around the grounds this morning. Do you think a spa treatment would help me to relax?"

Mr. Miller sighed. "Do it, honey. Book the works. Spoil yourself. But I hope that we can bring this untenable situation to an end as soon as possible, and fly home tomorrow." He lowered his voice. "It's obvious to me that none of the wedding party could possibly have committed this crime! Beyond a doubt, the guilty person is that serving woman at the winery, the one who was shooting her mouth off and saying that Terence should be punished."

Olivia jumped, banging against one of the coat hangers and sending a black jacket slithering off the rail. She grabbed it before the hanger clattered to the ground.

Mr. Miller was talking about her!

"What was that?" he asked, and Olivia froze again, feeling herself start to hyperventilate. How had she managed to get herself into such a perilous situation?

"What was what?" Angelique asked innocently.

"It sounded like a rattling noise."

"Oh, it's just the room's central heating turning on. The mechanism is rather noisy," Angelique explained.

Olivia had to give it to the blonde, she was a stellar liar who could dream up blatant untruths on the fly and without so much as a quiver in her voice! Olivia resolved to check and double-check Cassidy's story before believing it.

She clutched at the jacket, noticing it smelled strongly of wine. How was she going to get it, and the hanger, back on the rail without triggering Mr. Miller's supersensitive hearing again?

Perhaps the best would be to just hold it, Olivia decided. She tuned in again to the conversation taking place beyond the wardrobe doors.

"Anyway," Mr. Miller continued in a low, confidential tone, "I feel that the best for all of us would be if we can agree on a scenario. I know that everyone was confused and that is actually why I am going room to room, to see if anyone else remembers that serving girl heading out, soon after she told your husband-to-be that he was going to get what he deserved. I remember it clearly, as I was sitting in the restaurant with your mother and recall she seemed very murderous. She might even have stated she was going to kill him."

Olivia clamped her lips together to stop an astonished choke from escaping. This man was doing his best to get everyone to implicate her, so that they could all go home! How unfair was that?

"I am not sure that version will work," Angelique said carefully.

Olivia had the impression she was hedging her bets. No doubt, as soon as Olivia was gone, Angelique would tell her father she agreed with him, and that it was a good idea.

"Think it over, honey. Most people I've spoken to so far are happy with it," Mr. Miller reassured her. Olivia clutched the jacket in panic, and then loosened her grip as a paper in the pocket started rustling.

Luckily, Angelique's father was still in full conversational swing and didn't hear the small noise. "Tell me, have you tried the alfredo pasta al forno yet? Your mother is not sure whether to order that for lunch, or the prawn fettucine."

Paper in pocket?

Men's jacket, reeking of wine, in the honeymoon suite's wardrobe?

This had to belong to Terence! She remembered him wearing a well-cut dark jacket when he arrived. He had taken it off when the wild drinking and dancing began. Most likely, he'd hung it on the back of his seat and someone had brought it back.

A paper in the pocket could provide information she didn't yet have. It might even prove to be a clue.

Trying to move soundlessly, Olivia drew it out, conscious of every tiny rustle, and grateful that Angelique was loudly recommending that her mother should have the seafood pizza and a side salad with extra anchovies and Parmesan shavings.

Olivia clutched the paper in her damp palm. She'd gotten it out of the inside pocket where it had been stashed.

Carefully, she folded it over and placed it in her coat pocket.

A moment later, the wardrobe door flew open.

Blinded by light, Olivia let out a shriek.

Angelique stared at her irritably.

"Come on, come on. Don't make a noise, my dad might hear you and come back."

"I knocked this off the rail."

Scrambling out of the wardrobe, Olivia replaced the jacket on its hanger.

She was boiling hot after her confined ordeal, and her nerves felt shredded. So the Millers felt claustrophobic in the hotel and its enormous grounds? *Try spending time in here*, she thought resentfully.

"Thanks for the information," she said.

"Don't worry about my father," Angelique reassured her. "He won't be able to get everyone to agree on his version. Kyle and Rog are too stupid to be able to remember a different story, and the Joneses all hate him and will do the opposite of what he asks. Here, take my card before you go."

Olivia thanked Angelique again, shoving the business card safely into her pocket. Then she hustled out of the suite. The stairway to the rooftop bar was close by. She needed to get out of sight before any more of the family arrived to spend their imprisonment enjoying cocktails and delicious food.

Olivia's next destination was Cassidy's room, but when she tapped discreetly on the door, there was no answer. Perhaps Cassidy was having a nap after the stress of the previous night, or maybe she'd headed off for a few laps in the heated pool.

While Olivia was waiting outside, she heard women's voices from the room on the left.

Remembering that Angelique had said Alice was next door to Cassidy, she moved and knocked again.

It was opened almost immediately, and she found herself staring into Alice's surprised blue eyes.

Olivia couldn't help feeling fed up with Alice, who'd caused the entire evening to unravel when she'd irresponsibly kissed the groom, but she wasn't going to let personal feelings get in the way of her investigation. Taking advantage of the woman's confusion at finding a trench-coated apparition outside her door, Olivia pushed her way in and quickly removed her shades.

"Don't be scared," she told Alice, who was gaping at her in astonishment. "I'm the sommelier from La Leggenda. Remember me?"

"I remember you," the other occupant of the room said in a soft, threatening voice. "What are you doing here? The police mentioned you were a suspect. Surely suspects shouldn't be walking around this hotel and barging into people's rooms?"

The petite, dark-haired woman sat in a full lotus yoga pose on one of the twin beds, frowning dubiously at Olivia. She remembered this was Dinah, the bridesmaid who'd encouraged the others to be responsible. If only they'd taken her advice more seriously.

"I'm trying to help," Olivia explained.

"Help how?" Dinah wasn't buying her story. "You're not a cop. What right do you have to ask where we were and what we were doing? I think you should leave, right now, before *we* call the cops." She glanced meaningfully at Alice.

"I was working at the event all night, so I'm hoping that I might have seen or heard something that could identify the killer," Olivia said quickly. She knew she had only a few moments to change Dinah's mind before her patience evaporated and she made good on her threat. "The police didn't have the benefit of being on site at the time. Plus, I know how trapped you all feel here as you aren't allowed to travel outside of La Locanda. The sooner we find out who killed Terence, the sooner all of you can leave the hotel and go home," Olivia explained.

Alice burst into loud, hysterical sobs.

"It wasn't my fault! Everyone thinks so but they're all wrong! This whole situation got blown out of proportion. How could anyone think I would have kissed my own sister's husband-to-be? He simply hugged me and Angelique invented the rest! Nobody even cares how upset I am about this, apart from Lysander who comforted me after I was publicly humiliated!"

Sitting on the bed beside Alice and making sympathetic noises, Olivia wasn't sure she believed that version. She also warned herself that Alice's vehement denial could be because she'd committed the crime.

"Have a chocolate," she said, taking the Ferrero Rochers out of her jacket pocket. "Chocolate always makes things better."

"Thank you," Alice sniffed, unwrapping the chocolate. She appeared calmer as she ate it.

"I was in the ladies' bathroom at the time it happened," Dinah said, unwinding herself from her yoga pose and passing Alice a Kleenex. She seemed more cooperative now, to Olivia's relief. "Jewel was getting sick. I went to help her. When you drink too much, you need someone to hold your head steady and keep your hair out of the way."

Olivia was encouraged by this eyewitness testimony. This was important information. She remembered that Gramma B had seen Jewel heading for the bathroom, looking green. Jean-Pierre had been equally green after cleaning it. Undoubtedly, Jewel had been sick in there.

That ruled Jewel and Dinah off the list.

"I do have some other interesting information," Dinah added. She moved to the mat in front of the bed and stood on one leg, with her arms curved up above her. Olivia had no idea what that pose was called. Tree, maybe?

"What information?" she asked.

"It is just a rumor. But I was told that a month ago, while he was engaged, Terence went out with Madeline to a music concert while Angelique was at a college grads get-together. And I heard that they only got back in the morning."

She gave Olivia a sly glance and then serenely returned to being a tree.

"You mean that he cheated on her?" Olivia was appalled! A month before the wedding?

"Yes. Madeline told Miranda, who told Molly, who told me. And I told Cassidy, who told Jewel."

Olivia felt astounded, not only by the information, but by the fact that Dinah was composed enough to deliver the shocking revelation while balanced on one leg, without even wobbling.

Why had nobody spilled the beans to the bride? Had they all been too scared of being the messenger?

"Did nobody tell Angelique?" Olivia asked the burning question.

Dinah shrugged. "I guess none of us knew everything, except Madeline. So none of us said anything. Wouldn't be fair to either of them, would it?"

Olivia guessed there was cold logic in there somehow.

She couldn't help flashing back again to what a drastic error of judgment she'd made in planning to marry Ward. She was sure he had behaved exactly the same way as Terence in the weeks before the wedding. Like Angelique, she had been blissfully ignorant of his cheating ways.

"Do you know which room Madeline is staying in?" she asked.

Dinah nodded, moving into a kneeling position and then placing her hands on the ground and arching upward like a cat.

"She's on the second floor, first room on the right after the elevator. I'm not sure of the number."

"Thank you," Olivia said.

She hurried out of the room, encouraged that she was learning some important tidbits of information. She definitely knew more than she'd done an hour ago.

She got into the elevator and pushed the button for the second floor. But, as the doors were about to close, they pinged open again.

Olivia's heart stopped as Detective Caputi walked into the elevator.

# CHAPTER NINETEEN

Instinctively, Olivia ducked her head, pretending to rummage in her coat pocket as Detective Caputi pressed the button.

She couldn't breathe. For a start, her heart was jammed in her throat. Also, she was too terrified to make any sound that might draw the detective's attention to her.

Fortunately, the policewoman appeared impatient and preoccupied—at any rate, from her staring-at-the-floor vantage point, Olivia thought her feet seemed restless. She could see her black, polished ankle boot tapping on the elevator carpet.

Olivia would go straight to prison if her cover was blown. She'd been warned, and knew that by coming here, she'd be rubbing shoulders with the short-tempered detective.

Olivia just hadn't expected that she would end up trapped in the same four square yards of confined space!

She nearly jumped out of her skin as her phone gave a soft beep. Instinctively, she clamped a hand over her pocket. What a time to receive an incoming message.

The detective drew in her breath sharply and Olivia almost shrieked with tension. Had Caputi spied a stray blond hair adhering to the black beanie?

Olivia risked the tiniest upward flicker of her eyes, and saw the detective was staring at her own phone. She was frowning, tut-tutting to herself, clearly unhappy with the information she had received.

She heard a ping. Then boots clicked, retreating down the passageway.

Olivia lifted her head. Black spots floated in front of her eyes as she gulped in air.

She was on floor two, where she'd intended to get off. She couldn't now, of course. Not when the detective was prowling around that level. She needed to get out of this hotel immediately. There was too much risk that Detective Caputi would bump into her again, and next time, she might not be so distracted.

She punched the button for the lobby, feeling lightheaded with relief as the doors whooshed closed.

When they opened, she glanced immediately around to see where the police officer was.

He was outside, speaking to another officer who Olivia guessed must be taking over the next shift.

That gave her the chance she needed to sneak out and head home as fast as possible

But, as Olivia headed to the door, she saw Mrs. Miller and her son Lysander walk in.

They were talking together in soft, intense voices as they headed purposefully for the hotel bar.

Olivia felt literally torn. She hesitated, looking from side to side. The exit door on her left, the Millers on her right. Safety lay one way, and madness the other. She should leave at once, but the Millers seemed to be discussing a serious matter. This information could prove critical.

Olivia turned and followed them, berating herself for her stupidity.

Her actions were reckless, shortsighted in every way. Most probably, they would end in disaster. But for now, at least she'd have a chance to find out what they were debating in such hushed, yet fierce tones.

Olivia was glad to see that the bar was the epitome of old-fashioned grandeur. It had fancy high-sided seating booths that gave the illusion of complete privacy.

Unless, of course, someone sat down in the booth next to yours.

Olivia tiptoed in behind them and crept into the neighboring booth.

Perched on the soft, luxurious seat, she strained her ears to hear what the Millers were discussing.

"Did you do it, Lysander? Tell me! Did you lose your temper and stab him? I'm not going to tell anyone, but as your mother, I need to know the truth!" Mrs. Miller hissed, as Olivia leaned closer to the booth wall, enthralled.

This was proving to be even more eye-opening than she'd expected.

Lysander sighed.

"Mom, are you kidding? Stop slandering me!" he muttered querulously.

"Slandering you?" Mrs. Miller sounded affronted. "First of all, asking an innocent question isn't slander, and secondly, even if it was, I'm your mother and allowed to! Thirdly and most importantly, you are the one who's needed bailing out before now! Remember we had to get you out of jail after that graduation party where you ended up in a fight with the host? You were very fortunate that his family agreed to drop the charges after your father paid all his college fees."

Lysander grunted impatiently.

"You know you can act recklessly." Mrs. Miller's voice was quivering with earnestness. "But if you have, just tell me, and we can try to manage it."

"I didn't do it!" Lysander sounded exasperated.

"Swear to me!"

"I swear on—on everything! I did not do it, and I have no idea who did. Yes, I threatened Lance and those idiot groomsmen. They deserved it after insulting Alice. But I didn't take it further. I wish I had," he added regretfully.

"Well, all I can say is Angelique had a lucky escape," Mrs. Miller agreed. "I never thought Terence was good enough for her. He was arrogant and very disrespectful. She would have ended up being unhappy—but she's such a headstrong girl! Would she listen when I told her she was making the wrong decision? Of course not!"

"Yeah, he was a—" Olivia didn't catch the next word as Lysander mumbled it. From Mrs. Miller's gasp and shocked giggle, Olivia could guess what kind of word it was.

"Who could have done it?" Mrs. Miller mused, sounding thoughtful.

"What if it was Angelique?" Lysander asked. "You'll have to manage the situation just the same if it was her. I think it was her."

"No! Your sister would never do such a violent thing. She's a beautiful, gentle soul!"

Olivia clamped her lips together to stop a snort of disbelief from escaping. Angelique was the complete opposite!

"I think it was one of Terence's friends, Kyle or Rog. They are similar characters to him. Arrogant, opinionated, and aggressive." Mrs. Miller lowered her voice to a whisper and try as she might, Olivia couldn't pick up what she was saying.

"*Pronto?*" a man asked loudly, and Olivia almost fell off her seat with surprise.

The barman had arrived to take her order.

"Nothing, thank you," Olivia whispered. "I'm waiting for my friend."

The barman nodded, and moved on to the next-door booth.

While Mrs. Miller ordered cocktails, Olivia heard a chair scrape. Lysander had stood up and was heading to the men's bathroom.

He stopped when he saw Olivia and looked at her curiously.

Olivia felt her mouth go dry. This was twice in one short hour that he'd bumped into her, in her weird and memorable disguise. He must be wondering who she was, and why she was wearing such odd attire, and why she kept on being in the same part of the hotel as he was. Lysander seemed on the brink of putting two and two together. If he did, it would be disastrous.

She stared back at him as calmly as she could, given that panic was flaring inside her. She had to do something, quickly and subtly, to deflect his interest.

There was only one way that she could think of.

Olivia smiled politely at him.

"*Che bella giornata,*" she said conversationally, wincing inwardly at the awkwardness of her pronunciation of the Italian for "what a beautiful day."

Lysander gave an uncomprehending nod in return, the suspicion vanishing from his face. She could see him mentally pigeonholing her into the "just some random Italian woman" category and not the "who is this person and where do I know her from?" category. He continued on his way without looking back in her direction.

Olivia stood up and hurried out of the bar. It really was time to leave now as she couldn't risk any further close encounters. She decided to drive straight home, shed her sweltering disguise, and then go back to La Leggenda.

Luckily, the police officer was accepting a cappuccino from the hotel receptionist and didn't glance in her direction as she exited. Walking across the main parking lot, Olivia felt proud that for the first time since she'd arrived in Italy, she'd successfully impersonated an actual Italian.

Even though Lysander wasn't the quickest on the uptake, and the deception had only been for a moment, it was still an achievement and showed how she was progressing. While she hurried down to the golf course parking, Olivia mouthed the words she'd spoken over and over again, fine-tuning her pronunciation and accent. One day, she resolved, she would speak this musical language as well as it deserved!

As she drove out of the hotel, she mused over what she'd learned during this stressful foray.

Angelique's alibi needed confirming by Cassidy and she could not be ruled out as a suspect. Lysander was a hotheaded fighter with a history of assault. Terence had cheated on Angelique at least once, and

Mr. Miller was going door to door trying to persuade the entire wedding party to tell the police that she, Olivia, was guilty.

This was not looking good for her in particular, and after today's interviews, Olivia felt no closer to identifying the killer. All she seemed to be doing was unearthing more and more potential suspects!

"You have to start somewhere," she told herself firmly.

To Olivia's surprise, as she drove into the village, she spied the portly cyclist again. He was heading in the opposite direction this time, and despite his ample girth, setting a good pace up the steep hill.

This time Olivia made sure to give him a very wide berth. Driving on, and slowing to a crawl in the usual traffic jam on the village's narrow main street, she noticed something else that made conflicted feelings surge inside her.

Danilo was casually strolling into the Forno Collina bakery.

How could he be going out and about as if nothing was wrong, and he hadn't broken her heart with no further contact or explanation? She felt shocked to see that he was living his life as normal, and buying bread as if he didn't even miss her.

Not that she missed him either, she told herself, in a vain effort at denial.

Glancing at the displays in the window, she saw there were slices of Panforte di Siena. That was Danilo's favorite cake, and he'd introduced her to its rich yumminess. Made with generous quantities of nuts, dried fruit, spices, and syrup, and covered in powdered sugar, it was a dense, delicious treat. The spiciness gave it a unique and memorable flavor.

Since discovering how much he loved it, Olivia had made sure to buy a slice for Danilo every time she knew he would be dropping in. One time, she had even baked him a whole Panforte di Siena as a thank-you gift for helping to clear out her barn. He had been thrilled with it and had declared it even better than the shop-bought version.

She would never have the chance to bake another Panforte di Siena for him, thanks to the sudden termination of their friendship.

As he moved forward, Olivia spied a display of mini crostatas in the window. These sticky, jam-filled tarts were topped with a lattice of crisp, browned pastry. They had become her favorite and the treat she chose every time, even though Danilo had admitted they were a little too sweet for him.

Now, she saw him pause at the crostata display and stare at it thoughtfully before heading into the bakery.

Then the traffic eased and Olivia accelerated past. She felt discombobulated to have seen Danilo. His presence had triggered a disturbing rush of emotion, and worst of all, it was derailing her thoughts. She needed to focus on clearing her name and finding the killer.

Warning herself to stop obsessing about her ex-friend, she drove out of the village, keeping an eye open for any police cars, and in fact for anyone at all who seemed to be staring suspiciously in her direction. This behavior needed to become a habit, if she was going to avoid arrest. She didn't dare to relax until she'd turned down the quiet dirt road that led back to the farm and could see its open gate ahead of her.

Only when she drove through the gateway and parked in her spot near the farmhouse did she allow herself to let down her guard.

As soon as she was out of the car, Olivia tore off her stifling disguise, sighing in relief as the cool breeze tugged at her hair. Before she headed into work, she decided to examine the note that she took from Terence's coat.

Hurrying into the house, with a mound of bulky clothing over her arm, Olivia took the note from the pocket where she'd stashed it, and opened the page carefully.

"Well!" she said, as she read it.

It was written on a sheet of notepaper from the hotel and it said, "Babe, meet me @ 7 am in gym steam room, I will tell her I have gone 2 work out!"

Terence must have been intending to hand this to someone during the evening, setting up an assignation for first thing on his wedding morning!

What nerve!

Who had he been intending to give the note to? Alice? Madeline? Whichever of them it was, this provided more proof of his untrustworthy character.

Luckily, the outrage Olivia felt over Terence's cheating ways made her forget how upset she'd been to see her dark-haired ex-friend showing his face in the village bakery.

But it seemed she couldn't escape Danilo's presence in her life. When she opened her phone to read the message that had come through when she was in the elevator, she saw to her astonishment that Danilo had sent it.

# CHAPTER TWENTY

"Seriously?" Olivia said aloud, staring down at the unopened message with narrowed eyes, as if it might leap from the screen and bite her.

Annoyance, confusion, and hope—the hope made her even more annoyed—all surged inside her as she frowned censoriously down at it.

What was he doing contacting her now? Why had he suddenly gotten in touch via message? She didn't think Danilo was the kind of person who would send a text after what had happened between them. He would call, or come by to discuss things in person.

What, then, did this say?

She opened the message.

*"Olivia, I heard this morning that there were problems at the wedding rehearsal and that somebody was murdered. Are you okay? Say if you need any help. I can shop for you, just tell me what to get. D."*

Olivia read and reread the text, not at all sure what she should make of it. It seemed Danilo wanted to return to the friends-only arrangement that they'd had before love began to bloom—on her side, at least. But was that enough for her and did she want it?

Olivia knew the answer was no.

Probably, Danilo was just being kind. Despite his cold rejection of her, Olivia had to admit he was generally very considerate and usually thought of others. Narrowing her eyes as she read it again, Olivia took special note of the "shop for you." Clearly, Caputi's orders for the three suspects to go only home and to work, had already circulated around the entire village.

She sighed. That was another complication of their failed romance. What if everyone in Collina and the surrounding area now knew he'd rejected her advances? Hopefully he would keep that private.

However, the text was lacking a lot of important content. He had not mentioned their disastrous outing. He had not shared his feelings about her in any way, or explained his actions at all. That made her feel frustrated.

Olivia texted back:

*"Thanks. I am okay. All good 4 now."*

Short, polite, formal. She thought it hit the right note.

She read it twice more, just to be sure. Then she deleted the whole thing. There had to be better wording she could use!

Then she retyped the message, which ended up exactly the same as before.

Feeling as exasperated with herself as she was with Danilo, Olivia stabbed the Send button before she could spend any longer dithering over this unimportant subject. She had no time to waste. Her next urgent job was to go back to the winery and clear Marcello's name.

After pulling on comfortable and weather-appropriate clothing, and hanging her disguise in the wardrobe, Olivia headed to La Leggenda. As it was a fine afternoon, she and Erba walked to work. Marching briskly along the hilly route gave her a chance to clear her mind and think ahead. Olivia decided that she would not share her morning's adventures with Jean-Pierre. She didn't want him to have to lie on her behalf if the detective asked him any questions about her doings.

It would be better to keep this to herself, Olivia resolved.

When she arrived at the winery, she saw Jean-Pierre's car in the parking lot, although Marcello's car was not there. There was a small delivery van parked there, and her heart sank as she saw Gabriella's stylish Fiat. Olivia would have an unfriendly welcome when she headed through the doors.

For Marcello, being at work could mean he was busy anywhere in the winery's grounds. She was sure that he was with Antonio, doing winter maintenance in the fields. If he didn't return soon, she would have to find an excuse to call him.

To her surprise, when she headed inside, she saw that dozens of the pink-iced cupcakes had been placed in cellophane-topped boxes and arranged on the tasting room's back tables.

Gabriella was at the restaurant's reception desk, supervising the loading up of large foil containers. She seemed in a slightly better mood. When she saw Olivia, she waved expansively toward the tables.

"The cupcakes are for everyone. Eat, eat. Take some home. By tomorrow, all must be gone from here."

Olivia approached them cautiously.

These were the personalized wedding cupcakes, which she recalled numbered one hundred and eight, although there weren't so many now. Perhaps the Vescovis had already taken some.

She heard Gabriella liaising with the delivery person.

"Yes, here are the addresses. This food must go to these two orphanages—this box to the first, this to the second. And the third package to the children's village."

She smiled, seemingly satisfied as she prowled into the tasting room.

"The children will be feasting for a few days on this wedding meal," she said to Olivia, and added, "We decided to keep the cupcakes here. Orphans, I am sure, do not want cakes with other people's names on! So they have received the main wedding cake layers, and we must finish these."

She pointed sternly at the display and Olivia guessed her words were more of an order than a suggestion.

There were many names that she didn't recognize. But one of them stood out.

Kyle, the unpleasant groomsman.

Olivia took an empty box and put Kyle's cupcake into it. Then she took Rog's cake and added that to the box, too. There was a certain satisfaction in taking those for herself, she decided.

She looked for Don, wondering if she could complete a groomsman hat trick, but saw to her disappointment that Don was missing. Someone had eaten his already.

The name Terenzio caught her eye.

His cupcake was in the center of the display and Olivia was sure that nobody would feel comfortable taking that one and it would be left until last. Perhaps she could give it to Erba. She added it to her box.

"What a kind thing, to give the food to poor children. And to leave the small cakes for us." Jean-Pierre walked out of the storage room. He held a water bottle in his right hand and a large box of cupcakes in his left.

"I'm glad all the food is going to good use," Olivia said. "If you have time, we need to review the tasting list. It's time to update it."

But before she could attend to this work-related matter, she heard a car door slam outside.

Olivia's ears pricked up. She wasn't saying she had super-sensitive hearing, but she was attuned to certain sounds. Including the tinny noise of a gray Fiat driver's door being impatiently slammed by a certain short-tempered policewoman.

Olivia stared at the entrance door, feeling like a deer in the headlights. Even though she expected it, she couldn't stop herself from jumping as Detective Caputi marched in.

"*Buon giorno*," the detective muttered automatically. "Where is Marcello Vescovi? I need to speak to him urgently."

Olivia's eyes widened.

"He's probably out on the estate somewhere," she said, hoping to goodness that Marcello hadn't chosen this moment to take an illegal trip into town.

"I will call him," the detective replied, glaring at Olivia before taking out her phone.

But before she could do that, Marcello walked in.

He clearly had been working in the fields. His ankle boots were spattered with mud, and an old, well-worn corduroy jacket was slung over his shoulders.

Marcello looked preoccupied and not too happy. Although he stopped as soon as he saw the detective, and headed toward her with a charming smile, Olivia got the sense he was thoroughly fed up with the intrusion of the police into his business.

"Answer me a question, please, Signor Vescovi," Detective Caputi said. She spoke in a low voice, but Olivia could hear an edge of triumph in it. "I interviewed Mr. Jones just now. He said that he had forgotten to tell me an important detail last night. He said you had proposed a business arrangement, and he declined your offer and explained he could not do business with you. He said that your reaction was aggressive and in fact, combative, and he noticed you were especially angry with Terence, who was with him at the time. Now, explain yourself, because according to this testimony, you have a very strong motive for his murder!"

# CHAPTER TWENTY ONE

After Detective Caputi had delivered her accusation, the winery was filled with a ringing silence.

The only sound was faint chewing as Jean-Pierre, clearly also a stress eater, devoured Jewel's cupcake.

Olivia bit her lip. This was exactly what she had feared. It wasn't only the bride's father who was accusing the winery personnel. The dreadful Mr. Jones was also trying to spin the situation to make sure that the La Leggenda team got the blame and the families could leave the hotel.

Rattled as Olivia was, she admired how composed Marcello remained.

He nodded sympathetically.

"I apologize, Detective. Just as Mr. Jones forgot to tell you this, so, too, did I. I think he may be making too much of it in retrospect." His voice was soft and sympathetic. "As a bereaved father, of course he is looking for closure. However, at the time we spoke, I was not in the least angry. After I inquired about his business to find out if there was any common ground, he explained that he operates at a lower price point, which meant there was no reason to continue the discussion. We left the conversation there, and it was not significant to either of us."

Listening to Marcello's soothing account of the interaction, Olivia was stunned by his diplomacy.

She was the only one who knew how much Marcello was downplaying the situation, because she'd seen how enraged he had been. He had been furious at Mr. Jones's rejection, and the rude insults he and Terence had flung.

Now, he'd summarized the facts in such a calm way that even Detective Caputi was looking miffed, as if she'd hoped to unleash a bombshell but it had ended up a flickering spark.

"It is suspicious that you did not disclose it," she snapped.

"Detective, if I had thought it in the least important, I would have told you immediately," Marcello reiterated, his hands spread in appeal.

Olivia held her breath, hoping that Detective Caputi would believe him.

She wished she could explain to the obnoxious detective that she was looking in the wrong direction. Why was she back here at the winery, spoiling everyone's day, when she should be at the hotel and interviewing the bridesmaids to find out which of them had been cheating with Terence?

Olivia opened her mouth to spill the beans about Madeline's devious actions. Then she closed it again. It would only get her into trouble, because Caputi would ask how she'd found out.

"I will ask you more questions in private," the detective said to Marcello, sternly beckoning him down the corridor toward his office. Olivia guessed she would be looking for any inconsistencies in his story.

They left the office door ajar, so Olivia went to the back of the tasting room to see if she could overhear them speaking.

She pretended to be choosing more cupcakes to add to her stash, while straining her ears to overhear the murmured voices. Unfortunately, she couldn't pick up any clear words. Staring down at the sweet treats, she realized she didn't want any more of them. She was feeling all caked out for now.

Instead, after seeing the display in Forno Collina's window, she was craving a strawberry jam crostata, with its deliciously crispy pastry lattice and sumptuously sweet and sticky jam filling.

Still, there was no use craving one, because she couldn't go to the bakery. Putting thoughts of pastries out of her mind, Olivia went back to work.

She and Jean-Pierre headed to the storage room and prowled the shelves, deciding what changes to make to the tasting menu.

"Your rosé has been such a success," Jean-Pierre said. "We cannot remove it from the tasting menu, especially since it is the only one of its kind."

Olivia felt a flare of pride in the wine she'd formulated at the end of summer. How fortunate it had turned out so well.

"The rosé stays," she agreed.

"Then, we have four red wines on the menu already, but only two whites," Jean-Pierre observed. "Why do we not include three of each for a while?"

"The sangiovese could come off the list for now," Olivia agreed. "Nadia said they are battling to keep up with the demand for it, and quantities this year are low. So which white should we add? I keep wanting to include the chardonnay, but then I keep thinking people will prefer a varietal that's more Italian."

"Yes, the Italian names are part of the experience! I love the pinot grigio," Jean-Pierre said enthusiastically.

"Maybe we should taste the two quickly, and decide which will suit our guests' journey better," Olivia said.

"A good idea," Jean-Pierre agreed eagerly.

Olivia took four tasting glasses from the shelf and rummaged in the fridge. Luckily there were still a few open bottles of white wine from the wedding rehearsal—she was amazed any wine at all had escaped the guests' onslaught—and she found a bottle of chardonnay and pinot grigio among the small stash of survivors.

She poured a small portion of each into the glasses.

"Remember, this will be part of the journey after the vermentino, and before the white blend."

Olivia loved nothing more than swirling La Leggenda's fine wines, inhaling their sumptuous bouquets—first the volatile aromas of fermentation and then the more subtle ones of fruit, before tasting. She loved the way that the wine's nose, or aroma, contributed to the overall experience. Most guests were surprised to learn that the majority of the fruity flavors they picked up in wine were evident through smell, rather than taste.

"The chardonnay is quite light," Olivia noted. It was designed to be a more modern wine and this year, had been only briefly wooded in oak barrels. Rather than the heavier buttery, oaky flavor of traditional chardonnay, this wine had a deliciously complex taste that was soft and creamy, while alive with complex citrus notes.

Jean-Pierre nodded thoughtfully. "It is a magnificent wine. However, I wonder if it is too close in flavor to the white blend, which has a significant percentage of chardonnay."

Olivia nodded. "That's exactly what I was wondering, too. Guests might think them too similar, and then the impact of both will be lost."

They tasted the pinot grigio and Jean-Pierre sighed in delight.

"This variety of wine can be too dry for me to enjoy, but here at La Leggenda it is made with such character, richer than average, and I pick up a beautiful hint of peach."

"I agree. Pinot grigio can be very flinty tasting when it's too dry, but Nadia has managed to give ours such a depth of flavor, while still remaining true to the wine's character. It's different and distinctive when compared to the other two whites on the tasting list, and best of all, it has an Italian name!" Olivia praised it.

"Exactly." Jean-Pierre smiled. "Is there enough in stock?"

"Plenty," she confirmed. "So it goes on the list!"

Happy with the changes they'd made to the visitor experience, Olivia hurried to the back office to update the tasting sheets.

In a few more minutes, she heard the detective leave. You could feel the winery brighten up as her smoldering presence exited, Olivia thought. Seeing the printer was in Marcello's office, she now had the perfect excuse to go and bother him again.

She pressed the button to start the print run and headed purposefully to Marcello's half-open door.

"Yes, Olivia?" Marcello sounded pleased to see her—sort of. He looked frazzled, as if he'd seriously had enough of everything to do with the ill-fated wedding. "Oh, you have come to get the sheets."

"We're updating the tasting list to include the pinot grigio," Olivia explained. Having explained her presence, she continued. "I was wondering if you remember anything about what happened on the wedding rehearsal night. I keep on thinking that surely, between us, we should be able to work out who did this, based on what we saw."

Marcello nodded.

"I wish that my memories were clearer and that I had spent more time with the party. It was unfortunate that Mr. Jones declined my business offer so rudely. It was because of his actions that I stayed behind the scenes, thinking that my presence would only cause ill feeling. Plus, by then, I was not in a good frame of mind to be a welcoming host," he admitted.

Olivia was sure he hadn't told Detective Caputi any of this. She felt encouraged to have gotten some insight into his thought processes. From what he said, murder hadn't been on his mind.

"Were you in your office the whole time?" she asked.

Marcello nodded. "The noise was excessive and that music was awful, so I put in earphones and listened to opera and caught up on work. It was only when I was changing to a new playlist of songs that I realized it was quiet outside, and then I heard you announce over the microphone what had happened."

Olivia nodded.

The problem was that Marcello had spent the evening alone. How could she confirm his whereabouts?

"Did anyone else come into your office, looking to have a quiet moment?" she asked.

He shook his head. "You were the only one. Unfortunately, the detective also said this means she cannot clear me and may need to interview me again."

His lips tightened in annoyance and Olivia felt a surge of sympathy. Perhaps he also needed to go to the grocery store.

"I wish you'd been outside for more of the time," Olivia said. "I'd better go now. Everything is all organized for tomorrow."

Marcello nodded. "Thank you. Remember, we are only opening in the afternoon."

Olivia had forgotten that they'd planned for a late reopening, thinking they would need time to get everything cleaned up after the wedding.

"I'll see you tomorrow afternoon," she told her handsome, but sadly alibi-free, boss.

Feeling conflicted, she left his office to walk home. She wished that between herself and Detective Caputi, one of them had been able to clear Marcello. It was terrible having him on her suspects list, and seriously problematic that he was still on Caputi's.

*

When she reached her farmhouse, she was charmed to see Pirate snoozing in the sun on top of her car. She greeted the cat and spent some time petting him.

When she looked up, her attention was caught by Erba. Instead of heading off for an afternoon roam on the farm, the goat seemed captivated by Olivia's front door mat.

There was something on the mat, Olivia saw, hurrying over.

"Erba! Get away!"

There was a brown paper bag on the mat, and Erba actually had it in her mouth!

After a brief and unsuccessful wrestle with her goat, Olivia managed to rescue the bottom half, as the bag tore.

Looking pleased with herself, Erba headed off, munching playfully on a large portion of brown paper.

The bottom half of the bag contained a cardboard box. Luckily, it was still intact. Olivia headed inside, went to the kitchen, and put the bag on the counter.

Then she took out the box.

To Olivia's astonishment, she drew out a Forno Collina bakery container. Opening it, feeling utterly mystified, she found four mini strawberry jam crostatas!

She stared down at them in total confusion. Danilo must have bought them and left them here. There was nobody else who would leave that specific treat on her doorstep.

Olivia shook her head, flummoxed by his behavior. He'd shunned her romantically and hadn't called or explained. But he had messaged to ask if she was all right, and had dropped off her favorite pastries for her.

She had no idea what was going on!

Quickly, before she could think better of it, she dialed his number.

To her exasperation, it rang and rang unanswered and eventually went through to voicemail.

Olivia didn't leave a message. She had absolutely no idea what to say. Why on earth hadn't he answered his phone? Was he hinting that their relationship could only continue via texts and dropped-off gifts, and not through any actual, spoken communication?

Placing her phone on the counter, Olivia heard a noise behind her.

She turned to see Erba at the window. The goat was standing on her back legs, with her front feet on the sill and her nose pressed hungrily against the glass.

"I'm not giving you a crostata," Olivia told her. "They are mine, all mine. But I brought you something you'll enjoy even more."

She took Terenzio's cupcake out of its silver foil casing and fed it to her goat through the window.

Erba looked thrilled to be gifted this sugary treat, and devoured every crumb.

Then Olivia changed into shabby clothes, fetched her wheelbarrow, and headed over to the barn. Seeing she couldn't solve any of the mysteries currently in her life—not Terence's killer, not Danilo—she was going to focus on an easier and more practical task, and clear some of the remaining pile of rubble.

It was hard, tedious work clearing the pile, especially since every shovelful had to be delicately eased from the rubble, or else she might risk breaking a hidden treasure. To her alarm, upon entering the barn, Olivia thought the pile looked bigger again! Or maybe it was just the challenging day she'd had that was making it seem bigger.

She filled the first barrow load, feeling the familiar ache in her arms and legs after wielding the shovel, and wheeled it outside, closing the door behind her—an important and necessary step because although she couldn't see where Erba was, she could sense her goat watching and waiting for a chance to get in!

When she'd first cleared the pile, she had used the rubble to flatten the area where she parked her car. Her next job was to fill in a deeply eroded section of stony ground where she planned to lay one of her cobbled pathways.

Carefully, Olivia tipped the barrow load into the crevasse, pleased to see the difference it was already making.

Encouraged, she returned to the barn. This time, as soon as she dug into the pile again, the rim of her spade made the clinking noise that she'd come to associate with glass.

Feeling excited that this might be an important find, she put the spade down and continued to clear around it by hand, working cautiously in case whatever the spade touched had a sharp edge.

Olivia drew out a short, chunky shard of glass.

She felt breathless from excitement as she stared at it. This shard was the same color as the previous one she'd found. She and Danilo had taken that fragment to an expert to examine. He had said it was from a rare and ancient bottle made in the late 1600s. The distinctive dark green marbled glass could be traced all the way back to a specific manufacturer. Apart from her one splinter, there were no bottles or pieces still in existence.

Olivia felt dizzy with excitement. She'd become tired of working through the pile and uncovering only dust and stones and fragments of brick. This find proved to her that there might be more treasures in the small heap of rubble that remained.

Every splinter meant she knew a little more about her farm's forgotten history. Perhaps one day, she would have answers to why it had been abandoned for decades after having been one of the area's top vineyards in earlier times.

This was more than just a lucky find. Olivia decided it was a sign she shouldn't give up. Not on the historic mysteries of her farm, and not on the current, more troubling mystery of the murder.

Whatever it took, she had to keep striving until she uncovered the truth.

Feeling encouraged, Olivia resolved to go back to the hotel first thing in the morning. If she dug carefully through the secrets and lies,

123

she hoped she might find the equivalent of this curved glass shard, and identify Terence's killer.

# CHAPTER TWENTY TWO

The next morning, wrapped in her cumbersome disguise, Olivia climbed into to her car and drove determinedly out of her farmhouse. Heading into the village, she was immersed in her thoughts and preoccupied with the difficult day ahead.

She made a mental list of whom she should interview first—and, just as important, whom she should avoid at all costs. If the wrong person saw her at the hotel, they would call the detective and get her locked up.

Kyle, Rog, Don, Lysander, and Lance were all on Olivia's "wrong person" list, together with Mr. Miller. Given his master plan to blame Olivia for the murder, she'd be playing right into his hands if he recognized her.

As she drove out of town, a familiar sight jolted her from her musings. There was the portly cyclist, riding again. He was facing away from her, pedaling determinedly up the hill. Again, she noted he was going surprisingly fast.

She decided to wait until the road widened before trying to pass him. There was nobody behind her and it was better to be careful. But as she cruised along, the cyclist hit a pothole.

His bike jolted and rattled. Olivia swung the wheel to avoid the hole herself, noticing as she did so that the cyclist seemed to have dropped something.

What was it? It looked like a big, white, bulky shopping bag.

The next moment, a cloud of feathers filled the air.

Feathers flew up above her car, landed on her hood, and settled on her windshield. Olivia jammed on brakes and as she did so, something else hit the glass with a loud splat, and stuck there.

It was a false mustache!

Olivia scrambled out of the car, feeling mystified.

The cyclist climbed off his bike and hurried toward her. He looked slimmer now, and without the mustache, she was shocked that she recognized him.

It was Jean-Pierre!

What on earth was he up to, defying Detective Caputi's stern threats and heading out and about on his bike?

"What are you doing?" she asked incredulously. She turned and unpeeled the mustache from her windshield.

Of all the surprises she'd thought the day might bring, getting hit by a flying mustache had not been on the list.

Jean-Pierre stared at her in confusion.

"Olivia?" he asked. "That is you?" To her astonishment, Jean-Pierre started giggling. "You look so big! And so funny!" he spluttered.

"I do?" Olivia felt outraged. "What about you? You're the one who stuffed a feather pillow under your shirt! A *leaky* feather pillow. And what's with that mustache?" Her voice was quivering. To her surprise, she found it was because she was also suppressing a laugh. The next moment, it spilled out, just like the feathers. Olivia found herself cackling uncontrollably as Jean-Pierre bent over, wiping tears of mirth from his eyes.

"It was from a fancy dress party. I thought it made me look different," he managed, before exploding into laughter again.

"It does," she admitted. Then, finally containing her giggles, she added, "But why are you even risking going out?"

Jean-Pierre turned and picked up the feather pillow, folding it over so that the rip didn't leak any more feathers. Then he stuffed it back under his shirt.

"I had to go to football," he explained. "These practices are very important. The team cannot replace me at this stage! Our first match is next week."

"Well, be careful," Olivia cautioned him, giving him back the mustache. "Try and stick it on more firmly. It's very windy today. You don't want it coming off and hitting Detective Caputi's windshield!"

Imagining how the detective would snort in shocked disapproval at the sight set Olivia off again. She clapped a hand over her mouth to stifle the chortles, as Jean-Pierre leaned on his bicycle, his shoulders shaking.

When they'd finally gotten their laughter under control again, Jean-Pierre pressed the mustache against his top lip, rubbing it hard to affix it in place. He took his sunglasses off and cleaned them with his shirt.

"Where are you going in your disguise?" he asked curiously.

"To the hotel," Olivia said. "I have a few questions to ask."

Jean-Pierre raised his eyebrows.

"You be careful also. There must be many police around."

126

"I will," Olivia promised.

She climbed back into her car and headed on, feeling energized by the amusing start to the day. She hoped Jean-Pierre would travel safely, and was sure that Detective Caputi would be too busy at the hotel to drive around checking the school playing fields.

She was the one venturing into the dragon's lair!

As she turned into the now-familiar gateway of La Locanda, Olivia found herself hoping that the detective would treat herself to a lie-in this morning and start work later. After the crazy day she'd had yesterday, surely she deserved it?

She headed to her usual spot in the golf course parking. Walking up to the hotel's entrance, she looked carefully for Detective Caputi's Fiat but didn't see it anywhere.

This was a positive sign, she thought.

She strolled into the hotel looking casual, as if she'd just returned from a visit to the vineyard. The officer in the lobby didn't give her a second glance as she walked to the elevator and went up to the second floor.

The bridesmaids were her first and most important stop. She decided to start with Cassidy, and see if she could confirm the story Angelique had told her. Olivia tapped on the door, hoping that she would be in the room.

"What is it?" a voice called.

Olivia didn't have to think up an excuse, because a moment later the door opened and Cassidy looked out at her.

"Oh, you're here again? Angelique said you were asking questions yesterday. You don't need to ask me any, do you?" Cassidy sounded both worried and rushed.

"May I talk to you for just a moment?" Olivia asked quickly. She felt exposed in the corridor, but Cassidy didn't look eager to invite her in. Next time, Olivia reminded herself, she must seize the element of surprise and simply barge her way inside.

"What about?" Cassidy stared at her dubiously.

"I want to check what happened when you and Angelique went out for your walk. I'm sure you can provide details."

"Is it really necessary?" Cassidy frowned.

"Just one or two facts. It should take a minute." Olivia gave her a winning smile that she hoped concealed her growing desperation.

"Can't you come by later? I need to go to breakfast," Cassidy said, looking unmoved by Olivia's friendliness.

"Later won't be possible as I have to go to work," Olivia replied, thinking quickly.

Waiting out here in the corridor was making her increasingly jumpy. Cassidy wasn't being in the least cooperative, but Olivia's only remaining hope was to outlast her by standing in front of her until the tall brunette decided answering the questions was easier than shoving her out of the way.

Clearly, Cassidy was reaching this conclusion about Olivia's seemingly immovable presence outside her door.

She sighed impatiently and opened it wider, stepping back into her room.

"Be quick, will you? I'm starving, and need to get to my massage at the spa."

Relieved that Cassidy had capitulated, Olivia sidled quickly in and closed the door. She hoped this interview would yield solid information. She needed to start striking suspects off her list, instead of adding more and more of them on.

"You ran out of the restaurant after Angelique, when she was so upset about what Terence had done," Olivia said, deciding to get to the point as fast as possible.

"Yes, that's right," Cassidy said, turning to her dressing table and spritzing perfume on her wrists. "I caught up with her almost immediately. She couldn't go fast in those high-heeled sandals. She wanted to walk back to the hotel, but I told her it wouldn't be a good idea. It was dark, and the hotel was far away, and we were in a foreign country. Plus, what if she got a blister? So we ended up wandering around the winery's grounds. She was very angry and I thought it would be better for her to calm down before we went back."

"Did you meet anyone along the way?" Olivia asked.

"No." Cassidy crinkled her forehead, as if replaying their movements. "We walked along this long, sand road which seemed to end up at the main road, or maybe it was a different main road. We were really confused by then! So we decided to turn back, but somehow we overshot the path down to the winery building and we ended up at the goat dairy."

Word for word, this was pretty close to what Angelique had said. Olivia guessed from her knowledge of the winery that the two women had taken the service road, which was a sand road and ended up at a different tarred road. But they could have invented the story easily, after looking at a map of the winery.

"How did you know it was the goat dairy?" Olivia asked, identifying a potential weakness in her version.

"Because a goat came out!" Cassidy said. "This cute little orange and white goat jumped through one of the windows and came scampering along to meet us."

Olivia's eyes widened. Cassidy was describing Erba—not only her coloring, but also her friendly, sociable behavior!

"She really cheered Angelique up," Cassidy remembered. "She nibbled on her dress and actually bit one of the ribbons off. By the time we left, we were both feeling better."

Olivia was thrilled that Erba had managed to confirm this important alibi. What a clever goat she was.

"I'm glad you were cheered up, and it's just as well you didn't head out of the grounds. Those roads are very dark," Olivia agreed.

"Is that all?" Cassidy asked, grabbing her purse and heading toward the door again in a way that told Olivia it had better be all.

"Thank you for helping me," Olivia said, hustling out ahead of her. "By the way, it will be best if you don't tell the police I was here. That detective loses her temper if you mention my name. You don't want her to be angry at you."

She was pleased that finally, two important suspects could be struck off the list. Thanks to their lucky arrival at the goat dairy, Olivia was convinced that neither Cassidy nor Angelique would have had the chance to murder Terence.

Olivia replaced her shades and waited in the corridor until Cassidy had jogged around the corner. Then she knocked on the room next door.

The door was opened by Jewel, the plump, redheaded wine-drinking champion.

Quickly, Olivia whipped off her shades.

"Hi, could I possibly come in and chat for a minute?" she gabbled, hustling Jewel into the twin-bedded room. Wearing a bulky trench coat gave her a lot of pushing power, she realized.

Jewel was dressed in sweatpants and a tracksuit top. Since she looked pink-cheeked and tousle-haired, Olivia guessed she'd just finished her morning's exercise.

"What's this about?" she asked suspiciously.

"Nothing serious." Olivia smiled disarmingly. "I happened to be passing this hotel and I suddenly thought about Terence's murder. I feel very upset about it and am looking to set facts straight."

Jewel nodded absently. "We're all upset," she said, sounding not in the least upset. "But I unfortunately can't help you with any information. I became very ill that night. Like, seriously. I got so sick the last thing I remember is the groomsmen juggling the champagne bottles. I personally think that I got food poisoning from the chicken. My mother always warned me never to eat fish or chicken in a foreign country."

"What a shame," Olivia said. If Jewel could overlook the industrial quantities of wine she'd drunk, and the fact that nobody else had gotten an upset stomach, so could she. "It's awful to feel unwell on vacation," she added sympathetically.

"I think I must have spent more than half an hour in the bathroom," Jewel said, clearly enthusiastic about describing just how sick she had been.

Olivia decided to head her off before she shared too many gory details.

"Was Dinah with you? Someone said she went to help you."

"Look, it's a bit of a blur," Jewel explained. "I believe salmonella poisoning does that to you. I had a terrible headache the next day, and feel lucky I didn't have to be hospitalized. But someone was definitely with me in the restroom, and it must have been Dinah, because I do remember she helped me to leave once she was sure I'd finished throwing up."

Olivia nodded.

Given Jewel's highly inebriated "salmonella poisoned" state, she guessed she wasn't going to get more information, as there was no more to give.

"There is one other fact I wondered if you could confirm," Olivia said. "I was quite shocked when someone told me Terence cheated with Madeline. I wanted to find out if that was true."

"Er," Jewel said. She looked embarrassed. Her face, already flushed, turned a deeper shade of crimson.

The bathroom door opened and Madeline walked out.

# CHAPTER TWENTY THREE

"I heard that," Madeline said, stomping over to sit on the nearest bed. The steamy scent of shower gel filtered from the open bathroom door.

Olivia didn't know where to look. She felt herself turning even redder than Jewel. She'd made a terrible faux-pas. It had been a rookie error not to ask Jewel if she was sharing with anyone.

An apology was in order, she decided.

"Sorry," she said. "That was rude of me, Madeline. I didn't know you were in the bathroom."

Madeline glared at her, running a hand through her damp chestnut hair, which was cut so that it curled just below her ears.

"As it happened, Terence and I had a moment," she admitted. "It was about a month ago when he and Angelique were having problems in their relationship. My feeling is that they should never have gotten married. There were too many unresolved issues between them."

Olivia felt like asking Madeline if she thought that "having a moment" had helped the unresolved issues. But she didn't. She wasn't here to judge, but rather to tactfully ask questions. Even if it was a little too late for tact.

"Was it a vulnerable time?" she asked.

Madeline nodded. "Of course it was. I was extremely annoyed with Angelique, and felt that she'd betrayed our friendship and insulted me by insisting we wear a one-size-fits-all bridesmaid outfit."

Olivia raised her eyebrows, remembering her first casual thought upon seeing the very different bridesmaids.

Jewel nodded. "It was deliberately nasty of her. She had a made to measure wedding gown, by a top designer, that looked absolutely stunning and was as flattering as could be. And then the rest of us had to wear these dreadful, shapeless, calf-length frocks in a hideous shade of pink. Me? A naturally redheaded, curvaceous woman, in a pink sack?"

"It must have been traumatic," Olivia agreed.

"We all cried at the fitting. Not that any of the dresses fit," Madeline remembered. "And Angelique was horrible about it. Very uncompromising. She said it suited her color scheme and that it was her wedding and she would be the pretty one."

"Vindictive," Jewel said. "I mean, photos are forever! And she gets really aggressive if you untag yourself in her pics. Like, in the past she's completely blocked people over that!"

Olivia was confused by how cheating with Angelique's fiancé was a lesser crime than untagging yourself in a photo, but she kept quiet, realizing that she didn't understand the dynamics of this social group, which were clearly very complex.

"Anyway, Terence was upset over something else she did, and I was angry about the gowns, so we comforted each other," Madeline explained. "It didn't mean a thing!"

"No, I'm sure not," Olivia agreed, feeling that she was learning to lie almost as well as Angelique. For the sake of finding out information, she had to play along.

"I guess you think it might have something to do with the murder," Madeline snapped, sounding suspicious. "Like I told the detective, I was with Molly and Miranda when you made that announcement. We'd been dancing, but then the music was turned off. After you said Terence had been killed, I saw Dinah come out of the restroom, with Jewel leaning on her."

Olivia nodded. At this point, it seemed none of them were guilty and all could be taken off the list.

Madeline folded her arms, clearly still on the defensive.

"If you're going to question everyone who slept with Terence, I hope you'll also ask Cassidy," she said.

"Cassidy? Why?" Olivia asked.

"She and Terence also had a fling," Madeline said.

Jewel nodded. "It was about two weeks ago, wasn't it?"

Two weeks? Olivia couldn't believe what she was hearing!

She stared wordlessly at them, with no idea what to say or how to conceal her incredulity at the goings-on of this group. Was there anyone Terence hadn't slept with? she wondered. Perhaps that note in his pocket had been meant for another woman altogether!

Even though Olivia was silenced by shock, Jewel seemed eager to elaborate on the details.

"Cassidy and Angelique had a fight over the photographer. Cassidy wanted her to use her brother, because she'd promised she would. But Angelique said she had changed her mind, and was using some other person who was a friend of a friend and supposedly very cutting edge," she explained.

"So Cassidy got upset and went out for drinks with Terence and cried on his shoulder," Madeline said. "Of course, it ended up being more than that. You don't go out for drinks with Terence and expect him not to make a move on you. He has a reputation that way. He's a player, everyone knows. Or rather, he was a player."

"A player," Jewel agreed.

"Exactly," Madeline confirmed. "Anyway, Cassidy told Dinah, and Dinah told Jewel, and Jewel told me. Then I told Molly and Miranda."

If Olivia hadn't already cleared Angelique, she would have suspected her all over again. She certainly had a reason to be furious with her fiancé. And with her bridesmaids who were her supposed BFFs.

How could any group of friends keep so many secrets from each other? It was a mystery.

Yet again, Olivia felt relieved that she'd called her own wedding off. Look where serial cheating with your fiancé's friends led, she thought. It didn't just stop with the act itself. It precipitated lies and further betrayals, and created tensions and fault lines within a group, as each person decided what information they would hide.

"Did you tell the police about you and Terence?" Olivia asked, wondering if Detective Caputi was privy to the viper's nest of deviousness that characterized Angelique's social circle.

"No, of course not!" Madeline said, sounding horrified. "I wouldn't dream of telling the police! It wouldn't be fair to Angelique, as they would only suspect that she was the killer if they knew."

"We also didn't mention the incident with Cassidy," Jewel added. "For the same reasons."

"Loyalty is important to all of us," Madeline explained, sounding pleased with herself, and Olivia had no words in reply.

"Well, thank you for your time," she got out eventually. "I hope that the killer will be arrested soon."

"We're all supposed to say it was you," Jewel told Olivia, as she reached the hotel room door.

Olivia turned to face her, feeling consternation fizz inside her.

"Who told you that? Angelique's father?" she asked.

Jewel looked uncomfortable.

"No, actually, it was Angelique herself," she said.

133

"It was?" Olivia felt horrified. The blonde was even more devious than she'd suspected! Not only had she bought into her father's version, but she was doing her best to sell it to the rest of the party. That wasn't what she'd told Olivia! How two-faced could you be? she thought angrily.

"Angelique mentioned it when we were having cocktails at the rooftop bar last night. She said that we should think it over, and if we coordinated our versions, it would mean we could all leave this afternoon. That was when we were supposed to check out. It's a nice hotel but I'm bored of it. When Angelique went on her honeymoon, we girls were booked to fly to Milan for some fashion and food!" Jewel explained with a grin.

"We're still going to go, right?" Madeline said.

"Absolutely!" Jewel said. Then she added, hurriedly, "If the criminal is arrested by then. None of us think it was you, of course, and none of us would report you to the police as she suggested we should do."

"It was just a theory," Madeline confirmed.

"It might not have worked anyway," Jewel said.

"Especially after what that detective mentioned about the head injury," Madeline mused. "There must have been an actual fight for that to happen."

Head injury? In the midst of her panic, Olivia grasped at this important fact.

"What do you mean?" she asked Madeline.

Madeline frowned thoughtfully.

"Well, the second time she interviewed me, which was late yesterday afternoon, she asked if I had seen anyone strike Terence on his head with a blunt object."

"Really?" Olivia filed this nugget of information away.

"I think the postmortem results had come back and they'd picked up a wound there," Madeline explained. "But I don't remember him being in a fight, and I didn't even notice him knock himself accidentally."

"Thank you for the information."

Olivia let herself out and closed the door, feeling as if she needed to have a cold shower after what she'd heard. With friends like those, how could you turn your back for a second without discovering a knife in it? she wondered.

Her predicament was getting more and more serious. If she didn't find the killer in the next few hours, the impatient guests would overcome their differences, united in their desire to leave the hotel for more interesting parts of Italy. They would find a way to blame everything on Olivia, and she would find herself in jail, with nineteen metaphorical knives stabbed into her back.

How could she carry on investigating, she worried, when every guest had already been told that she was the killer? Was there a way to continue at all, or was she hurtling toward certain arrest?

# CHAPTER TWENTY FOUR

Alarmed by how the situation was unfolding, Olivia decided to hide in her car to regroup, away from watching eyes. There, she could assess what she'd learned, and plan how to continue asking questions without being caught.

As she left the hotel and passed the bowling green, she saw Gramma B standing on the manicured grass, wearing a pleated navy skirt, leather brogues, and a black Cannibal Corpse T-shirt. She was practicing her bowls while speaking on her cell phone.

In these desperate times, Olivia needed to overhear what she was saying. Casually, she strolled toward the bowling green, where she pretended to tie her shoelace while tuning in to Gramma B's one-sided conversation.

"I know, I know, Agnes. It's all very sad, but I can't help feeling it's for the best."

The blue-haired lady picked up the bowling ball and eyed the small white jack which looked to be miles away, on the far side of the green.

"My husband built the wine import business, you see. Terry Senior, as he was known, was always entrepreneurial, and for him it was all about relationships and quality. Good old-fashioned values. Then he brought in our son Terry Junior—he's Terence's father. I didn't agree with a lot of his decisions and felt he was chasing the money. Then, when my husband retired, and Terry Junior told me that his son Terence was going to be employed with the vision of running the company one day, I don't mind telling you, Agnes, I was appalled!"

The elderly lady leaned forward and with a practiced flick of her wrist sent the black bowling ball curving in a true arc across the green. It slowed, touching the white ball just before it stopped.

"Why was I appalled? Because my grandson Terence was useless, that's why. He was lazy, extremely arrogant, disrespectful, and a little know-it-all who refused to learn. Plus, he was never focused on business. He was a skirt chaser!"

Olivia nodded in agreement. She'd never heard a grandmother describe her grandson in such brutally concise terms.

"I told Terry Junior time and again that he should groom Lance for the role. Lance is not without his flaws. He has a dreadful temper on him and is hotheaded, but so was Terry Senior at that young age. He calmed down suddenly at the age of twenty-seven. When I saw he had a good head on his shoulders after all, I married him the next year."

Olivia couldn't help grinning in admiration when she heard that. Clearly, unlike herself and Angelique, Gramma B had been way too streetwise to make any disastrous decisions in her youthful folly.

"In addition, Lance has a better business head on his shoulders and he's also a more humble person than Terence could ever be," the elderly lady continued as Olivia listened, fascinated, to her sharp assessment of her family's personalities.

"Yes, Agnes, I tried to convince him," Gramma B continued. "But Terry Junior was obsessed by the idea that the business should go to his eldest, no matter what, and that was how the rule of inheritance worked. I reminded him my husband wouldn't have approved! Handing a business down to someone who has no ability, and receives it on a plate, is how it can go from success to ruin within a single generation!"

Gramma B threw another bowling ball. It, too, described an accurate path to the white ball, as if magnetically drawn there. It clipped the side of the white before rolling to a stop.

Olivia was impressed, and rather intimidated, by Gramma B. The lady was hardcore! She aspired to be like her one day but even at this early stage of her own life, she wasn't sure she had what it took.

Certainly, Gramma B far surpassed her in the bowling ball category. In fact, with her incredible aim, she was nothing short of legendary.

As Olivia retied her shoelace for the fifth time, she found herself wondering exactly how far Gramma B's mettle, and her determination to see the family business in responsible hands, had taken her.

Though senior in years, she was clearly feisty, and from her bowling ball prowess Olivia could see she had steely strength in her wrists and fingers, and perfect coordination.

Would she...? Had she...?

Shocking though it was, Olivia had to acknowledge that if Gramma B had been hell bent on her goal of having Lance inherit the business, she could have made it happen.

At that moment, an annoyed male voice spoke from behind her.

"What are you doing? You've been lurking there, listening to my grandma on her call. I've been watching you!"

Appalled, Olivia jumped to her feet and spun round.

She found herself staring at an angry-looking Lance.

"I—I was just—" Olivia began stammering out the flimsy beginnings of an excuse, but it was too late. Up close, and in the brightness of daylight, her cover had been blown.

"I know who you are!" Lance sounded outraged. "You're the woman from the winery! Everyone's saying you hit my brother over the head and then stabbed him with a corkscrew. Why on earth are you here?"

How had this rumor escalated so quickly? Olivia felt appalled.

She heard a loud click as Gramma B's third bowling ball connected with the jack. Then the blue-haired lady turned and strolled over to her grandson.

"So this is the person that did it?" she asked, affixing Olivia with a penetrating gaze.

"No! It wasn't me. I'm trying to find out who it was. There's false information being circulated that I was the culprit."

"Oh." Gramma B sounded disappointed, as if she had planned to take Olivia aside and thank her for her role in saving the family business. "But you were listening to my conversation?" she added, sounding sterner.

"I'm not the guilty one. I'm trying to catch the killer!" Olivia protested.

She felt as if Gramma B's gaze was scouring her.

After a long pause, the elderly woman snapped, "I can see you didn't do it. I can always read a face. But if I ever catch you eavesdropping on me again, you'll be sorry. And now, I'm going to head in and fix myself a Bloody Mary. You two carry on and sort your issues out."

She stomped away, resuming her conversation with Agnes as she powered up to the hotel.

Olivia stared apprehensively at Lance. She was in big trouble now. Gramma B's stabilizing influence had departed, and she was face to face with a hotheaded, tempestuous youngster who hadn't yet reached the pivotal age of twenty-seven where reason would prevail. Her cover was totally blown. All she could do now was try to talk her way out of the situation she'd landed in.

"If I really was the killer, why would I be here?" she asked Lance soothingly. "The police told me I could only go home, or to work, so I'm taking a big risk by showing my face at the hotel at all. I'm doing it because I'm desperate to find out the murderer's identity. All of us at the winery are shocked by this terrible deed."

Gazing at Lance in earnest appeal, Olivia had no idea what he thought about her version. She would have to take Gramma B's word that he was a better, less flawed person than his elder brother. Right now, he seemed intimidating, angry, and unpredictable.

"Can we sit down somewhere?" she continued. "Maybe the rooftop bar?"

That would provide a quiet place for them to speak. At this early hour of the morning, people wouldn't be drinking. Apart from Gramma B, who clearly lived by her own rules, but Olivia was sure she'd use the downstairs bar with its private booths, to continue her chat with Agnes.

"All right," Lance agreed grudgingly.

Olivia headed swiftly into the hotel and made a beeline for the elevator, with Lance following. They made it up to the top floor without anyone else recognizing Olivia, and hustled into the bright, airy, and modern space. Her guess had been right. The bar was empty.

Glancing around as the barman fixed her a coffee and brought Lance an Aranciata San Pellegrino, Olivia noted that this bar was a magnificent venue. With huge, sheet-glass windows around three sides, Olivia thought she might have been able to see as far as Pisa when the morning mists lifted. Certainly, the hazy outline of the faraway hills was hypnotic. Looking the other way, she saw to her amazement that she had a clear view of the local village. She could see all the way down the main street, and if she'd had a pair of binoculars, she was sure she could have spied the two rival bakers glaring at each other, with tourists ready to film them as they shouted angrily at each other across the road.

In reality the bakers were the best of friends, but their fake vendetta brought so much business to both their shops and the village that they maintained the pretense of enmity.

Olivia decided she would have to take a leaf out of the bakers' book. She must pretend to be calm, even though she was panicking inwardly.

The barman brought their drinks and she quickly paid, hoping that this gesture would prove her good intentions. She sure needed Lance on her side.

"So, what have you picked up so far?" Lance asked her in a low voice.

Olivia felt as if she was walking a tightrope. She didn't want to offend Lance. How much did he know about his brother's philandering ways? she wondered nervously as she stirred her rich, dark coffee.

"All the bridesmaids have alibis," she said. "Jewel was getting sick, Dinah was helping her, and the other three were dancing. Cassidy was with Angelique. They went for a walk after it happened. All the parents were in the restaurant. So that basically leaves the groomsmen, and Angelique's brother and sister, Lysander and Alice."

And Gramma B, she thought, wincing. It might be better not to mention Gramma B at all to Lance, who seemed protective of her.

"What do you think happened?" Lance asked. Clearly, he was pushing her to confess what she knew.

"I understand from some of the bridesmaids that there might have been a few—er—uncontrolled moments between them and Terence in recent weeks, where passion took hold," Olivia explained, watching Lance carefully. He seemed calm as he poured his Aranciata San Pellegrino over ice. Olivia could smell the orange, sugary sweetness of this drink, the Italian equivalent of Fanta.

"I heard that it was Cassidy and Madeline," Lance told her. "I'm not sure about any others."

"Yes, that's what I heard, too," Olivia said, relieved that he already knew what his brother had been up to, and with whom.

"My theory is this," Lance said. "I think that Angelique was so angry when she found out what he'd done that she killed him, and Cassidy helped her. After all, they only have each other's story to confirm where they were."

"And my goat," Olivia added.

"Your goat?" Lance stared at her as if she was mad.

"Yes. They went for a walk past the goat dairy and met my goat."

"And your goat can confirm what time this happened?" Lance asked incredulously.

"Well, no," Olivia admitted. "But Angelique and Cassidy did go out together just after Terence left."

"Exactly!" Lance raised his index finger as if this point proved his argument. "They went out! And that's clearly when they did it. Maybe they visited the goat dairy afterward, for an alibi, or they had been there earlier and decided to use it in their story."

"But why would Angelique trust Cassidy, when Cassidy had cheated with Terence?" Olivia asked, confused. She saw Lance's eyes narrow, as if he hadn't thought about that.

140

"Angelique might not have known about Cassidy. She could just have heard about Madeline, or maybe they didn't tell her that either, and what happened with Alice was enough," Lance suggested. "Those girls are weird. One minute they're like colanders, with secrets pouring out of them, and the next moment they're locked up tight, like a high security safe."

Olivia had to admit this was an accurate insight into how the group behaved. And, after all, Angelique had seemed ready to kill Terence over the incident with Alice. She might not have needed any other reason.

Had the two friends conspired together to commit murder?

But their encounter with Erba had sounded so authentic!

As Olivia struggled with this alternative theory, she heard the familiar sound of officious footsteps approaching.

To her horror, she realized she wasn't the only one who had decided to use this place as a quiet meeting spot.

Detective Caputi, accompanied by a uniformed sergeant, walked in and took a seat at the corner table.

She might not have noticed Olivia if she hadn't choked on her coffee. Upon seeing the stern, steel-haired detective, Olivia inhaled her mouthful instead of swallowing it.

Cupping her hand over her mouth, Olivia did her best to splutter quietly, but the detective's head snapped around at once. Her radar was perfectly tuned to pick up any Olivia-sounding noise.

Upon sighting her, Caputi jumped up and made a beeline for their table. This time, her laser gaze seared straight through the flimsy disguise of coat, scarf, beanie, and shades.

"You!" she exclaimed.

With a sense of doom, Olivia watched the triumph light up her face.

Olivia tugged off the beanie. It was boiling and scratchy and had failed in its job of turning her into an anonymous stranger. She stuffed it into the coat pocket, staring at the detective with dread as she waited for the inevitable.

All too soon, the hammer blow fell.

"Olivia Glass, you are under immediate arrest. You have broken your restrictive conditions. As such, you will now accompany me to the police station where we will book you into jail," Detective Caputi announced, in loud, satisfied tones.

141

# CHAPTER TWENTY FIVE

"No!" Olivia begged Detective Caputi, her voice still hoarse from the close encounter with her steaming Americano.

To her amazement, her plea for clemency was echoed by Lance.

"No! She did nothing wrong!" he appealed to the detective.

Olivia nearly fell off her chair in shock. Why was Lance saying this? She struggled to remain poker-faced, and not show how flabbergasted she was by his words.

The detective turned to Lance, fixing him with a piercing glare. Olivia could see she was itching to arrest him, too, for his defiant words.

"You are questioning my decision?" she asked, in a voice that made Olivia want to hide under the table. Luckily, Lance had less history with this intimidating woman, and was able to hold his nerve.

"I asked her to come to the hotel," Lance said. "I've been desperate to work out who killed my brother. Knowing that Olivia was working in the winery all night, I wanted to speak to her. I thought, if we put our heads together, we might be able to remember more about the evening."

Lance must seriously believe Angelique had committed this crime, Olivia thought. At any rate, he was doing his utmost to stop her from being carted off in the back of a police van.

The triumph disappeared from Detective Caputi's face. She looked furious as Olivia swiftly backed up Lance's story.

"I'm sorry. I know I wasn't supposed to be here, but Lance seemed so hurt and vulnerable," she lied.

Detective Caputi stared at her cynically. It was clear she didn't believe a word of Olivia's story, but had to give Lance the benefit of the doubt.

"Leave this hotel immediately!" the detective ordered. "Go now! If I see you anywhere other than home or work again, I will arrest you instantly. This is your last chance, and you do not deserve it!"

"I'm going. I'm very sorry," Olivia said, standing up hurriedly and abandoning her coffee. "Thank you for inviting me here, Lance."

Detective Caputi wasn't taking her word for it. Barking out an order, she instructed her officer to accompany Olivia.

She crowded into the elevator with the policeman. He stood right next to her even though it was a spacious cubicle, and stuck to her like glue while she headed out of the hotel and back to her car.

Only when she had unlocked the car did he take a few paces back, watching her with his arms folded.

Before Olivia climbed in, she removed her scarf, and her too-warm coat, and three of the four jerseys.

The policeman's expression became increasingly perplexed as Olivia shed layer after layer. She didn't know what to say to him. It wasn't a situation where easy conversation could flow. So she said nothing at all and simply stripped off her piles of clothing in a businesslike way, as if this was a perfectly normal routine for her.

Then she scrambled into her car, flinging her deconstructed disguise onto the back seat. Her face was bright red, and not just from the heat of her bulky outfit. This had been a harrowing experience.

Olivia drove obediently home, with the uneasy certainty that Detective Caputi was monitoring every inch of her progress from her lookout point in the rooftop bar. She cruised slowly, but at a steady speed, through the village where the bakeries were doing a brisk morning trade. Smiling warmly at their customers, the bakers occasionally took a break to glower theatrically at each other across the narrow road.

Watching the familiar spectacle of their fake feud made Olivia feel comforted. After the near-disastrous morning she'd had, and her total lack of viable plans for getting back to the hotel, she was grateful to be surrounded by normality—or at any rate, what passed for it in Collina village.

When she pulled up at the farmhouse, Erba capered over to meet her, making her laugh by gamboling around her in circles as she headed to the house. Pirate was in a Sphinx-like pose on her doormat, exactly where Danilo had left the pastries.

A cat was just as welcome a sight as a crostata, Olivia thought. She felt her tension dissolve as Pirate stretched into a perfect arch before meowing a friendly greeting.

Glad as she was to be home, she couldn't help a pang of disappointment when she checked her phone and found there was still no return call from Danilo.

143

Even though she was perplexed by his behavior, there was no point in worrying over it, because it was now in the past, she reminded herself firmly. She needed to move forward, and not allow herself to remember how much fun his company had been, and how they had laughed together, and how she'd enjoyed cooking for him.

Pondering on her situation with another pang, she wondered if the strawberry crostata had been a goodbye gift.

"Enough of this," she said. She could waste hours theorizing what it all meant. Instead, she needed to use the time productively by checking on her fermenting grape juice—or, as she thought hopefully, her bestselling wine-to-be.

Olivia headed up to the barn and pulled open the doors, feeling pleased by how smoothly they moved on their enormous, well-oiled hinges. Being able to open a door easily made such a difference. It felt like walking into a brand new winery, even though the building was more than a century old.

But, as Olivia headed optimistically into the cool space, she stopped and stared at the ground in horror.

The rough concrete blocks that she'd swept so carefully were no longer pristine. A dark stain was spreading across them.

It could only be wine.

"Nooo!" she said aloud in a high, squeaky voice.

One of her fermenters must have sprung a leak.

Feeling as if she was jumping out of the starting blocks, Olivia raced across the barn. She stared down at the fermenters, anxiety flooding through her.

It was the far one! It must have been faulty or damaged. How was such a thing even possible? The wine was slowly leaking out and it would continue to do so, pint by precious pint, until her hopes and dreams were no more than a rusty stain on the floor.

Worse still, Olivia had nowhere else to put the wine. Both fermenters were full, she had no other containers in the house, and she couldn't go out to buy one.

Her stomach clenched as she realized she couldn't ask anyone to help her! It would be wrong to expect anyone at La Leggenda to save her own private batch of wine, and calling Danilo was an absolute no-no.

Olivia practically danced from foot to foot in anxiety as she stared down at the wine. Action was needed—immediately! She could hear the tiny dripping noise as it flowed out of the leaking container. Every moment counted! If she delayed, she might lose the entire fermentation vat, but where on earth could she put all the wine?

The biggest receptacle in her house was a kettle. That was far too small and in any case, not renowned for its effective fermentation properties.

Briefly, Olivia had a vision of pouring the wine into her bathtub. It wouldn't ferment there, either, but it would stop it from spilling out onto the floor.

"Think sensibly," she chastised herself. If she applied calm logic to this problem, surely she could solve it.

She glanced at the back wall, and her gaze rested on the two oak barrels she'd purchased.

They were clean and ready for use. The problem was they were not supposed to be used for at least another month. Her wine was intended to be briefly oaked, but only after the initial fermentation was complete.

Now, there was no choice. She would have to decant the remaining contents of this vat into the barrel straight away. It might ruin it, but it wouldn't ruin it as badly as having it leak out all over her barn.

Olivia marched over to the barrel and removed the cover.

Then she headed back to the fermentation vat, picked it up in a bear hug, and staggered over to the barrel with it, feeling the slow leak seep into her fourth and last jersey. She didn't care. Firstly, because she had managed to save a substantial amount of her potential end product, and secondly because at this early stage of fermentation, Olivia was reassured by how her wine smelled.

Having had a little experience of wine at various ages and stages, thanks to Nadia's guidance, Olivia thought her wine was maturing perfectly.

There was nothing wrong with it. She couldn't predict what the end product would taste like, but she was confident that the processes were on track.

The problem was that the early contact with oak would derail it completely. This would introduce an unknown factor into the delicate process.

Olivia tipped the last of her precious wine into the barrel and replaced the lid, crossing her fingers that it would work out for the best. After thoroughly checking the other vat for any signs of leakage, she left the barn, trying her hardest to put her worries aside.

For now, she had an urgent date with her washing machine.

While the wash cycle ran, Olivia took a long shower and made herself a light lunch, using the last slice of ciabatta bread, the last fragment of mozzarella cheese, the last tomato and the final drop of olive oil. She'd had no chance to find out about grocery deliveries. Her fridge looked as empty as it had done the day she'd bought it.

She put her washing in the basket and took it into the courtyard, where she'd set up a washing line against the back wall. It was the ideal place to air-dry her clothes in the glow of the afternoon sun. Enjoying the rays as she hung the clothes, Olivia thought about what she'd learned at the hotel that morning.

The most important piece of information was that Terence had been hit on his head before being murdered.

Presumably there had been a mark there, and most likely even an open wound. She remembered how mussed his dark hair had looked when she'd seen him in the car. Now she knew it was because of the injury.

If she could find the weapon, it might help her to piece together what had happened, and how.

"Erba, we must go to work," Olivia called through the kitchen window to her goat, noticing she was perched on top of the Wendy house's roof. It didn't look like a comfortable spot, and Olivia had no idea how she got up there. Thinking about it, she wasn't sure she even wanted to know!

She ran out to her car, as Erba scampered eagerly from the courtyard. They climbed inside and sped away, heading purposefully to the winery. If there was a clue to be discovered, Olivia resolved she was going to find it before opening time.

# CHAPTER TWENTY SIX

It was seldom that La Leggenda's parking lot was completely empty, but the notice by the front gate, "Closed for a Private Function Until 2 pm on Sunday," had effectively deterred any visitors.

Olivia scrambled out of her car, feeling determined as she headed over to the winery building.

She decided the best plan would be to retrace the route that Terence had taken as he drunkenly staggered out of the restaurant, cradling his bottle of red wine and that lethal corkscrew. The problem was that nobody knew what the route had been.

Olivia tilted her head back, staring up at the bright sky. To follow his steps, she needed to think the same way as he had, and to put herself into his drunken frame of mind.

She mimed the action of gulping down a shooter. Then she pretended to knock back a few glasses of wine. Terence had also drunk a whiskey. Then, of course, he'd gotten impatient with the half-glasses available and he had demanded a sparkling wine bottle.

He'd spilled a lot on purpose. Olivia pantomimed him, staggering slightly as she pretended to shake that bottle to within an inch of its life!

Then she imagined draining the contents that remained after the froth had spurted out. She imagined the bubbles, cold and fizzy. Probably some of the Metodo Classico had spilled onto his shirt, and a little might have gotten up his nose.

Olivia was in the zone. She felt she'd become Terence! Her head was whirling, her feet unsteady, her thoughts were jumbled and incoherent.

In this state, he'd reeled into the winery where he'd been accused of kissing the matron of honor.

Closing her eyes, Olivia imagined that kiss.

Danilo's face materialized in her mind, and she imagined his strong hands cupping her face, pushing her hair aside as he leaned toward her...

Her eyes flew open again and she huffed out an angry breath.

147

That was not the direction she needed her out-of-body experience to take.

Closing her eyes again, Olivia customized her experience to be Danilo-free. So after that head-spinning kiss, and the walk back to the winery, the anger and accusations and the realization that he was now in big trouble, Terence had staggered out.

Olivia took a step forward.

She'd successfully channeled him!

Her vision was blurred, her feet were stumbling. And it was dark, she reminded herself, very dark.

Olivia reeled forward in the imaginary darkness. She ricocheted off the stone pillar outside the restaurant door and let her feet take her on a weaving, winding journey.

Although the body had been found in the parking lot to the left of the restaurant, when Olivia staggered away from the doorway, she found herself lurching in a righthand direction. Why, she didn't know.

Perhaps, if he was so drunk, there was no reason for Terence to have headed directly to the car. He could have wandered around first. After all, the gardens to the right of the restaurant were a pretty place, and in the nighttime spotlights gleamed among the shrubs and flowers and the crisscrossed tiled paths. The light had attracted him, she decided, like a very inebriated moth to the flame.

Olivia allowed herself to stumble into the garden, letting incoherent angry thoughts flit through her mind. She held an imaginary bottle in her right hand.

She came to a cross path. Most definitely, Terence would have lost his balance and reeled along it. Olivia reeled, too. As she weaved down the narrow, tiled strip she kept an eye open for anything that might possibly have been used as a weapon.

A piece of metal, perhaps, or a sturdy wooden branch. Perhaps even a large stone, although she couldn't see any large stones in this garden.

As she passed a clump of bushy ferns, a faint shimmer caught her eye.

She stopped, abandoning her pretend drunkenness as she pushed the ferns aside. For a confused moment, she stared down.

Her brain began to race. This must be it! The missing evidence was lying here in the dirt, concealed by the greenery.

Then a concerned shout wrenched her from her thoughts.

"Olivia! Are you all right? You seem to be dizzy!"

Feeling mortified, Olivia spun round to see Marcello watching her from the restaurant doorway.

From his puzzled expression he'd probably been standing there for a while, watching her stagger around and probably wondering why he'd ever hired such a madwoman!

Quickly, she reassured her boss that she did, in fact, have a plan.

"I was trying to retrace what Terence might have done when he left the restaurant. And I've found something, Marcello! Come and see!"

Marcello ran to join her in the garden as Olivia pushed back the stiff, bristly fern leaves.

"Look, it's a wine bottle."

"The one that Terence took with him?" Marcello asked.

"No, it isn't! He took a bottle of red wine. This is the vermentino white."

Olivia moved more of the ferns aside and bent down, looking closely. The bottle had a smear of dirt on the rim, except it didn't look like dirt. It was rust colored and as she stared at it, Olivia had no doubt in her mind that this was the weapon that was used to hit Terence.

Hit with a bottle of vermentino white?

With a flash of insight, Olivia realized beyond any doubt how this had happened, and who had done it. At last, she found herself able to piece together the evening's events in a way that made sense.

She gasped, feeling as if her world was spinning again, but from excitement and adrenaline this time.

"I need to get to the hotel as fast as I can." The ferns sprung back into place as she jumped up.

"Why go there? Why not bring the police here?" Marcello asked.

"Because I don't want the murderer to offer an alternative story," Olivia said firmly. "I want this to be an ambush, and I need the element of surprise."

Marcello squeezed her arm. "Please be careful. Shall I come with you?"

"No," Olivia said reluctantly. Even though she longed for Marcello's support at such a critical time, she couldn't place him in the firing line when Detective Caputi still suspected him. "It's better for all of us if I do this alone," she insisted.

He nodded reluctantly. "Call me if you need me. I will go there immediately to help."

Feeling breathless with expectation, Olivia headed for her car, dialing Angelique's number as she walked.

"Guess what?" she said, as soon as the other woman picked up. "I've made a breakthrough in the case, and I now know who the killer is."

There was a short silence.

"Really?" Angelique asked, sounding suspicious. "And who is it?"

"I'm coming to the hotel to explain everything," Olivia said. "I'll be there in fifteen minutes. Please, can you gather the families? Maybe in the hotel lounge? Make sure everyone is there."

"I'll do that!"

Olivia thought Angelique sounded motivated. She was sure that by the time she arrived, the wedding party would be assembled as per her request, waiting to hear what Olivia had to say.

The guilty person would be part of that group. Olivia felt a twinge of doubt as she thought about that. She hoped her impromptu plan would work out. She only had one chance. If the murderer didn't confess, Olivia would be arrested. The wedding party would be long gone before she could clear herself.

She had to get this right!

*

As soon as Olivia arrived at the hotel, she dialed the detective's number.

She answered, sounding characteristically short-tempered.

"*Pronto?*" she snapped.

"Detective Caputi? It's me, Olivia."

There was a surprised pause.

"Why are you calling? Where are you?"

"I'm at the hotel. I'm about to head into the lounge."

Quickly, Olivia jumped out of her car and began power-walking in that direction.

"The lounge?" Caputi sounded furious. "Did you not listen to what I told you? You think I was talking for my own fun? Olivia Glass, this is a blatant defiance of police conditions and I am going to arrest you immediately!"

"Please come and arrest me. It's the downstairs lounge, next to the bar," Olivia added helpfully. "But before you do, you might want to hear what I have to say. I've solved the case, and I'm going to prove it by telling the wedding party what happened!"

Disconnecting the call, Olivia sped up and ran the rest of the way.

She burst into the lobby breathlessly, seeing the police officer glance at her. His curious expression hardened into suspicion, but before he could do anything more, she was past, heading through the ornate double doorway and into the large, opulently furnished lounge.

Her footsteps sank into thick, plush carpet. Muted lighting gave an intimate and warm feel to the spacious room, even though the pristine glass windows were bright.

The families were present, Olivia saw with relief. Angelique had done her job.

To her astonishment, though, they were not waiting for her with the quiet decorum that Olivia would have thought appropriate for this serious occasion.

Everyone was fighting with each other! Everyone!

Angelique and Alice were head to head in the middle of the room, screaming at the tops of their voices. Mr. and Mrs. Miller were yelling at each other, and somehow the Joneses had joined in, fighting with both of them. Meanwhile, Lysander looked ready to come to blows with Lance, and Cassidy was throwing such a temper tantrum at the groomsmen that they had retreated all the way to the far window.

Apart from Don, Olivia realized. Don was surrounded by the rest of the bridesmaids, who were shrieking insults at him.

Angry words resonated around the room.

"You're to blame for bringing Alice up with loose morals!" Mr. Miller roared.

"You're to blame for letting Angelique date that dreadful man!" his wife shot back.

"Dreadful man? What do you mean, dreadful man? Both your daughters are tramps! Our son would have married down! Shameful!" Mr. Jones sneered.

"This would never have happened if you'd held the wedding somewhere sensible like Florida!" Mrs. Miller protested angrily.

"Don, did you insult my friend Jewel and call her a cheap date? She got sick from salmonella! Not wine!" Madeline hissed.

"If you look at my sisters that way again, Lance, I'm going to punch you in the nose!" Lysander threatened.

"Look at them how? I wasn't looking at them! I was trying to hear what my parents are shouting about!" Lance argued back.

"Kyle and Rog, you two are losers! Horrible, revolting, bullying losers! I have never seen you say anything nice about anyone! You are toxic and awful and deserve to—to—never go on a date with any girl who's interesting and pretty and has a personality!" Cassidy shrieked.

As Olivia stared around, appalled by the magnitude of the conflict, she noticed that the only two people who weren't fighting were the two grandmothers.

They were sitting side by side on a sofa, watching the pandemonium with interest. In fact, as Olivia looked more closely, she realized that Gramma B was helping Granny Petra understand what was going on, pointing to the different groups and repeating the insults to the deaf woman in a loud, clear voice.

Gramma B was nursing what looked like a strong whiskey, and the barman was presenting Granny Petra with a small sherry.

The hotel receptionist hovered in the far doorway, shifting from foot to foot and clearly wondering whether she'd get into more trouble for calling the manager, or for letting this conflict rage unchecked.

Olivia needed to take control of the situation urgently. If the manager called security to disperse the group, her chance would be gone.

"Hey, everyone!" Olivia began.

She tried again, louder.

"HEY EVERYONE!"

Nobody took the slightest notice. It was as if they hadn't heard her at all, and she didn't have a convenient microphone to use this time.

Olivia had no idea what to do. Should she jump on a table? Flick the lights on and off?

A silver bell on the bar counter caught her attention. Perhaps if she rang it, the warring factions might hear and stop yelling at each other.

Olivia headed across the room, weaving in between the combative groups. She punched the bell as hard as she could. Its silvery *ting* sounded loud and piercing.

The closest group—the groomsmen and Cassidy—paused their argument and turned to glower at her instead. Kyle and Rog looked shocked to see her there. She guessed they'd bought into Mr. Miller's story about her being the culprit.

Before they could start a new fight, Olivia capitalized on her progress by punching the bell three more times.

*Ting, ting, ting,* the high-pitched note rang around the room.

Gradually all the knots of arguing people turned to look, and silence descended in the lounge.

"Good afternoon, Joneses, Millers, and friends," Olivia began, hoping a polite and personal welcome might break the ice. "I would like to speak to you as a group. Angelique, could you come here please?"

Angelique didn't look too pleased to be dragged away from the shouting match with her sister, but as she took her place beside Olivia, she brightened, clearly remembering why she had come here.

Her father felt the opposite way.

"What are you doing in this hotel?" Mr. Miller roared. "You killed my daughter's fiancé! Everyone knows you are the murderer and you should be in prison!"

"Yes," Kyle muttered in surly agreement.

"Can't believe it's taking these Italian cops so long to lock her up," Rog snapped.

"Surely it's illegal for her to be at large, especially with corkscrews visibly displayed in the bar area!" Mrs. Miller confided to Mrs. Jones in a stage whisper. She sounded friendlier than she had. Olivia was glad that her visit had achieved one successful outcome already. The Millers and Joneses had decided they hated her more than each other.

She cleared her throat, feeling apprehensive about the bombshell she was going to unleash on this already conflicted party.

"I have come here to explain which one of you is the killer," she declared to the assembled families.

# CHAPTER TWENTY SEVEN

Olivia's announcement was met by a brief, stunned silence as everyone turned to stare at each other. Kyle was the first to break it.

"Looked in the mirror, did you?" he jibed. Pretending she hadn't heard this heckler, Olivia continued.

"Let me take you through what happened after Terence left the winery and went outside," she said. "We all thought he went straight to the car, but during the autopsy, they discovered that he had been hit hard on the top of his head. Now, that couldn't have happened in the car. There's no room. The roof is too low. So since it didn't seem logical, I went looking for more evidence, to see if I could find any sign of a fight, or even a weapon. And I found something."

Now the room was very quiet. Everyone was looking at her in anticipation. Although she knew that the expectancy she saw on one person's face was for a different reason. That person would be hoping that she hadn't worked out the truth.

"I found a discarded bottle of wine in the gardens nearby the restaurant. It has a smear of blood on the rim and it was clearly used by the killer. I think that Terence and the killer had a fight in the gardens. Then the killer pursued Terence to the car."

She gazed around at the now-shocked faces.

"The bottle that was used to hit Terence over his head is not the same one he took out with him. The bottle Terence held was our internationally award-winning La Leggenda Miracolo red blend, which sells out every year and is featured on numerous wine lists at leading restaurants worldwide. However, the bottle that was clearly used as a weapon is our incredibly popular vermentino white wine, which is highly sought after as an alternative to sauvignon blanc, and becoming a top seller in many international markets, including the States."

Olivia stared meaningfully at Mr. Jones while she spoke. Even though it was a slight digression from her storyline, she felt it was important. He needed to acknowledge what a big mistake he'd made in rudely declining Marcello's overtures, as well as insulting Italian wines in general!

She guessed that Mr. Jones got the message because his face reddened and he looked down at his hands.

Satisfied, Olivia continued.

"Anyway, my point is that the bottle I found will have someone's fingerprints all over it, and that will confirm their guilt. I didn't touch it, so the evidence is undisturbed. The police can take it directly from where it was dropped, and examine it properly."

Everyone was following her story. She didn't see any sign of confusion in anyone's face. In fact, she saw a few nods. The Millers were agreeing with her, which was a massive relief since Mr. Miller had been the one spearheading Project Blame Olivia.

And one person, the guilty party, looked appalled.

Olivia hoped that Detective Caputi would arrive soon. She was about to publicly announce the killer's identity. After that, she had no idea what might happen. She feared that without the icy control the policewoman wielded, things might erupt into a huge, stand-up fight.

Anyway, she was committed to her story now. Hoping that the detective was walking into the hotel at that moment, Olivia resumed speaking.

"Terence was hit over the head, and then placed in the car by his killer before being stabbed. So instead of being a crime of passion, this was actually a premeditated action."

"But who was it?" Mr. Miller asked, sounding impatient. "You've explained a whole lot of theories to us, but where's the identity of the murderer? Where's the proof?"

"Yes, I agree. Stop wasting our time!" Kyle said angrily.

"Let's get onto the motive," Olivia said. "There were many tensions among everyone in this party, and many reasons why Terence could have been killed. But the main motive ended up being jealousy. Jealousy that an older brother, who was arrogant and incapable, would end up inheriting the family business and destroy it."

Gasps came from around the room as some of the quicker thinkers realized who Olivia was referring to.

"The killer is Lance!" she announced, for the benefit of those who were still looking puzzled.

Olivia stared directly at him as she spoke, aware of Mr. Jones's disgusted exclamation and Mrs. Jones's indrawn gasp. Lance himself was very pale. He'd been looking more and more uneasy as she spoke. As soon as she accused him, he stared down at his hands.

Clearly, it was a family trait.

155

"Why do you say that?" Angelique asked, sounding curious.

"Lance spotted me earlier this morning outside the hotel. He accepted right away when I told him I wasn't the killer and he was very interested to find out what I had learned and asked a lot of questions. I think he was trying to make sure I didn't suspect him. Then, even more suspiciously, he proposed a wild theory of his own, which was that you and Cassidy conspired to murder Terence. He tried to convince me that you were the criminal."

Olivia pointed at Angelique.

"Me?" she gasped, sounding outraged. She glanced at Cassidy, who gave a dramatic shrug of disbelief.

"I think he did that to throw me off the scent, as he was worried that he might be caught out," Olivia explained.

"Do you have any other evidence? This is my friend's brother you're accusing!" Rog shouted.

"As a sommelier, I notice who drinks what wine. At the time of the murder there were only two people drinking wine straight out of the bottle. One was Terence, who started with champagne and then grabbed the bottle of red on his way out. And the other was Lance, who was drinking the vermentino white."

After a few more beats of shocked silence, the room erupted. Everyone was shouting at each other all over again. The Joneses and the Millers were back into full-scale warfare. Confusingly, Kyle and Rog now seemed to be fighting with each other, and Alice and Angelique had taken sides together, and were now screaming at Lysander.

Everyone was shouting at everyone else, except Lance.

Olivia saw to her horror that Lance was taking advantage of the melee. He stood up and walked swiftly toward the courtyard exit door.

"Wait!" Olivia shouted.

He was going to escape, she was certain of it.

"Hey!" she yelled, but her voice was drowned by the deafening arguments.

Olivia pushed her way through the throng, getting elbowed in the shoulder by Cassidy, who'd started pulling Jewel's hair. She was almost knocked off her feet by Don, trying to escape an enraged Madeline.

The two grandmothers were still in their seats, Olivia noticed, as she shoved her way through the crowds. So was Dinah, sipping a sparkling water as she stared calmly at the chaos.

"Come back!" she shrieked at Lance, and this time he heard her. He glanced over his shoulder and then broke into a run.

As Olivia flung herself after him in pursuit, all the shouting ebbed away and in its place an eerie silence fell.

A familiar silhouette stood at the courtyard exit. Backlit by the afternoon sunshine, Detective Caputi's slim build and sharp bob were unmistakable.

"I heard all of that," she said. "In fact, I was able to record it."

Lance skidded to a halt, staring at the detective in horror.

"No! Don't arrest me!" he pleaded.

Then, his nerve breaking, he turned and dashed the other way, heading to the opposite door.

"Stop him!" Olivia cried.

Angelique made a grab for his jacket as he passed, but Lance pulled free.

"Come back, you lying murderer!" Lysander roared, getting into the spirit of the chase. He dived at Lance, clearly intending to grab his knees and take him down in a tackle, but missed and landed belly-first on the floor.

Panicked, Lance jumped onto a table, sending the salt shaker rolling off the edge. He vaulted onto another table which rocked dangerously, and then with a desperate leap, he landed on the plush carpet by the door.

"He's escaping!" Olivia cried, hoping that the lobby officer would hear her. She rushed for the door, arriving at the same time as Jewel, Angelique, and Mr. Miller.

The four of them jammed together, wedged in the doorway for an uncomfortable moment before Lysander cannoned into Jewel from behind. She staggered forward and uncorked the blockage.

"Catch him!" Feeling as if she was in the hundred-yard dash, Olivia raced along the carpeted corridor. "Catch him!"

The officer in the lobby had been alerted by the pandemonium.

As Lance hurtled desperately toward the main entrance, the officer broke into a run. Like a charging bull, he stampeded across the carpet. Just as it seemed Lance would outrun him, the officer dived for his ankles.

Clearly, he was highly trained in the art of tackling. Lance plunged to the ground, with the policeman's hands clamped firmly around his Disney socks.

A moment later, two other police joined the fray. By the time they all stood up again, Lance was in handcuffs.

"It wasn't me, it wasn't me!" he shouted breathlessly, casting appealing glances at the officer, and at his parents, and even at Olivia.

"I hit him over the head with a bottle, yes."

Detective Caputi nodded in satisfaction. Olivia guessed this was clearly enough of a confession for immediate arrest.

The police officer escorted Lance to the waiting car. He was not a cooperative prisoner. Followed by his anxious-looking parents, the young man was struggling, shouting, protesting as he went.

"I didn't do the other stuff! I hit him and then I got scared about what I'd done, so I dropped the bottle and ran back inside. I never killed him. He was still on his feet when I left. In fact, he insulted me and said I'd have to beg and scrape if I even wanted a job as janitor when he took over the company. You're lying!" Since he couldn't point a finger at Olivia thanks to being cuffed, he jerked his head in her direction.

Olivia forced herself to remain calm, even though she heard genuine desperation in Lance's tone. It didn't mean he really was innocent, she reminded herself. Not when all the evidence pointed to him. This was a last-ditch attempt to avoid the consequences of what he had done.

Olivia nearly jumped out of her skin as a heavy hand clapped her shoulder from behind.

She turned and found herself staring at Mr. Miller.

"Congratulations, young lady," he said, in tones loud enough to reach Detective Caputi, who was walking toward the police van. "You have solved this crime with great aplomb, and the police should be thankful for your hard work. Without a doubt, the killer has been caught. I always believed Lance was guilty myself," he lied, without so much as a blush. "Now we can all pack up and leave this Tuscan hellhole!"

Olivia decided this was good advice. After all, until the investigation was formally concluded, she was breaking her restrictions and at risk of arrest. With one empty space still available in the back of the police van, it would be wisest for her to get back to the winery as quickly as she could.

# CHAPTER TWENTY EIGHT

When Olivia arrived back at La Leggenda, Nadia and Marcello were waiting expectantly at the winery's entrance.

"You have done it again." Nadia sounded elated. "You have caught a killer! I hope that he will spend a long time in prison. Imagine murdering your brother. I have never been angry enough to think of doing that." She glanced at Marcello with a sideways smile. "Hitting you over the head with a bottle, yes. Killing you, no."

Nadia laughed—enough for two, which was lucky, because Marcello seemed distracted and didn't pick up on her joke. Olivia thought he still looked worried, and nowhere near as thrilled with the outcome as Nadia was.

"The police have just left. They took the bottle away and told me we are now cleared, and free to come and go once again. But we still have a serious situation, in that another murder occurred at our winery. Even though it was solved, I am concerned that this incident will affect our reputation," he said.

"I understand," Olivia said in a small voice.

She hated seeing Marcello upset. It was the worst feeling in the world, but as she searched for the right words to console him, he explained that the situation was even direr than she'd thought.

"The bride's father has just messaged me to say he will pay nothing more. All we received was a small deposit, and we spent thousands preparing our venue and the food. And we lost out on two days of tourist trade as a result of closing." He sighed.

"Marcello, I'll make it up to you!" Olivia promised. "Now that we've started wine tourism events, we can do more of them. We can market La Leggenda as a destination for weddings, celebrations, milestone birthdays. I'll add it to the website and put it out on our social media, and sign up the winery on a few of the influential sites. I promise you, business will flood in! It will be an incredible new income stream that will reap big rewards down the line."

Marcello's stern expression softened, to Olivia's relief.

"I trust you," he said. "I know you will work your hardest, and I look forward to seeing what your ideas bring."

Olivia squared her shoulders, proud that Marcello had faith in her. She would rise to the challenge! Over the next week, she decided, she would focus all her attention on wine tourism opportunities and promote La Leggenda into this important market. If she did her work correctly, they should have the first bookings in the next couple of months, and then a flood of business in spring and summer.

They headed into the winery, where Jean-Pierre was completing a tasting for a group of guests.

"*Buon giorno*," he told them. "Thank you for your wonderful orders. These delicious wines will be shipped to your homes in Canada, and we hope that when you drink them, you will remember, with happiness, the flavor of Italy!"

He smiled and bowed. Then he turned to Olivia with a concerned expression, lowering his voice.

"Gabriella said that we are out of milk, eggs, vanilla extract, stone-ground flour, caster sugar, tinned tomatoes, dried oregano, and black pepper. As a result of the wedding," he explained. "She has given me a list of products, together with the stores where I must purchase each one, as Paolo has the day off today. May I go now and shop for her?"

Anything to get Gabriella on her side again, and evict her from her position as Olivia's public enemy number one!

"Of course. Go right away. I'll handle the tourists, and Marcello can help if needed," Olivia agreed.

"There is one other thing." Jean-Pierre frowned at her anxiously.

"What?" Olivia asked.

"As you know, I have been using my bicycle today. I brought it to the winery, and it is under a tree outside. I am worried that if I use the bicycle to shop, I may be too slow in my errands, and also the eggs might be damaged."

Olivia nodded. She didn't want to incur Gabriella's wrath by having even one cracked eggshell.

"Take my car." She handed him the keys. "Make sure you get everything on the list!"

"I will do. Thank you."

Looking relieved, Jean-Pierre jogged out of the tasting room, leaving Olivia alone.

She stared across the pristine and elegant high-roofed space, with the tasting tables returned to their original positions, the framed posters on the walls, the tiled floor gleaming with polish and care. It was difficult to believe it had been the scene of so much drunken debauchery such a short time ago.

Olivia was battling to accept that this drama was now all in the past. She felt as if she needed to spend time processing what had happened, and catch up mentally with the crazy rush of events that had resulted in Lance's arrest.

Her hunch had been correct and the risk she'd taken had paid off, but she still felt conflicted about the outcome. Why she wasn't feeling happier that justice had been done?

Rather, she was uneasy. In fact, deep down, she didn't believe that it was fair.

It must be fair, she told herself. Lance deserved punishment, even though he'd certainly drawn a short straw in terms of brothers. Not to mention fathers! Terence and Mr. Jones had seemed like worse people than Lance, but they couldn't be, since he was the one who had committed the murder. What had prompted him to act in such a strange way? she wondered.

Olivia couldn't help recalling Nadia's words. She would cheerfully have bashed Marcello over the head with a wine bottle, but would have drawn the line at killing him. That innocent comment had planted a seed of doubt in her mind.

She remembered Lance's odd reaction after being accused. He'd admitted to the bottle hitting incident immediately, but he'd vociferously denied the murder.

What if—she started wondering, and stopped herself abruptly.

This was no time for what-ifs! The suspect had been arrested, the mystery had been solved, and the dreadful guests would hopefully be checking out any minute.

Now, she needed to bring her best self to the afternoon's work and be fully present for the tourists who would arrive soon. Remembering that she'd had a torrid morning and that more than likely her mascara would have borne the brunt of it, Olivia grabbed her purse and hurried to the ladies' restroom.

Luckily, her eye makeup had managed to escape the pandemonium with minimal smudging, easily corrected. And her lipstick needed a refresh, too, Olivia decided, staring at herself critically.

Rummaging in her purse for the Rose Sunset shade, she leaned on the counter, getting close to the mirror so she could ensure that all the details were accurate.

Her elbow squeaked loudly as it touched the porcelain surface.

She reached for a Kleenex in the box on the counter, ran it under the tap, and wiped carefully under her eyes.

The counter squeaked again as her hand touched it.

Jean-Pierre had done a fantastic job of cleaning, Olivia thought, as she carefully reapplied her makeup. This restroom was sparkling. It was always hygienic and well maintained, but Jean-Pierre had definitely taken the cleanliness to another level. Even the walls looked to have been scrubbed down.

Putting her lipstick back in her purse, Olivia frowned.

Something wasn't adding up.

She touched the gleaming tap, glanced at the floor.

Jean-Pierre had been told to clean up the sick, but he'd ended up sanitizing the whole restroom to within an inch of its life.

She'd assumed that Jewel had been sick in one of the cubicles and all that would have been necessary would be to clean the toilet thoroughly, and possibly wipe the floor if the drunk (or salmonella poisoned) woman had missed the bowl.

Tapping her fingers on the counter, Olivia pondered over whether a highly nauseous Frenchman would have spent time doing unnecessary cleaning, when the job was turning him bright green around the gills.

She didn't think so. Not if it wasn't essential.

The fact that Jean-Pierre had clearly attacked the entire restroom meant that there had been a big mess. Grimacing, Olivia imagined the vomit equivalent of Armageddon, strewn around the room. Not an image she wanted in her mind, but now it was stuck there.

How could it have happened when Dinah had been helping Jewel? She'd said specifically that she'd held her friend's head and kept her hair out of the way.

Curious, she decided to call Jean-Pierre. Perhaps he had been over-dramatizing.

She dialed his number and he answered immediately.

"Olivia! I am glad you called. What size eggs does Gabriella prefer? They have large and extra-large here."

Olivia thought back, trying to recall what the fussy restaurateur favored.

"Large," she remembered. "She says they are tastier than the extra-large. I called because I wanted to ask you about when you cleaned the ladies' restroom."

There was a pause.

"I prefer not to think of that again," Jean-Pierre pleaded.

162

Olivia decided to ignore his plea. "Was the sick really everywhere? Or had it just spilled over the toilet bowl? As I notice you cleaned the entire restroom."

Jean-Pierre drew in a stressed breath.

"Now I am nauseous once more! It was everywhere. Throughout the restroom, and two of the cubicles! As if a bomb had exploded, a bomb made of vomit! Never have I seen anything like it in my life. I did not know one person could—"

"I'm so sorry," Olivia interrupted him. "That's all I needed to know. Go back to your eggs."

If Dinah hadn't been there the whole time, and had only arrived later, that changed the entire timeline. Even more seriously, the new evidence proved that Olivia had been told, and believed, a massive lie.

"Oh, no," Olivia told her reflection, sounding stressed. "I've made the most terrible mistake! Thanks to me, Detective Caputi's arrested the wrong suspect!"

Adrenaline gave her feet wings as she sprinted out of the restroom.

# CHAPTER TWENTY NINE

"Marcello, please will you look after the tasting room?" Olivia called, as she raced down the corridor, heading for the exit. "I've got to go out urgently!"

Guilt churned inside her as she powered across the floor. She'd been such an idiot! Why hadn't she correctly analyzed all the evidence, instead of leaping to the wrong conclusion? What would happen if she was too late?

She reached the main doorway and skidded to a stop.

Her car!

Jean-Pierre had taken it! There was no sign of Marcello's SUV and she guessed Antonio was using it to run an errand.

Olivia glanced at Gabriella's stylish silver Fiat.

Their current relationship didn't allow for cars to be borrowed. Gabriella would most likely refuse, especially when she found out why Olivia wanted to use it. And she would find out! She'd interrogate Olivia for hours before deciding whether to grant permission, and Olivia didn't have hours.

That left only one possibility.

She stared dubiously at Jean-Pierre's bicycle, propped against a tree.

It had been a long time since she'd ridden a bicycle. She didn't even have a helmet with her.

Olivia shook her head. Enough quibbling over the details, she resolved. Lives were at stake. She was the one who'd missed critical facts and made a drastic misjudgment. Helmet or not, she had to fix it, without a moment's delay.

Plus, on the bright side, the village was almost all downhill and there was only a short, if steep, climb on the other side to the hotel.

"Let's go!" Olivia declared.

She jumped on the bike and wobbled her way along the paved driveway.

She was shocked by how hard the seat was compared to what she remembered from when she was a teen. She would have thought modern technology would have meant greater comfort, but it seemed the gold standard for today's riders was to make the seat as small, narrow, and brick-hard as possible.

When she reached the main road, she turned right. This was easier than pedaling along the flat. It was a long, winding downhill ride.

"Whee!" Olivia said, as the wind from her increasing speed blew her hair back. She leaned into the curve and then leaned the other way for the next bend. She felt like a Tour de France rider. This had been a brilliant choice, and was going to get her to the hotel in no time at all. She was sure of it.

The road flattened out in the village and Olivia pedaled steadily along, swerving to avoid a minibus parked outside the bakery, and noticing the hardware store clerk glance curiously at her. No doubt, her impulsive ride along the main road would soon be the talk of the town.

Determinedly, Olivia exited the village, gasping as she stared at the road ahead.

Why had she never noticed before the hill was practically perpendicular?

As her aching legs trembled and the bike wobbled more and more violently, she started to wonder if this slope was even legal! Weren't there rules about what gradient a road could be?

Her breath was coming in hoarse gasps, her backside was burning, and as for her legs, she simply hadn't known they possessed so many different muscles, all of which were screaming at her to stop.

She changed gear yet again. She was all out of gears now. The only other option she had was to get off and push.

"Keep going!"

Olivia's head whipped round as another cyclist passed her. The elderly man on his heavy, old-fashioned bike was pedaling steadily, yet at a surprising speed. On the back of the bike was a basket piled with shopping bags.

She glanced at him desperately.

"Help me!" she mouthed, but she didn't have any air to get the actual words out, and in any case, he was already several yards ahead of her and the gap was widening.

Then, like a beacon of hope, Olivia saw the hotel's driveway ahead of her. One more minute of unbearable torture, and she would reach it.

And the driveway was flat.

Encouraged that she'd almost achieved her goal, Olivia lowered her head and drew from reserves inside her that she hadn't even known about.

Finally, she swung left into the flat driveway. Here, she sped up again, feeling encouraged. Level roads were definitely her forte, she decided. This was where her cycling strength lay.

Best of all, she was just in time. Ahead of her was a large taxicab, stopped outside the hotel's front entrance.

Kyle and Rog were piling their bags into the back. Olivia stopped beside them and they looked at her inquiringly. It took a few moments before coherent communication was possible again.

"Where—where are the—bridesmaids?" she asked.

The two men exchanged a puzzled glance.

"What do you want to see them for? You're not still investigating, are you?" Kyle asked suspiciously.

"I need to confirm a small detail," Olivia hedged.

"You need to stop interfering," Kyle chastised her in critical tones.

"The girls have all left, anyway," Rog added.

"Left?" Olivia felt crestfallen. Her efforts had been in vain.

"Just left." Rog laughed callously. "They took the first minibus to the airport. Good luck in catching up with them!"

"No, they went into the village first," Kyle corrected him. "Angelique wanted to pick up some cookies from the bakery."

"I—oh, no!"

Olivia was appalled.

She hadn't given that minibus a second glance as she'd freewheeled past it. She'd wasted pointless, muscle-burning minutes pedaling up a sheer mountain side for no reason at all! They would have bought their treats by now.

"Thank you," she said, turning the bike around.

As Olivia headed back, hope blossomed inside her again. She knew what that bakery was like. Any normal woman—and Olivia classified Angelique as normal in that regard, would be spellbound by the lavish displays of sugary cookies, breads, savories, pies, and other delights that crowded the shelves.

You could easily spend an hour hypnotized by the exquisite detail on the sumptuously iced cakes, wondering which one would taste the best.

It simply wasn't possible to make a quick trip in and out of the bakery, Olivia decided, as she turned onto the main road.

This, then, was the final push. She allowed the gradient to take her forward, puzzled by how much steeper it had seemed on the way up.

This downward slope was very gradual and in fact, she wasn't going fast enough.

With a sigh, Olivia started pedaling down the hill as fast as she could.

There was the cab! It was still outside the bakery. Her suspicion had been right, and Angelique had been unable to tear herself away from the deliciousness on display.

Letting out a breath of relief, Olivia coasted toward it.

Then she uttered a cry of dismay. The minibus was pulling off. She was too late!

Olivia slowed down, feeling crestfallen, knowing that she'd failed in her mission and only a miracle could save her now.

Then, in front of her eyes, the miracle occurred. Another tour bus approached, traveling in the opposite direction. The narrow roads in the village made it almost impossible for two buses to pass. They had to squeeze by each other at a snail's pace.

As the buses edged along, with the merest inch between their wing mirrors, Olivia caught up.

As soon as the maneuver was complete, the minibus sped up again, but so did Olivia. A bicycle could pull off quicker than a large van loaded with passengers and luggage. Even if the rider was reaching her physical limits and suspected she had a nasty blister forming on her backside.

Olivia made it past the minibus, the bike's wheels juddering over the cobbled section of the road.

"Stop!" she cried.

Worried that the driver might ignore her or not hear her at all, she swerved to the left and rode in front of the bus.

"Stop!" she yelled, raising her hand authoritatively. This caused her to wobble so badly that she and the bike fell over in front of the van.

Brakes squealed as the driver hastily stopped.

Olivia scrambled to her feet. She'd been going so slowly that the only injury was to her dignity. She was okay with that because she'd achieved her goal. Now, a bigger challenge lay ahead. This was her last chance to accuse the murderer, obtain a confession, and make sure that justice was done.

# CHAPTER THIRTY

The minibus's sliding door opened and Angelique climbed out, looking curious.

She was followed by Cassidy, Jewel, Dinah, Molly, Madeline, and Miranda. All of them were dressed to the nines, ready for their onward flights.

"What are you doing?" Angelique asked, staring at Olivia critically as if judging her mussed hair and her dusty pants and her flushed face.

Judging her and finding her wanting, Olivia had no doubt.

"I was wrong," she began.

"Wrong about what?" From Angelique's condemning expression, it seemed she thought Olivia's entire life had been a mistake.

"Wrong about who committed the murder," Olivia told her, picking up her bicycle. Its sturdy frame gave her exhausted legs some much-needed support.

"But how can you be wrong?" Jewel challenged her. "You explained everything to us in the hotel lounge."

"Yes, that's true. But I left out an important detail. I didn't consider all the information. I nearly caused a catastrophe," she admitted, deciding she needed to own her weaknesses. After all, that was the only way to grow. She couldn't imagine Gramma B whitewashing over the sins she'd committed. Gramma B would have jutted her chin and spat out the truth!

"How?" Angelique probed.

"I didn't assess what happened next. There was a part two, after Lance and Terence had their fight."

"A part two?" Angelique crinkled her nose in confusion.

"Yes. Lance followed Terence outside. He hit him over the head with a bottle, but he didn't kill him. Someone else did."

"Who?" Jewel asked.

"Dinah." Olivia pointed to the petite, dark-haired woman who was standing all the way at the back of the group.

Jewel placed her hands on her hips and jutted her chin defiantly.

"Dinah? You can't be serious! She is my best friend and you're a liar!"

168

"No, she's the liar and you tried to cover for her, by saying that you thought she was with you the whole time you were getting sick. She wasn't."

Dinah stared at Olivia through narrowed eyes. Her gaze was darkly hostile and her lips were pressed tightly together. Clearly, she was taking the Fifth Amendment, and Olivia could expect no easy confession.

"So what do you think happened?" Jewel sounded angry.

"After Lance hit Terence over the head, he went and sat in the car. Dinah found him there and some kind of argument must have ensued. Anyway, she stabbed him with the corkscrew, wiped it off, and then hotfooted it back inside to get away from the scene. She headed into the ladies' room, probably to wash any evidence off her hands, and saw Jewel had been sick all over the place. So Dinah stayed with her, knowing that it would be an excellent alibi. But it wasn't." Olivia pointed at Dinah. "Because if you really had helped your friend, she wouldn't have made such a mess!"

Jewel was still simmering with outrage.

"And why would Dinah do such a thing? What reason could she possibly have?"

That particular question flummoxed Olivia, because she didn't know. There must have been a reason. Some conflict must have played out between the two of them, but what? She wished she could have been a fly on the wall, or rather on the car door.

Glancing at Dinah, she saw the petite brunette nod knowingly, as if she guessed that Olivia wasn't psychic and had no idea.

Olivia was about to admit to this gaping hole in her theory, but then Angelique spoke thoughtfully.

"I can think of a reason," Angelique said. "Dinah's always had a crush on Terence, ever since school. He was never interested in her, though. But Dinah has this weird character flaw. She hates it if somebody else has something she can't have." Propping her chin on her pearly-pink fingernail, Angelique stared thoughtfully at Dinah.

"I've just remembered another detail," Molly said. "Dinah, a few minutes after Terence stormed out of the restaurant, you said you were going to look for Alice. But I saw Alice just outside the restaurant, crying on Lysander's shoulder. You marched straight past her and headed out into the night. I thought that was strange, and I noticed at the time you seemed purposeful."

169

Olivia nodded. Molly's words confirmed the timeline and clarified her own memories. Now she recalled that Dinah hadn't followed Jewel straight to the restroom, but had hurried outside.

Everyone turned to stare at Dinah.

Finally, the slim, dark-haired woman spoke.

"You have no proof," she insisted in a sharp voice, directing the comment at Molly but glaring at the group in general.

Angelique leaned threateningly toward her. "Maybe my fiancé being murdered is all the proof I need," she retorted.

"You don't falsely accuse my friend!" Jewel shouted. "Dinah is a better person than you'll ever be."

"How can you say that?" Cassidy entered the fray. "Angelique is my best friend!"

Molly raised her voice. "If that's the case then why did you sleep with Terence two weeks ago, Cassidy?"

"And why did you sleep with him a month ago, Madeline?" Cassidy hissed.

Angelique let out a cry of rage. Shoving Cassidy aside, she lunged at Dinah, grabbing her by the lapels of her white designer jacket.

Madeline launched herself at Cassidy, kicking and punching in fury. Jewel piled into the conflict, pulling Molly's long chestnut hair as if she wanted to tug it out by the roots.

In another moment, they were all fighting with each other.

Screams and yells reverberated around the street as the women vented their anger.

"Please stop!" Olivia cried. "You'll get into trouble!"

Nobody paid her any attention at all.

Then she saw the group of tourists pile out of the other bus, which had stopped just beyond the bakery.

"Hey, this is what we read about," a bearded man said, as he eagerly pointed his phone at the scene. "Bakery fights! I thought it was just the bakers that shouted at each other across the road, but it seems that a whole lot of ladies get involved too. I had no idea. This is such great entertainment!"

"Quickly, do a live broadcast," the woman following him advised, scrambling out with her phone in hand. "How amazing is this? It's so authentic, I feel at one with the locals and enmeshed in their culture. I am giving both these bakeries five stars on Trip Advisor."

"Which bakery do you support?" a lanky youth asked, moving forward and ducking away from Cassidy's clawing hand to shout the question in her ear while he filmed. "Are you on Team Mazetti's or Team Forno Collina?"

Cassidy was too busy trying to jab her fingers into Madeline's eyes to reply.

"Please, stop!" Olivia shouted again.

She grabbed hold of Angelique's hand, trying to pull her out of the fight, but Angelique was too quick for her. She yanked Olivia toward her, screaming in anger.

"This is all your fault! Why did you interfere?"

Olivia's bicycle crashed to the ground. A moment later, her weakened legs gave way and she sprawled onto her side.

Clearly sensing that victory was hers, Angelique leaped in for the attack.

Olivia rolled away as the blonde made a grab for her hair. She wished she was still wearing her beanie. This woman was mad! Olivia could actually hear her teeth snapping like a shark. What would happen if they snapped shut on one of her fingers?

"Stop it!" she squealed as Angelique pinched her shoulder hard. Olivia windmilled her arms in self-defense and got in a lucky blow. Angelique shrieked.

"That was my nose!" she cried in aggrieved tones. "You hit me on my nose!"

"Ouch!" Olivia yelled, as Cassidy kicked her in her thigh. She didn't think Cassidy had even meant it, because she was on her back at the time, flailing to get away from an enraged Madeline.

Olivia managed to jackknife past Angelique's onslaught. She scrambled to her feet. This was madness. The most sensible thing she could do was put some distance between herself and this melee, and then call the police.

"Where are you going?" Angelique called as Olivia began to run. "Wait! I haven't finished with you yet!"

Olivia managed to find the reserves of speed she needed to escape the maddened bride-no-longer-to-be. She couldn't outpace the lanky tourist, though. He was matching her step for step, phone in hand, turned to landscape mode for optimal filming.

"Mazetti's or Forno Collina? Can you give me a clue? Nod for yes!" he shouted at her. Then, yelling to the woman behind him, he called, "Hashtag Bakery Blondes! This is gonna trend! Hashtag Bakery Blondes!"

What was the world coming to? Olivia wondered in confusion. Here she was, in a life-or-death situation, trying to escape the blond, human version of an attacking shark, and was this young man trying to help? No! He was filming!

If she'd had any breath to spare she would have told him off.

But then the man slowed suddenly and vanished from her view, leaving Olivia on her own. Glancing up, she saw the road in front of her was blocked.

She stumbled to a halt. Behind her, the sounds of the fracas died down, as if someone had twisted a volume knob, and then abruptly unplugged the stereo.

Clad all in black, and poised in front of a police car, Detective Caputi blocked the road. Her arms were folded as she surveyed the scene.

She spoke briefly into her walkie-talkie. To her amazement, Olivia's newly attuned ear for Italian immediately translated the words, "Bring a ten-seater van."

Then she turned to freeze the ex-fighters in her accusing gaze.

"You are all arrested," she said in tones of quiet satisfaction, as if this was turning out to be a milestone day for her not only professionally, but personally. "You will accompany the officers to the police station at once."

As if it had been a life goal that she'd strived for ever since joining the police, Detective Caputi unhooked a pair of handcuffs from her belt. Then she stepped forward and clamped them shut over Olivia's wrists.

# CHAPTER THIRTY ONE

The prison cell was cold and unwelcoming, Olivia thought, as she stared around her austere confines for the hundredth time. No effort had been made to put innocent people, wrongfully arrested, at their ease.

She was seated on the plank-like bed and her view ahead was of a blank wall and a high, barred window.

To her right was a metal toilet and sink, but the cold stainless steel was so depressing that she hadn't paid that part of her environment much attention. Rather, her gaze, and her hopes, were focused on the left side. That was where the door was!

At the moment, the solid door was firmly locked and there was no movement visible through the tiny, barred section.

But this would change, Olivia thought hopefully, for the hundredth time in what must have been two hours. Surely it would change. Someone would have to come along soon. If she was here overnight, they would at least feed her?

She touched the blanket again, feeling doubtful. It was very scratchy. If she was here overnight, it wouldn't be comfortable at all, and the cell was chilly even now. The inch-thick pillow looked to have been made from the same material as Jean-Pierre's bicycle saddle, probably chipped out of a block of local granite.

Her lips were dry, but her Chapstick was in her purse, which was now in police custody, together with Jean-Pierre's bicycle.

Obviously, a public fight provided grounds for arrest, but Olivia had been trying to break up the fight! All she needed was a chance to prove the purity of her motives. So far, she hadn't had that opportunity. In a whirlwind of confusion, she'd been ferried to the police station with the rest of the chastened group, and then locked away on her own.

She sighed, hoping that her involvement wouldn't give the detective the ammunition she needed to accuse her of an actual crime! After all, now that she was finally in jail, she was sure Caputi would be racking her brains for ways to keep her there.

"Hello?" she called again. She'd called a few times, hoping for a response. Angelique and the bridesmaids must be somewhere, but they weren't replying to her. She hoped Detective Caputi hadn't placed her in solitary confinement.

Then she heard the ominously familiar clicking heels approach.

Olivia's stomach twisted. This was scary! She hadn't realized how vulnerable you felt in a locked cell, at the mercy of the police.

A key rattled in the door and then it swung open. Detective Caputi stood in the doorway. Olivia tried a nervous smile but it wilted on her lips.

A few moments passed in silence. They felt like eons. Finally, the policewoman spoke.

"I am sure you are wondering what will happen to you now," she said in harsh tones.

Olivia's eyes widened. This was worse than she'd feared. The other woman's voice was filled with finality. Not the tiniest room for hope remained.

"Yes, I'm very worried," Olivia admitted. "Will you listen to my version?"

The detective's lips tightened briefly.

"I will not," she said.

Olivia clutched at the rough, fibrous blanket. Her hands felt icy cold. It was too late, and the moment to speak in her defense had passed.

"You won't? Are you sure?" she pleaded. She guessed she'd be cuddling up to this scratchy covering for some time. Days, at best. Years, at worst!

"I am sure, yes," Detective Caputi retorted.

Another silence followed. Olivia's mind was churning with useless ideas, starting with leaping to her feet, pushing Caputi out of the way, and making a run for it. That was the best she could come up with. It showed how hopeless her situation was. In any case, her legs couldn't sprint as far as the cell door, after all the cycling they'd done.

She let out a despairing sigh. She should have known that it would end this way eventually if she kept interfering in police business.

Then, to her astonishment, Detective Caputi's face softened. She looked friendlier than Olivia could ever recall her being. In fact, Olivia was stunned to see the tiniest gleam of humor in her previously stony expression.

"Your version will not be necessary," she said. "After questioning Angelique Miller, I immediately interviewed her bridesmaid, Dinah

Todd. In due course, Ms. Todd broke down and confessed to everything."

"She did?" Olivia asked incredulously. She couldn't believe her ears! She'd never dreamed that Dinah would end up confessing, and was filled with respect for Detective Caputi's lethal questioning techniques. She wished she'd been able to sit in on the interview and watch.

Olivia felt breathless as she realized how close Dinah had come to getting away with her crime, and escaping Italy. Every agonizing turn of those bicycle pedals had been worth it, she thought.

"Did she say why she killed him?" She risked the question, hoping that the detective might be willing to share the back story.

"Ms. Todd explained that she had been enamored with the groom, Terence Jones, some time ago. He never returned her affections and although she felt insulted by his rejection, she forgot the incident. But then he contacted her again and seduced her three days before the party flew to Tuscany."

"He did?" Olivia's mouth dropped open in shock.

"He told Ms. Todd before sleeping with her that he was regretting the wedding plans. He said that he had been feeling desperate, and had already had a weak moment with Madeline and Cassidy, but that he now knew he had found true love with her. He promised he would call off the wedding on the morning itself, and that he and she would elope together."

"And she believed him?" Olivia asked, confused.

Detective Caputi shrugged. "He convinced her using more than his charm. Ms. Todd, as the least well-off of the circle of friends, was highly motivated by the thought of marrying into his family's extreme wealth."

"Ah." Olivia nodded wisely. Money had no doubt been a strong persuader.

"On the wedding rehearsal night, Ms. Todd was horrified to hear that Terence Jones had been seen kissing the bride's sister. As soon as she could find an excuse for going outside, she left the winery and went to look for him. She found him in the car clutching his head."

"What happened then?" Olivia asked, spellbound by the story.

"He laughed at her, and said his promises had been a lie, and had simply been used to achieve his life goal which was to seduce all the bridesmaids—the Magnificent Seven as he referred to them, including the six bridesmaids and the bride's sister Alice—by the time the

175

wedding party left Tuscany. He congratulated her on being number three of seven."

Olivia's mouth fell open.

Hell hath no fury, she thought.

"Ms. Todd was outraged by this. She saw he was holding a corkscrew and it suddenly occurred to her to murder him," the detective explained. "She said that although she is usually a calm and controlled person, a red mist enveloped her and she acted in the moment."

Olivia nodded thoughtfully.

"After committing the crime, her reason returned. She wiped the weapon carefully down and then hurried to the ladies' restroom to make sure there was no trace of blood on her. She said she was thinking logically once again," Detective Caputi explained. "In the restroom, she found her friend Jewel getting sick. Deciding to wait there until someone found the body, she realized that helping her friend would give her the perfect alibi. Which it almost did. So we have released Lance. The family asked us to allow him to go home, and said they will deal privately with the incident of assault."

Olivia was stunned by what Detective Caputi was telling her. What a lucky break she'd had, gazing around that restroom and putting two and two together. If she hadn't, Dinah would have gotten away and traveled home, clearly without a twinge of remorse that the wrong person was locked up for the crime.

Talking of crime, Olivia remembered with a guilty start that she had been imprisoned for a reason, even if wrongfully so. She'd been arrested for causing a public disturbance. She was still in trouble with the law and was confused why Detective Caputi was even speaking to her in such a friendly way.

"You may be wondering what happens now," the detective said, as if reading her mind.

"Er—yes. I was, in fact, wondering," Olivia admitted.

The detective paced out of the cell and stood, holding the door open.

"You are free to go."

Olivia stared up at her. Was this a trap? Did the detective really mean it? Or was she waiting for Olivia to stand up before slamming the door in her face and laughing evilly?

Well, she'd have to find out!

Scrambling to her aching feet, she tottered hesitantly to the door, which remained open.

"Ms. Angelique Miller emphasized that your role in the proceedings at the bakery was that of a peacekeeper. However, we are not pressing charges on anyone involved in the fight. The bakers have requested it. They said it will adversely affect tourism, and that the fight took place in a spirit of fun."

The detective's words dripped with disbelief, but she didn't seem angry. Olivia guessed she was simply relieved to have a full confession from the right suspect.

"You may collect your possessions from the front desk upstairs," she advised.

"Thank you very much," Olivia said gratefully.

As she passed the detective, she heard her murmur something.

Heading upstairs, Olivia puzzled over what the almost-inaudible words had been.

They had sounded a lot like "Thank you, too."

Surely that was impossible?

Olivia felt very confused. Most probably, she'd misheard. But if she had heard correctly, it meant that Detective Caputi actually appreciated her efforts, and that made Olivia feel ten feet tall with pride.

She climbed the stairs—after the Leg Day she'd had, every step was torture—and when she finally reached the top and limped toward the front desk, she was taken aback to see Angelique there.

To Olivia's surprise, she gave her the friendliest of smiles.

"Wasn't that an experience? Do you know we're trending on social media as Hashtag Bakery Blondes? I've just got my phone back and seen the footage."

"Is that so?" Olivia said. She wasn't sure she welcomed this fame and hoped it would blow over quickly.

"Yes. It's all been tremendously exciting. I had a feeling that coming to Italy would be an adventure but I never thought it would be quite so intense. I mean, life-changing. I feel I've awakened a new personal strength within myself. I owe you a lot of thanks for everything."

"You're welcome," Olivia said politely. She was glad that Angelique was taking the incident in such good spirits.

"I'm looking forward to a solo honeymoon," she added. "It's going to be exciting staying in magnificent accommodations in the Seychelles for two weeks, and doing exactly what I want!"

"I'm sure it will be the experience of a lifetime. I think you're very brave," Olivia said, glad to have a reason to praise her.

"You know, I wasn't going to change my mind about calling the wedding off. Even if Dinah hadn't killed Terence, I wouldn't have forgiven him for what he did," Angelique said, her chin jutting.

"It was the best decision to call it off," Olivia agreed. "You need to be sure someone's right for you before you marry them. My experience with Ward taught me a hard lesson."

She felt filled with thankfulness that she'd been able to turn her back on the incident and move on to new directions. Thinking back, she had managed to grow and learn from her mistake, becoming a stronger person after the ordeal, just like Angelique.

Angelique looked cheerful. "I feel my future is brighter now. Who knows where I will end up? At least it won't be in the Jones's hideous family compound back in Alpine, New Jersey. I was dreading having to live in that modern, soulless, chrome-and-glass monstrosity. Tuscany is definitely on my list of places I want to see again. I can't wait to come back to your winery and learn more about tasting, or even hold a birthday party there! Maybe next summer," she said blithely, and Olivia's heart plummeted.

"That would be wonderful," she said in tones of artificial joy. "Next summer I believe we are almost entirely booked up, but perhaps the following year, or the one after?"

Inwardly, although she wished her well, she hoped that Angelique never set foot in the area again. She was convinced that if and when the blonde returned to La Leggenda, she'd bring trouble all over again.

*

Olivia wheeled the bicycle outside, staring at it resentfully. Her backside throbbed at the mere idea of climbing onto its saddle again.

It was four p.m. and the winery would be open for another hour and a half. Her sweaty, torn, and tattered clothes bore witness to the active afternoon she'd had chasing down suspects and getting involved in street fights, but she had no option. She had to go back there and help out for the rest of the afternoon. She'd bunked for far too long already, and now had to pitch in and help.

Wearily, Olivia swung her leg over the brick-hard saddle. She had no idea how these Tour de France riders did it.

Luckily, the police station was on the winery side of the village, so although there was a challenging uphill, at least the distance wasn't too far. Deciding that dignity was far less important than survival, Olivia

178

climbed off and pushed the bike when she reached the steepest slope. Only when she was over the crest did she mount up again, pedaling along the short flat section and then turning the bike down the winding driveway.

As she neared the winery buildings, she saw Nadia standing outside, peering in her direction. Pulling up, she saw Nadia's expression combined consternation and awe.

"Olivia, what is this I hear? I was phoned by three different people to say that you were involved in a massive fight outside the bakery, and arrested!"

Her gaze traveled up and down Olivia's scuffed, rumpled frame.

"Yes. It was very unfortunate. I had a last-minute brainwave about the case. I realized I was wrong, and there was more to it. So as a result, Dinah, one of the bridesmaids, made a full confession. And Detective Caputi even thanked me!"

Nadia's eyes widened.

"No!" she exclaimed.

"Yes. I feel very proud."

"You can be proud in other ways," Nadia informed her with a conspiratorial grin. "You are an Instagram celebrity, they say. The bakers want to give you a gift as Collina town and their bakeries are now trending all over social media. What are those pastries you like? They say you can have a free one every time you visit them."

Olivia stared at her in concern. "That's so kind, but I'll never get down a dress size!"

Nadia waved a dismissive hand. "Dress size? Who cares? Curves are beautiful! But now, you must come to my house and shower and do your hair. There is a bus load of tourists arriving in half an hour for a wine tasting. Luckily, a friend gave me a pretty top as a gift, but it is too large for me. It will fit you perfectly, and you can wash the stains off your pants, as they are black, and the wet spots won't show. You can use my makeup, perfume, hairdryer, whatever you need. My home is yours."

Swept up in Nadia's organizational whirlwind, Olivia found herself ferried off to the vintner's house.

After wiping down her pants and hanging them over a chair to dry, she climbed into the shower, grateful to be soaping away the sweat, dirt and grime with Nadia's gorgeous-smelling shower gel, and washing her hair with Nadia's expensive shampoo. She dried herself and headed into Nadia's bedroom.

As quickly as possible, worrying that the tourist bus might arrive early, she styled her hair, did her makeup, and spritzed on some perfume. Olivia had to admit, as she looked at her new, improved self in the mirror, that she felt like a new woman. Washing off the smell and feel of that jail cell was a rejuvenating experience.

And, as an unexpected bonus, her aching backside felt firmer than it had for months!

She headed back to the winery and arrived in time to see Marcello hurry out of his office. He nodded approvingly when he saw her.

"I understand that you valuably assisted the police in making a new arrest of the correct suspect. I am glad that this matter is now resolved."

"Like I said, I wanted to set things right. Now we can put this behind us and focus on our wine sales and the new events initiative," Olivia explained.

"It is going to be a fresh and exciting chapter for us," Marcello agreed, with an expectant smile.

Jean-Pierre beamed at her from behind the counter.

"Olivia, you have saved me! The local news site is writing an article on our soccer team tomorrow. All the players will be interviewed and are having a group photo taken. I was going to have to miss the whole thing, because Detective Caputi would arrest me if she saw it. The coach will be so glad to hear I can join in. I cannot thank you enough."

"That's wonderful! I can't wait to read it." Olivia felt thrilled that Jean-Pierre could glory in his fame as a key member of the village team.

As she walked around the tasting counter to join Jean-Pierre, she heard the tour bus pull up outside.

Hurrying to take her position beside him, Olivia felt filled with warm satisfaction that her day had turned out so well after such an unpromising start. In fact, she was almost totally content.

Almost.

Despite the success of her investigation, her love life was still fraught with unanswered questions.

Standing ready to welcome the guests, Olivia squared her shoulders and tried to put the unhappy thoughts aside. Solving the impossible was out of her control.

# CHAPTER THIRTY TWO

It was fully dark when Olivia and Erba arrived back home. As she drove through the farmhouse gate, Olivia's thoughts were hungrily focused on dinner.

She was drawing a complete blank on her nighttime menu, and regretting that she hadn't thought to stop in at the bakery before it closed.

Racking her brains, she remembered that there was a half pack of pasta in the cupboard, and a quarter tin of tomatoes in the freezer. Perhaps her herb garden would yield something tasty to marry these sparse ingredients together. She was completely out of cheese and olive oil. And after her agonizing ride, she was starving!

"We're going to need to be creative tonight, Erba," she told the goat, who was staring over her shoulder, entranced by the drive.

Olivia cruised to her parking spot, wondering where Pirate was.

Then she let out a surprised gasp.

Pirate was perched happily in front of her, washing his tail in a relaxed and contented way.

The fact that he was washing his tail didn't worry her at all. Pirate was a tidy cat with a strong focus on hygiene. She was happy for him to groom himself as often and thoroughly as he preferred.

What was astonishing was that he was doing it while on top of Danilo's car.

"What is going on?" Olivia asked herself incredulously. She stared at the pickup, which looked to have been freshly washed, as a torrent of emotions resurged inside her.

A faint light was visible through the small, high barn window. Danilo must be in there, working on the pile. Why?

She headed over to the barn, her mind spinning with confusion. She felt self-conscious and apprehensive about confronting him at last. She dreaded that he'd only come to confirm, in person, that things were over between them.

Danilo was filling the wheelbarrow by the light of a lantern he'd placed at the foot of the pile. As soon as he saw her, he put down the shovel and turned to her.

"Olivia. It is good to see you. Are you all right?"

Olivia hesitated in the doorway.

"I'm fine," she said, keeping her voice as neutral as she could. "I worked out who the murderer was. I spent some time in a prison cell before being released. And the detective thanked me!"

Danilo's eyes widened. He walked toward her hesitantly.

"I am so glad. And your wine? I notice one of the fermenters is empty and lying on its side."

"It sprang a leak, so I had to decant it into the oak barrel. I'm hoping it won't ruin it."

She stared at him warily. Danilo hadn't come all this way to ask about her wine. Why, then, was he here? Her stomach churned as she waited for him to speak.

"I wanted to—" he began, but as he got out the words, Olivia saw out of the corner of her eye that her opportunistic goat had taken advantage of her highly distracted state.

"Erba!" she reprimanded her goat loudly. She was trying to sneak into the barn again, under cover of the low lamp light.

"We'd better go outside," she said, as the goat edged through the doorway, flattening herself against the wall. Her first ever vintage had managed to survive one disaster, but not a drop would be left in the morning if Erba was accidentally shut in overnight.

"Of course, of course," Danilo agreed, grasping his lamp.

They hustled outside, and after double-checking that Erba really was capering back to her Wendy house, and hadn't managed to sneak in again, Olivia closed the door firmly.

Then she led the way up to the farmhouse.

She walked in first, and Danilo followed. Third in line was Pirate, who was meowing in welcome and winding himself ecstatically around Danilo's ankles.

"Come to the kitchen," she said, inwardly berating herself for having invited him into her home, because most likely, this discussion would be better held in the hallway. "Would you like a drink?" she added.

No matter what direction the conversation took, Olivia knew she needed a glass of wine to help her get through it.

"Actually, I brought a bottle of rosé." Danilo produced it, like a magician brandishing a white rabbit, from inside his jacket. "It is for you. But if you like, we could pour a glass now."

In the bright kitchen, she saw he was wearing a deep red shirt that complemented his dark hair and olive-tinged skin. His hair had been shaved on one side and a perfect seam cut into the hairline, before the rest was swept to the other side.

Normally she would have commented on his hairstyle but of course now, she couldn't.

Despite having filled a wheelbarrow of dusty rubble, his shoes were shiny enough for Olivia to see her face in them. She'd never seen Danilo with such mirror-like shoes before.

"A glass now sounds like a good idea," she admitted.

Looking relieved, Danilo took two glasses down from the shelf, and the next moment, Olivia was holding a glass of icy cold, deliciously pink rosé.

"I don't know how to start saying what I need to. Olivia, I treated you badly," Danilo said.

"Please, help me understand why? What happened at Sovestro was—was unexpected. And hurtful. Then things got even more confusing, because you messaged me and left a bakery treat on my doorstep, but you didn't answer your phone when I tried to call!"

Danilo was staring at her with concern.

"Did you not get my note, Olivia?"

"Note?" Olivia felt completely disoriented. What was Danilo talking about? There had been no note!

"I left it on the bakery bag. Taped to the top."

A ray of enlightenment pierced her confusion. "I wouldn't have seen it then. Erba ate the bag. I only got the bottom half."

Danilo pressed his lips together. Olivia wondered if he was trying to stifle a laugh. That would be crazy, as this was no time for laughter. This was an extremely serious situation!

"The note said I would come back tonight, and that we needed to talk. I said I had made reservations at Ribollita for seven p.m. and hoped that you would accompany me there."

Olivia's heart leaped. Dinner reservations at one of the area's most stylish restaurants? Then bewilderment descended again.

"And the missed call? What if I'd been phoning to say I couldn't go?"

Danilo looked embarrassed. His cheeks flushed a dull pink.

"I was—I was confused and emotional after leaving the note. I was not thinking clearly. After leaving your farm, I had to send a batch of paperwork to my accountant in Milan. Only after I had couriered the

183

envelope, I realized I had slipped my cell phone inside the file. It arrived in Milan two hours ago. He will send it back to me tomorrow."

"Oh," Olivia said. She felt like giggling because that was hilarious! But it would be wrong to express mirth at such a time, after Danilo had explained how emotional he was, so she simply nodded as he continued.

"I behaved terribly when we were at Sovestro. Please understand that I was shocked. I thought my world had ended. But it did not excuse my actions, and it does not change my feelings, which I cannot deny. Just tell me, Olivia, tell me so that I know and I can try to prepare— when are you going to leave Italy and go back home?"

Olivia stared at Danilo, feeling as if her world had pivoted on its axis and she was living in a strange alternate reality.

"But I'm not going back home," she said.

She was perplexed to see that Danilo looked just as thrown as her.

"You said you were. You read it to me, in writing. In black and white."

A dark suspicion had started to form in Olivia's mind.

"You don't mean—" she began.

"The postcard," Danilo said. "It was from your mother, and it clearly said—"

"No!" Olivia shrieked. "You didn't take that seriously?"

"Of course I did!" Now Danilo sounded as guilty as if he was being accused of a crime himself. "Should I not have done?"

Where to start? Olivia's head was whirling. That stupid card was still in her purse. She'd kept it as a reminder she needed to reply. This entire conversation was a wake-up call to her that others perceived her mother differently than how she really was.

"My mother has this fixation that I will come back one day. She pursues it tirelessly. Every time she calls me, or emails, or sends a postcard, it's with a job opportunity, or a reminder that she knows my 'extended vacation' will end soon. That's how she is! She can't help it and means no harm, but it's super-annoying. That annoyingness is one of the reasons I'm kind of glad to be here, and not there," Olivia ended, feeling ashamed of what she'd said.

She didn't want to speak badly about her family, but she needed to be honest at this critical time.

Danilo propped his elbows on the counter and buried his head in his hands. He was muttering in Italian.

"I never thought it was untrue. I was devastated." Straightening up, he stared at her with a wide and honest gaze. "I came back from my work on the ships because my father was unwell; he had a chronic illness that worsened suddenly. When I arrived, I became involved with a teacher who was spending a year in Italy before going back home to Australia. By the time we met, she had three months left. And at the end of the three months, she went home. Our bonds were not strong enough, she had no roots. Her stay had been an adventure, and so had the relationship with me. I thought—when you read that card to me, I thought you were telling me you were going to do the same."

Olivia felt her eyes stinging. This heartfelt confession was stirring all her emotions. She could understand why Danilo had shut down so badly, why he'd behaved so weirdly.

"I'm here to stay," she said softly. Then she added, trying to lighten the situation. "After being caught up in so many murders, I'm not sure the police would let me leave!"

She was glad to see Danilo grin at that.

"I've been studying the language and everything, because this is my new home. I haven't spoken it much, because I've been worried about my terrible accent. But here you go," she said.

She took a deep breath. The words milled around in her mind. Could she string them together in the right way and produce a coherent sentence that would not humiliate herself, or the Italian language?

Danilo was watching her closely, his gaze dark and intense. Glancing at the kitchen window behind him, Olivia saw that even Erba was taking in the drama, with a beady eye pressed against the glass.

In Italian, Olivia said, "I hope we understand each other better now. I feel you and I are becoming more than friends and I would like us to be closer. And I am looking forward to going to dinner with you tonight, as I have only had one slice of bread for lunch, and am very angry."

The next moment Olivia realized she'd used the wrong word! She'd meant to say *affamata* and instead had used *arrabiata*.

"Hungry, I mean. I am very hungry. Not angry at all."

The tension in Danilo's face melted away, replaced by the warmest smile she'd ever seen. He stepped forward, closing the awkward two-yard distance they'd kept from each other while they spoke, and embraced her, his arms tight around her.

"That was the most beautiful, perfect Italian I have ever heard," he said, his voice unsteady. "My feelings are the same."

Looking at the expression in his eyes, Olivia knew with heart-stopping certainty that this was it. It was the shift in their dynamic that she had dreamed of for so long, the start of a new, wonderful, romantic chapter in her life.

It hadn't followed the path she'd expected and had certainly taken longer than she'd ever thought it would. As Danilo's lips touched hers, Olivia had only one coherent thought in her mind.

This moment had been worth the wait.

By the time the kiss ended, Olivia was sure that Danilo must be able to feel her heart pounding, all the way through her borrowed shirt. He took her hand in his, squeezing it in a tender gesture.

But wait. It wasn't just a tender gesture. Danilo had been holding something, and now that item rested in Olivia's palm.

It felt like a slim, angular, cool piece of metal, and she was confused why he was passing it over to her.

"I picked up what I hope might be an important treasure this evening, while working in the barn," Danilo explained.

Gasping in excitement, Olivia opened her hand and stared down at the object. Her eyebrows shot up as she took in exactly what it was, and what the implications of this amazing find might be.

In her hand was a long, rusty, old-fashioned key.

# NOW AVAILABLE!

## AGED FOR VENGEANCE
### (A Tuscan Vineyard Cozy Mystery—Book 5)

"Very entertaining. I highly recommend this book to the permanent library of any reader that appreciates a very well written mystery, with some twists and an intelligent plot. You will not be disappointed. Excellent way to spend a cold weekend!" --Books and Movie Reviews, Roberto Mattos (regarding *Murder in the Manor*)

AGED FOR VENGEANCE (A TUSCAN VINEYARD COZY MYSTERY) is book #5 in a charming new cozy mystery series by #1 bestselling author Fiona Grace, author of Murder in the Manor (Book #1), a #1 Bestseller with over 100 five-star reviews—and a free download!

Olivia Glass, 34, turns her back on her life as a high-powered executive in Chicago and relocates to Tuscany, determined to start a new, simpler life—and to grow her own vineyard.

**A high-end wine tour comes into town, led by a world-class museum. When they stop at the winery, it seems like the winery's big break—but when one of the tour members ends up dead, it jeopardizes everything.**

**Can Olivia find the killer and save their reputation?**

Hilarious, packed with travel, food, wine, twists and turns, romance and her newfound animal friend—and centering around a baffling small-town murder that Olivia must solve—the TUSCAN VINEYARD is an un-putdownable mystery series that will keep you laughing late into the night.

Book #6 in the series, AGED FOR ACRIMONY, is now also available!

## Fiona Grace

Debut author Fiona Grace is author of the LACEY DOYLE COZY MYSTERY series, comprising nine books (and counting); of the TUSCAN VINEYARD COZY MYSTERY series, comprising six books (and counting); of the DUBIOUS WITCH COZY MYSTERY series, comprising three books (and counting); of the BEACHFRONT BAKERY COZY MYSTERY series, comprising six books (and counting); and of the CATS AND DOGS COZY MYSTERY series, comprising three books (and counting).

Fiona would love to hear from you, so please visit www.fionagraceauthor.com to receive free ebooks, hear the latest news, and stay in touch.

## BOOKS BY FIONA GRACE

**LACEY DOYLE COZY MYSTERY**
MURDER IN THE MANOR (Book#1)
DEATH AND A DOG (Book #2)
CRIME IN THE CAFE (Book #3)
VEXED ON A VISIT (Book #4)
KILLED WITH A KISS (Book #5)
PERISHED BY A PAINTING (Book #6)
SILENCED BY A SPELL (Book #7)
FRAMED BY A FORGERY (Book #8)
CATASTROPHE IN A CLOISTER (Book #9)

**TUSCAN VINEYARD COZY MYSTERY**
AGED FOR MURDER (Book #1)
AGED FOR DEATH (Book #2)
AGED FOR MAYHEM (Book #3)
AGED FOR SEDUCTION (Book #4)
AGED FOR VENGEANCE (Book #5)
AGED FOR ACRIMONY (Book #6)

**DUBIOUS WITCH COZY MYSTERY**
SKEPTIC IN SALEM: AN EPISODE OF MURDER (Book #1)
SKEPTIC IN SALEM: AN EPISODE OF CRIME (Book #2)
SKEPTIC IN SALEM: AN EPISODE OF DEATH (Book #3)

**BEACHFRONT BAKERY COZY MYSTERY**
BEACHFRONT BAKERY: A KILLER CUPCAKE (Book #1)
BEACHFRONT BAKERY: A MURDEROUS MACARON (Book #2)
BEACHFRONT BAKERY: A PERILOUS CAKE POP (Book #3)
BEACHFRONT BAKERY: A DEADLY DANISH (Book #4)
BEACHFRONT BAKERY: A TREACHEROUS TART (Book #5)
BEACHFRONT BAKERY: A CALAMITOUS COOKIE (Book #6)

**CATS AND DOGS COZY MYSTERY**
A VILLA IN SICILY: OLIVE OIL AND MURDER (Book #1)
A VILLA IN SICILY: FIGS AND A CADAVER (Book #2)
A VILLA IN SICILY: VINO AND DEATH (Book #3)

Made in the USA
Las Vegas, NV
28 September 2022

56177490R00114